MW01235607

THE ELECT

LAURA WADSWORTH CARTER

CLEAN READS

The Elect
by Laura Wadsworth Carter
Published by Clean Reads
www.cleanreads.com

Dedicated to my best friend and husband, Evan Carter

1

Hunt. Confront. Detain. Deliver. Those are my orders. I repeat them over and over to myself as I prowl through the streets of the village. My boots make no noise on the dusty road as I weave between towering grey buildings, and my eyes scan every shadow and alley for movement. I can sense the presence of other Young Ones over my shoulder, searching like I am. We're on a mission. Someone is breaking protocol, and we're supposed to find him and turn him over to the Men in Red.

Frustrated that I'm missing something at ground level, I take three bounding steps and throw myself onto the roof of a two-story building. I land with ease and roll my neck, trying to relax. The early autumn sun creates a sheen of sweat on my tan skin, and my uniform clings to my back, but it doesn't bother me. A short, red-headed girl lands on the roof beside me, and she leers, sizing me up. She's a few years younger than I, maybe eleven or twelve years old, and she's no match for me. We don't speak. Nobody speaks. I move forward again, compelled by my very nature to follow orders.

I trace the edge of the building, scanning the empty streets below for clues as to the man's whereabouts, but there are none. I leap over the road to the next row of buildings and try again. Across the village skyline, small uniformed bodies do as I do, bounding from one building to another, but there is no sound in the air. The light breeze coming down from the northern mountains carries no noise, which is what the Foundation prefers. I'm preparing to move to another street when the flutter of a white curtain in a red-framed window catches my eye. I pivot and immediately drop down to the road, landing in a soft crouch before moving towards my prey. I've found him.

I lift a leg and slam my foot through the front door of the five-story apartment building, and the wood splinters and explodes backwards into the hallway. I'm greeted by warm, stale air and sterile, white stairs. Footsteps shuffle in the stairwell overhead, and I can tell he's moving upwards, towards the roof. I lunge up the steps, taking them four at a time until I reach the roof access. Light floods into the stairwell as he throws himself through the exit, and I tear after him, slamming against the weighted, metal door so hard that it breaks off its hinges and slides across the gritty roof.

He runs from me, pumping his legs as fast as he can so that his shaggy brown hair bounces around him, but he's not fast enough. He looks over his shoulder at me and trips, landing on his side with a grunt. I don't run to catch him now. The chase, uneventful and short, is over. His narrow chest heaves with each breath, and his gaunt eyes widen as I close in on him. He rolls onto his back, shuffling his hands and feet beneath himself to scramble away from me, but it's no use. I lean over and grab the collar of his black shirt and tug him up so he's standing in front of me, pain wincing across his bearded face.

"Citizen, you are in violation of Protocol Three, Section Two," I tell him as I twist him to the side and pull his arms behind him. I retrieve a set of handcuffs from my belt and click them around his wrists.

"Please, kid," he says. "Don't do this! All I did was visit a friend."

"Did you have authorization?" I ask, knowing already he didn't. The sole authorized movement within the village is given to citizens going to and from work. Social calls are not permitted.

"N- no," he stammers, dropping his head.

"Then you are in violation of Protocol Three, Section Two," I restate. I lift my fingers to my mouth and let out a shrill whistle that cuts through the air. Several Young Ones on nearby roofs turn towards me. When they see I've apprehended the man, they drop back to the streets, disappearing beyond the ledges to head towards the Compound. I shove my prisoner towards the broken doorway, and he stumbles through and heads downstairs to the street. When we exit the building, he looks back at me with desperation.

"Towards the main road, Citizen," I say, motioning with my head towards the center of the village.

"What's going to happen to me?" he asks, shoulders slumping in on his thin frame.

"That is for the Men in Red to determine," I reply and direct him to move with a flick of my hand.

We walk in silence from here on until we reach a main road where a single black van waits for us. Two Men in Red get out of the cab and one rounds the back of the vehicle and yanks one of the doors open. The other nods at me and grabs the man's arm and tugs him away. I don't watch them put him in the van. My job is done, so I head back to the Compound along with the other Young Ones, all of whom heard my whistle to stop the search and now walk ahead of me.

It takes about fifteen minutes at a controlled pace until we reach the Compound gates, and I file in line with the others close to my age. We wait without speaking for our turns with the nurses as we reenter the controlled zone. It's standard protocol for us to receive a new dose of vaccine to protect us from outside elements whenever we return from a mission. I don't question it. I have no reason to.

After a few minutes, only four of us are left — two girls, another boy, and myself. I can't identify them by name, nor have I ever talked to any of them. One of the girls — petite and fair-skinned — reaches the nurse's station when a deafening explosion roars from the far side of the Compound. A feathery cloud of dust spews into the air, and the ground trembles beneath me. Inside of the gate, nurses and Men in Red grapple for their balance, waving their arms and widening their stances.

I, on the other hand, do not even flinch, nor do the other three Young Ones in front of me. Instead, we all stand blank-faced with our hands by our sides as a tower of medical vials tumble from its formation and crashes to the ground. Sparkling shards of glass fly out like tiny, bouncing slivers of light while a mournful siren wails from further inside the Compound. A few of the Reds rush forward and push us inside the gate, locking it behind us in case the rebels are attacking. In all of the chaos, I am ordered to go straight to my standard position in the main courtyard amongst the hundreds of other Young Ones. Reds buzz around us, checking the buildings for anything suspicious, and I assume they find nothing since we are eventually dismissed to retrieve our dinner.

The sun has set by this point, and I take my place in line to retrieve my bar. It takes a couple of minutes before I reach the table, behind which stands a nurse dressed in all white.

"No water tonight," she says. "Something's up with the tower. You'll get it in the morning."

"Yes, ma'am," I reply, taking my food. I step aside and go sit cross-legged in my designated spot. I rip the wrapper off with one swift tear and consume the bar in two bites. It tastes the same as ever — like nothing. But this bar is what gives me my strength, so I don't complain.

When everyone has eaten, we are sent to our barracks for sleep. We all proceed in synchronized movements as we shower, change, and lie down on our cots. Tomorrow, I will wake up and repeat this same choreography, because it's the same thing I've done every day for as long as I can remember. Nothing ever changes.

———

THROUGH NO EARNEST INTENTION OF MY OWN, I FIND myself awake and lying on my back. A network of gray, steel rafters weave across the ceiling above me, and a lacy netting of cobwebs and dust flutter against them from the cold draft in the room. To my right, a Man in Red grips a thick rope hanging from a bell, and he pulls downward with a huff, sending the bell into a fit of clanging to awaken us. Though I would like nothing more than to remain beneath the wool blanket that's tucked around my chin, my body propels me into a sitting position as a groan escapes my lips. The cool grit on the floor bites into my bare feet, and my bunkmates, a few dozen boys around my age, mirror my movements with almost identical timing. But when they proceed to stand and straighten their bedding, I hesitate.

I'm caught up in a strange cycle that I know I've repeated thousands of times, but it feels new today. In this moment, something has changed. I stand up and run my fingers over my cropped hair and release a slow breath. I've spent years in this building, sleeping on this very cot, but the memories are wavy, like my mind has been flooded with fog. I press my palms over my eyes, squeezing them shut.

Most of the boys have now begun to change their clothes. None of them speak, and the silence leaves an eerie pall in the air. Across the room, my behavior has caught the attention of a middle-aged Man in Red. I lock eyes with him, and his expression narrows, folding his dark brows inward as he studies my face. It's my first indication I'm doing something wrong, and I swoop down and tug the sheet and blanket over my cot, smoothing the wrinkles. I glimpse up and see him now speaking to another Man in Red, and they both watch me. The pistols on their hips and the menacing sneer on their faces remind me that they're here to keep us in line. And right now, I am out of line.

Not wanting to draw more attention to myself, I hustle to the trunk at the end of my cot and withdraw my uniform. I shrug into the routine brown button-up shirt and matching pants and shove my feet into wool socks and a pair of black boots that pinch my heels. As I reach down to tie the laces, a black mark on my right wrist draws my attention from beneath the cuff of my sleeve. I tug the fabric back and see the thick outline of a triangle tattooed into the tender skin above the tendons and veins. The fingers of my left hand trace the symbol as I search my mind for its significance, but I find a murky void instead of a memory.

Annoyed, my fingers tie the laces, and I stand. I'm a few seconds behind everyone else now, and I scan the room to find them all clicking various weapons onto their belts. In the top of my trunk, beneath where my uniform had been placed, I find a sling and several perfectly smooth gray stones. The pad feels worn and familiar in my hands, and I stroke the braided leather handles. Beside me, a pale-skinned boy with dull eyes and a wild patch of freckles attaches his own sling to his waist.

The shrill screech of a whistle cuts through the room, and I flinch. The trunk lid slips from my fingers and slams shut. I suck in a breath and wait for a reaction from someone, but there is none, so I drop the stones in my pocket as though nothing is out of the ordinary. The boys around me are falling into line, and I step forward to join them as we prepare to leave the building, somewhat aware that we should be heading to retrieve our breakfast now.

Just as we begin to move forward, a firm hand grabs my right arm, and I'm jerked to the side. Panic snarls in my chest as a heavy arm pins me against a cool wall, and I struggle to not grimace as the back of my head smacks into the unforgiving cinder blocks. In front of me stands the same short, stocky Man in Red who had been staring at me earlier. His greasy, blond hair is slicked over to one side, and his deep-set eyes are dark and shifty as they bore into me. He wears a scarlet shirt and black pants, and a small golden triangle is pinned to the left side of his collar. As he opens his thin lips to speak, I inhale the scent of stale alcohol and tobacco, and my stomach clenches with nausea. He grabs my face with a calloused hand and squeezes my cheeks so my lips squish together, and I can't help but feel like an animal being inspected for slaughter.

"What are you doing, boy?" he asks with a sniveling, high-pitched tone. My face drains of blood, and my heart picks up speed as the Red's expression grows more furrowed. The surprise of the encounter has my mind reeling, but I know better than to reply. I feel awake for the first time since I can remember, and I intend to keep it that way.

"What's wrong with this one?" the Red mutters to himself. My heart pounds in my chest with such speed and voracity that I begin to worry the guard will hear it, and my own body will betray me. All at once, the guard releases my face with an apathetic grunt and pushes me towards the door by my shoulder. I'm startled by my sudden propulsion, and I stumble forward into line as relief floods my body.

I follow the silent parade of students as it streams out of the doors and into an alley. The buildings on either side of me are identical — long, gray, and void of visual interest. The only features that stand out against the monochromatic scheme are the doors, which are blood red and resemble nicks and cuts in the buildings' exteriors. I'm tempted to look around, but I train my eyes forward and focus on blending in with the group. The crunching cadence of our boots against the unpaved dirt road fills the otherwise silent air.

"You, too?" a voice whispers to my left. We are now entering a courtyard, and before I can stop myself, I whip my head around to search for the source of the voice. A pair of warm, blue eyes set below a short curtain of straight, black hair meets my gaze. My own eyes widen as I jerk back to face the front. I scan the courtyard and find it swarming with Men in Red. Now is not the time to have a conversation.

"You missed it, too," the voice whispers again, this time as a statement, not a question. There's an urgency to the boy's tone, and I feel the need to respond, but I don't want to get caught again. I mull over his words, wondering what he meant. I begin to dismiss them when something rushes back to me — the gate, the line, the explosion, the vials.

Holy crap. I missed my vaccine. But why would that make a difference in my mental clarity? Is that why I can remember things now? Or did I catch something from the village when I touched the man? That couldn't be it, because this boy didn't touch the man, and he's as aware as I am. The thought triggers an image of the man's pleading face in my mind, and my stomach drops. What had I done to him? And why? I shove the memory down, knowing I need to focus on the bigger issue at hand.

Stealing a glance at him, I wonder if the blue-eyed boy was the one at the gate with me, but I don't speak yet. If I answer his question, I will be admitting that I have broken protocol. And yet I can't convince myself that this is a bad thing.

Even still, I don't want to lose track of one of the only other students who could have answers. Clenching my fists by my sides, I muster my courage and decide to answer him in the briefest way possible. My lips are parched with apprehension, but I turn my head anyways and whisper, "Later."

The boy tilts his head in agreement, his eyes filled with a knowing glint, and then we separate into two different columns that lead to a row of rectangular, black tables. On the other side of the barrier stand female nurses in a white uniform of cargo pants and pressed shirts. Like the Men in Red, they also wear a golden triangle pinned to their collars.

The lines move at a brisk pace, and I am soon handed a tin cup of water and a small, plain brown package. I take my ration and go sit on the ground in my assigned spot within the rows of students in the courtyard. The sky above us is clear and still has the lingering golden-pink hints of dawn at its far edge. The air itself is crisp with the chill of autumn and void of all sounds beyond the shuffling of feet and ripping of packages as everyone eats their breakfast. This place — my home — is desolate and sterile.

I set my cup down and tear at the edge of the wrapper that encases my food. Inside is a skinny, beige block that has no discernible scent. I already know what it will taste like, and I lift it to my lips and take a bite, ripping off a third of the bar. For how little flavor it has, I might as well be chewing the wrapper itself. It settles like a boulder in my stomach and leaves me parched, especially after not receiving my ration of water last night for some reason. As I reach for the cup by my side, a figure casts a shadow over me, and a large boot unceremoniously knocks my cup over with a loud clamor, spilling its contents across the dusty ground. My lips begin to part in protest when I notice the color of the shirt the person is wearing. It's red. I stare out across the quadrant, waiting for whatever comes next.

"Here, kid," the Red says with a smooth voice. He kneels beside me and places a new cup of water in my hand. "Sorry about that." I dare to look at the face that is now inches from mine. The Red's skin is dark brown, and his black hair is clipped short. A faint shadow of stubble hangs over his thin cheeks and sculpted jaw. This man is strong and fit — that much is obvious. And to my horror, there's something in the guard's expression. He knows.

I gulp despite the dryness in my mouth and turn away as fear seizes my body. I don't want to be captured or re-vaccinated, assuming that's the reason why I can all of a sudden remember things. I consider running off, but that's a foolish idea. One glimpse at the guns strapped to the belts of the Reds is enough of a warning. I sigh and prepare myself for the worst, and then the Red grabs the knocked-over cup, stands back up, and walks off without another word. I blink repeatedly, unsure why he didn't say anything. I know better than to speak after him, so instead I tear off another bite of food and stare at my shoes.

2

"What's the news for today, Colonel?" the Man asks as he stares at the spiraling flames that rise deep from the heart of the fire that heats his office. It's early autumn, far too warm for a fire for most people, but he enjoys the crackling sound and earthen smell it produces and is content to sit shirtless in front of it for hours on end with little regard as to the comfort of his staff.

"Everything is status quo, sir. But..." the Colonel begins, and he pauses to relax the trembling in his voice. Typically, his updates included nothing unusual besides a few arrests throughout the country, but this one provides the looming effect one might feel when awaiting a death sentence. The stifling heat combines with his nerves and gives him the sensation that he's suffocating, and he yearns to loosen the collar of his starched shirt, but he knows better. Only his eyes move as they flick over the room's interior, filled with worn, imported furniture and covered wall to wall in musty, outdated books.

"But what, Colonel?" the Man prompts between raspy coughs, which he muffles with a tired handkerchief.

"We seem to have a slight problem, sir. There's been an incident on the Compound of Village K," he says. The Man cocks his head but does not move otherwise.

"What kind of incident?"

"Well, sir, some of the older students... well, they missed their vaccine. The process was disrupted following an explosion in the kitchen," he almost whispers.

"They missed their what, Colonel?" the Man asks, dismissing the news of the explosion altogether. The cooks on the compounds are notoriously dim-witted, and minor explosions such as this (often involving a cigarette and a gas stove) take place every once in a while to the surprise of no one.

"Their serum, sir. The Crystal. Should we round them up and proceed as usual?" the Colonel says. He's met with an extended period of silence while the Man weighs his options.

"Do nothing, Colonel," the Man replies at last. He pulls himself up from a faded, red armchair and scratches through his thick, black hair.

"Do nothing, sir?" the Colonel asks, the surprise evident in his tone. He had expected to be reprimanded for the carelessness of the staff.

"You heard me. This might be the type of experiment we've been waiting for," the Man replies. "But no one outside of our circle is to know about them, you hear? Not even the Reds on the Compound."

"Forgive me for asking, sir, but what do you mean by experiment?"

"You're going to watch those students, Colonel, the ones who missed the vaccine. I want them followed. I want to know their every move. But don't intervene with them unless they start to, how should I put it... test their limits. Do what you need to do, but don't let them know we're watching, or the consequences will fall on more than Village K, if you know what I mean." With that, he saunters past his companion and exits the room, leaving the Colonel to brace himself on the back of a wooden chair and calm his nerves.

————

When breakfast concludes, the courtyard fills with movement as students make their way through neighboring alleys and enter many of the buildings. It's time for classes to begin, I realize. Memories of various rooms and books slide through my mind as I recall the courses I've been forced to take, which include basic math, literature, history, and skill-based exercise... fighting skills, to be exact.

As I return my empty cup and discard the wrapper, the memory of yesterday's mission comes back again, and the desperation on the man's face as I shoved him towards the truck haunts me. I hadn't even flinched, as if I didn't care that all he did was visit a friend. Did I care? Was what he did *that* terrible? The hollow feeling in my stomach tells me something is wrong, and I shouldn't have done that. But those were my orders, right?

I remember the lead Man in Red, Clive, issuing them. I see him now, standing in the middle of the courtyard, as tall and broad as the side of a building, with narrowed eyes that slide over each of the Young Ones as they move to their first class. I look away before his gaze reaches me. Why did I follow his orders without question? It has to have something to do with the vaccine.

I mull over the idea as I walk to Block C, on the south end of the Compound, to attend my literature class. Each step brings back more and more information as images continue to pour out from my mental vault. I see faces of all ages and genders, etched with sorrow and mouths agape in silent screams as my hands close around their wrists and shoulders. I hunt people, chasing them down and fighting them when they resist, aware that their strength is no match for mine. I kick in doors and throw people around, telling them which protocols they have broken and ignoring their pleas for mercy. With every memory, my stomach continues to drop until I taste bile. I am a monster. I look at my hands as I walk, expecting my skin to be covered in blood, but they're clean, void of any blemish aside from the triangle tattooed on the inside of my wrist. It's an illusion, a lie.

I soon reach my classroom and choke back the urge to vomit as I pause beyond the doorway. Several other students — boys and girls — are already inside, sitting in their assigned seats. A stack of books rest on the wooden table by the door, and I grab one as I proceed to my seat, avoiding eye contact with Stern, the soft-spoken Man in Red, who teaches the class. I hope he didn't notice my hesitancy. Once I'm sitting, I dare to look at him. Hidden behind a bristly mustache and a smudged pair of thick, black-framed glasses, he seems to be in some sort of panic. He fidgets behind his desk, which stands at the front corner of the room, and he alternates between shuffling through a chaotic pile of papers and wiping his damp forehead with a white handker-chief. He doesn't seem to notice me, and a small bit of tension seeps from my shoulders as we await instruction.

Stern finally sighs and stands up, giving up his search. He takes attendance with a glance and begins the day's lesson. He instructs us to read a poem written almost thirty years ago when Belstrana was at war with its neighboring countries. We had lost the war and were forced to sign a treaty that sent our country spiraling into a decade of economic depression and political strife.

"The author remains unknown, but the message is as rele-vant as ever," he tells us with a soft voice, concluding his intro-duction. I flip through my book to the correct one and read the poem, which I realize in an instant I already know by heart.

When the sun sets over our forested land
And the flowers withdraw their bloom,
Turn not on each other or lose faith and hope,
For our leaders will perish the gloom.
Believe in your heart, and listen to me
That alone we don't know wrong from right.
But offer yourself for what's best for us all,
Your sacrifice will change night to light.

"You see, students. When you think not about yourself but about what's best for Belstrana, we all prosper. Don't be afraid to make the necessary sacrifices to lift up your fellow countrymen. We are all in it together, and without mutual sacrifice, we will all fail. Now, can anyone give me an example of some of the things the author encourages us to give up?" There is a quiver in his voice, which he tries to conceal by clearing his throat, but the grief in his drooped shoulders cannot be hidden. If I weren't already so annoyed by the blatant manipulation in the lesson, I might feel sorry for him.

Every student in the room raises his or her right hand. I mimic them, worried I will draw attention to myself if I do not participate. Stern focuses his attention on a homely-looking girl in the front, left desk of the classroom, closest to the door. "We'll go around the room, starting with Number One," he says as he points towards the girl.

"Family, sir," she replies and then withdraws her hand from the air. Without hesitation, the next student, another girl with a silvery-white ponytail speaks.

"Television, sir," she adds, and Stern nods his approval. The answers continue to flow through the room like a line of mechanical dominoes, and with each response, my irritation increases. I already know what each student will say before they speak. Trained in how to answer, they rattle off things like extra food, music, art, toys, and books. These are all items that can be sacrificed without raising too many eyebrows, I realize. I wonder if they were given up or if they were taken. Irritation begins to be replaced with anger.

When the series of choreographed answers lands on me, I know I'm supposed to say "cars," but my voice drops and I say, "Individualism, sir." Stern's eyebrows twitch, and I duck my head. But he doesn't move or correct me.

The line of answers continues with the boy behind me who adds jewelry to the list. I peek up from my book as the next student says, "computers."

Stern, now sitting at his desk again, has his eyes trained on my face. His hands hold his handkerchief in midair as though he was going to wipe his glistening forehead but was frozen before he could do it. I drop my eyes again, knowing he must have decided to wait until after class to inflict his punishment on me. I need to keep my mouth shut from now on... if there still is an opportunity for a "from now on" after Stern gets a hold of me.

After fifty minutes, the bell rings, and everyone stands up, places their worn, red textbooks in a stack by the teacher's desk, and files out of the door. I try to blend in as much as possible, and I almost make it to the hallway when Stern grabs my shoulder and redirects me towards the other side of the room. My pulse quickens as my dread increases, especially after the last student leaves the room. Stern closes the door behind him and then scurries around the room, pulling the white shades down over the two small windows on the far wall. If he looked upset at the beginning of class, he now looks close to hyperventilation, and I'm not sure if it's from fear or from anger. The sheen of sweat on his forehead glistens above his twitchy brow, and he removes his glasses to wipe the lenses with his handkerchief.

"I... I had heard... it must be true," Stern mutters. Unsure if he's speaking to me or to himself, I stay quiet and watch him pace between rows of desks. Stern jerks his head towards me and crosses the room in four large steps so his face is now inches from mine. It takes great effort for me not to step away from him, but for some reason, I don't think he means to harm me or turn me in.

"Tell me. What have you noticed?" he asks with a low tone, his eyes steady for the first time since class began.

"Sir?" I reply, not willing to expose myself quite yet.

"There's a rumor that some of you missed your vaccination. That amid all of the chaos yesterday afternoon, they forgot to finish the job..." He pauses for a moment and the corners of his mustache droop as he frowns. "Why wouldn't they find you later, after the crisis was dealt with? Surely they know who you are. Their records are immaculate," he adds.

I struggle to keep my expression indifferent. His questions could come from a place of genuine interest, or they could be a setup.

"Don't play dumb with me. I know you're a neutral right now. Speak up," he says. The handkerchief in his hands trembles, and his breaths are short and uneven. Stern is as nervous as I am right now, if not more.

"I don't know what a neutral is, sir," I say after several seconds. It's the safest answer I can think of.

"A non-vaccinated student. It doesn't happen often, and when it does, the students are caught well before they reach this point," he replies.

"And what point is that?" I ask. Stern stares at me with his head cocked to the side, measuring my words.

"Cognizance, August. You're thinking and aware of what's around you. I know you are. Your eyes give it away," he replies. I take a few hurried steps away from my interrogator and prepare to bolt. He must sense what I'm about to do, because he throws his hands up by his side, dropping the handkerchief. "Stop! It's okay. I'm not going to turn you in."

I pause mid-stride a few feet from the door. "Why?" I ask. He shuffles forward and closes the gap between us.

"Because they already know it's you. I can't figure out why they haven't cornered you yet. Like I said, we've had incidents like this before, but they've never gone on for this long before. Why would they let you and the others go neutral?" he mumbles. The rapid tapping of his foot fills the otherwise silent room.

"The others — do you know who they are?" I ask. I'm sure I met the other boy this morning, but I don't remember his name, much less who the girls were.

"I'm not sure who they are, of course, but I heard there were four total. Two boys and two girls." His description is the same as my memory.

"And you don't have any idea why they haven't caught us yet?" I ask, feeling my pulse tick faster.

Stern's frown drops even more as he says, "I don't know. It might seem like a good thing to you right now, but I wouldn't doubt there's something underhanded going on." My fingers involuntarily clench into fists. I can't get caught again. If what Stern says is true, I have to get off of the Compound before the Reds change their minds.

"What should I do then?" I ask, trying to suppress my panic by shifting my weight from one foot to the other.

"For starters, you can avoid idiotic responses like the one you gave in my class earlier. You're lucky it was me here and not someone else," he snips. I sigh and duck my head. He's right. I have to play by their rules if I want to remain unseen.

"I'm sorry, sir. Everything seems so prerecorded and trite." I sigh. "It won't happen again, sir."

Stern snorts. "Of course it's prerecorded and trite. That's what we do here. That's why they forced me here after they closed the universities. I didn't want to be a Red, unlike most of the rest of them. I didn't want anything to do with the Foundation, but they threatened to harm my family if I didn't come here and spoon feed you their garbage. No need to think for yourself when the Foundation can think for you." His voice is heavy with sarcasm, and he takes a deep breath to calm himself.

"Well, they've let you go neutral for some reason, and since I don't know what that reason is, you need to play along. Keep your mouth shut and act like nothing has changed since before the explosion. It's not likely, but maybe if you don't give them any indication that you are neutral, they'll let it go," he says. "But you've got to quit looking around so much. As far as they're concerned, you're a machine to be used at their discretion." His words send a chill over my skin, and I shiver.

"I can't help but think..." he begins. One of my eyebrows rises as I wait for him to finish his statement. He wrings his hands together and whispers, "If you can get away from the Compound, you might be perfect. Your strength alone could take out thirty Reds."

I move my head away, confused even more than I had been. After all, Stern is a Red. Why would I hurt him? "What do you mean?" I ask. Stern opens his mouth to speak, but a sudden rap on the door startles us away from one another with a panicked jerk. Worried it's another Red, I stand at attention, feet together and back straight while Stern scurries to open the door, picking up his handkerchief along the way. His face is pallid as he pulls the door open and reveals a towering, lean Man in Red out in the hallway.

"Clive needs to speak with you, Stern," the man snips. I can see enough of him via my peripheral vision that I can tell he's staring past Stern and at me.

"What... what for?" Stern stutters, halfheartedly blocking the door with his body. It does no good since the Red is at least eight inches taller than him.

"How should I know?" the Red says. "Now go on. He doesn't like to be kept waiting."

Stern takes one final glance back at me and then rushes from the room, leaving behind his papers and leather satchel. I stand motionless, waiting on the Red to make the next move. After several long moments of him staring at me, I begin to feel like his eyes are boring holes into the side of my face. I'm two seconds away from running when he speaks again.

"Shouldn't you be getting to your next class?" he asks. I take this as my cue to leave, and I turn my tightly-wound body to address him.

"Yes, sir," I say as I brush past him into the hallway.

3

The Colonel clears his throat. "Sir?"

"What now, Colonel?" the Man replies. He sits in his usual seat across from the mantle, and his damp, white undershirt clings to his chest. The hot smell of stale body odor mingles with the sweet scent of alcohol, and the Colonel fights the urge to cover his nose.

"I just got off the phone and wanted to update you about the situation in Village K's Compound, sir."

"Well?" he says and then slurps a swig of scotch from his glass and smacks his lips.

"It seems as though their minds are rewiring. Their memories are coming back, or at least it appears that way. But they have yet to act on anything," the Colonel replies.

"What does that mean, Colonel? The goal here is to see if they can lead us to the rebels. Are they going to do it or not?" He rattles the ice in his otherwise empty glass, and a skittish secretary enters the room, takes it from him, and refills it.

"I'm not sure, sir. As of right now, they are following our rules but are expressing a bit of curiosity. It's too early to tell how they'll react long term or if any of the rebel Reds are contacting them, especially since we don't know who the specific traitors are."

"Very well. Continue watching them. We need to stop this rebellion before it starts, and if I don't miss my guess, that explosion was no accident. Someone's trying to use them for the movement, and we're going to find out who they are. Understand?"

"Yes, sir."

"Let me know if anything changes."

"Yes, sir," the Colonel replies and rushes from the office, frantic for fresh air.

———

I'VE BEEN IN THE TRAINING ROOM FOR AT LEAST THIRTY minutes, and even though I know I risk revealing myself every time I do it, I can't stop looking across the room at a girl. Around us, Men in Red pace through the facility like disciplined fire ants, and every few seconds, she glances up and studies the scene. Her long, curly, brown hair is pulled into a low ponytail at the base of her neck, and it cascades over her left shoulder, shining against the faded, drab brown of her uniform. At this moment, her large eyes narrow around her thin nose, confusion clouding her face. None of the other students break from their bland expressions, so why her? Could she have been one of the other three at the gate with me?

I roll my fingers over the leather-wrapped handle of a dagger, and a flash of light from overhead bounces off the blade and snaps me back to attention. The room around me is divided into several sections based on our skill set. In the far corner, diagonal from where I practice throwing knives, other students train with ropes, making knots and lassos and other tangled entrapments. Beside them, more Young Ones take turns lashing out with thin, silvery chains or expandable, black bow staffs. Closest to me, a few yards away, some of the youngest students in the room test their skills with leather slings, which is my best weapon. Secured to my belt, it rests on my hip, and the weight of it provides a fleeting moment of security.

The brunette girl, whoever she is, stands on the other side of the sling group. Her slender fingers are clasped in a white-knuckled grip around the handle of a long, black whip, which hangs like a tense snake by her side. She eyes the series of targets placed on various ledges along the brick wall in front of her, planning her execution. Within ten seconds, the lot of them have been either shattered or knocked down, and pieces are still rattling on the floor as she coils the whip and clasps it to her belt. I clench my teeth together, afraid my jaw will fall open from awe. She made it graceful. It was violent and loud and harsh, but her fluidity and poise made it seem like a dance. None of the other students around her come close to her skill.

From the corner of my eye, I see a thick red figure — an approaching guard — and I jerk my head forward, narrowing my concentration on the paper outline of a human torso that hangs in front of a suspended, wooden wall. I don't even have to think about what I'm doing as I bring the knife up, feeling the cool blade between the tips of my fingers. I exhale and release the dagger, pitching it forward across the no-man's land between the target and myself. The blade slices straight through the center of the paper and sinks into the wall with a solid thump. The guard lets out a satisfied grunt and moves down the line to the next student.

I use the time it takes to retrieve the dagger as an opportunity to steal another glance at the girl. There's no mistaking her movements from across the room. She stands out, big time. I wonder if that's her natural state or if she's doped up like everyone else, but it doesn't seem possible. She's too alert. Her eyes skirt across the room until they unexpectedly lock with mine. I almost gasp but manage to clamp my lips together before the exclamation can leave my mouth. My cheeks grow warm as I remember Stern's warning. If I have any chance of getting out of here, I have to be careful and ignore distractions, even tempting ones. Even still, a small part of me hopes she's one of the three others.

As I jog back to my starting point, I study the movement within the different sections. Children, some of whom must be no older than ten, practice with the ferocity and skill of adults, and they use their weapons with lethal force. More memories of arrests and battles struggle to break free, but I shove them down. It's becoming more and more obvious that the lifeless expressions on the faces of the Young Ones have to be connected to the vaccine I should have gotten. It seems strange to me that it can suppress personal cognition without impeding our abilities to learn rudimentary skills like reading and simple math, let alone combat training. However it works, it's wicked and dangerous. I return to the line and roll my shoulders, trying to release some of the tense knots. It doesn't matter right now that I know how the vaccine works, because that information doesn't change the fact that I'm stuck here, acting like a brainless pawn. I might as well keep my head down and do what I'm told before they discover it's an act.

I spend the next hour throwing my dagger over and over again into the same notch so that with every strike, the divot gets deeper, exposing the fresh grain within. Uneasiness settles in like a canon shot in my gut, and it leaves a seething, angry hole in me that grows wider the longer I stay silent and wrestle with my thoughts. By the time the class ends, I'm so frustrated I can barely function. I need to know the truth. I hesitate for a moment before I set the dagger back on the table beside the others. I want to keep it with me, but I can't risk it in case a Red notices one missing. Besides, I have a pocket knife that I can use should I need it.

Just as I fall in line to exit the building, I catch a glimpse of the brunette girl. I had almost forgotten about her, and my pulse quickens as she approaches me. Determination is written across her face, and it's obvious to me now that she had to have been at the gate. I shoot her a quick glare, not out of menace, but because I don't want her to speak here. Not yet, anyways. There are too many people around. She tilts her head forward enough for me to notice, and her face relaxes while her pace slows. She sidles up beside me and looks straight ahead.

"We need to talk," she whispers as we walk through the door. I flick my eyes towards her and give her the faintest of nods. Still surrounded by a swarm of other students, I take the initiative and go off course, veering away from everyone else through a maze of alleys that connect barracks and classrooms, all the while listening for her soft footsteps behind me. When we are alone, I come to a stop and face her, keeping a few feet between us in case someone walks up on us.

"What do you know?" I ask her, getting straight to the point. It's not that I don't want to talk more with her. But now isn't the time.

"I... You first," she whispers. Her hands balance on the curve of her hips, and loose strands of her hair dance around her face. Golden sunlight falls perfectly over the rooftop behind me and casts her in a warm glow. Her eyes are a deep green, flecked with gold. I swallow and then stop breathing. A memory creeps past my eyes, of me as a small child, running through a field of sunflowers towards a woman with warm brown eyes and a gentle smile. Just as soon as it arrives, the memory fades, and I rub my temples with my fingertips. I had had a family. That woman was my mother.

"Are you okay?" the brunette girl asks, shifting her weight from one leg to the other. I drop my hands and shake my head, returning to the conversation at hand. There would be time to dwell on that memory later, or at least that's what I hope.

"Yeah, I'm fine. Look, there was an explosion at the gate yesterday. Do you remember that?" I ask, searching her face.

"I do," she says. "You were there, too. I knew I remembered you." Her lips purse as I nod.

"Listen, we shouldn't talk here. It's too risky," I say. She glances over her shoulder and shifts her weight again. I frown, hoping it's the circumstances that are making her uncomfortable and not me. "Can you meet me tonight?"

"How can I trust you?" she asks, brows furrowed.

I study her for a few seconds, trying not to let my gaze linger for too long, but I can't help myself. Truth be told, I'm not sure why she should trust me or how I can even trust her. I know nothing about her, but something inside propels me to believe she's as much of a victim in all of this as I am. I run my hand down my face and sigh.

"I can't give you a great reason why you should trust me other than the fact that you and I are some of the only people in this entire place who know something's up. And I'm betting we have a better chance of figuring it out together than we do apart," I say. Her shoulders relax a little.

"Okay," she says. "Where do you want to meet?" I pull my eyes from her and search the buildings around us. There's a red door several yards away, and a white sign above it reads STORAGE in crisp, black paint. It's as good a place as any.

I point at it and say, "There. We'll meet inside the storage room tonight two hours after lights out." She opens her mouth to speak but slams it shut as her eyes glaze over. Before I can ask her what's wrong, she walks away from me. I look over my shoulder. A small boy, dressed in brown, moves towards us, and

I take off in the opposite direction as the girl. I resist the urge to stare at him as we pass one another, but I get enough of a glance to know he has red hair. As soon as I'm out of the alley, I dart towards my Belstranan history class in which I'm reminded that, according to my instructor, Belstrana can do no wrong in the world of politics and socio-political decisions. I refrain from voicing my disagreement.

Lunch is an identical repeat of breakfast, including the spilled water and suspiciously kind Red. Though I know better, I dismiss it as a strange coincidence and then head off to another training class. This time, the room is filled only with boys, and weapons are not allowed. We focus on hand-to-hand combat, which includes a mixture of martial arts, boxing, and wrestling. Around me, boys pair off under the supervision of a host of burly-looking Reds. Some wrestle, some kick, some punch, but nobody winces when they're hit. It's bizarre... another effect of the vaccine, I guess.

When my opportunity comes around, I square off against a blond boy with a long nose and large ears that poke from the sides of his head like wobbly bowls. He appears to be a year or two younger I am, and he approaches me on the mat and waits with his hands by his sides. A Red approaches us and gives us the go-ahead to begin. Recalling years of close-combat lessons, I relax my knees and bring my fists up to protect my face.

Without hesitation, the boy lunges forward and swipes his right fist towards my chin, but I bob out of the way, and his punch rushes past me. I keep my hands up and wait, bouncing on the balls of my feet. I know that, given my larger frame and older age, I could crush this boy, but I don't want to do that. I have no reason to hit him other than the orders coming from the Reds around us. If I can let this kid wear himself out, then I can use his exhaustion against him and defeat him with less physical force.

The boy runs forward again, spinning the heel of his boot towards the back of my knee, but he never makes contact as I jump much higher than I think I should be able to and avoid the blow. As soon as my feet make contact with the mat again, the boy plants his feet and kicks once more. The one-sided fight continues for several more minutes, and I find myself astonished by my own speed and agility. When he staggers a little bit, I push forward and land a series of punches against the boy's firm gut. His spine curls in as he stumbles backward, but he shows no sign of pain. He catches his balance and ambles towards me. I take the opportunity to flick my eyes across the room and see we're the last ones fighting in this round. One person from every other pair has either been pinned or knocked out. I need to end this now to avoid suspicion, especially as the Reds around us begin to pace with impatience.

I don't want to knock the boy out, so I wrack my brain and choose a less abrasive method to end the fight. I crouch low and wait for the boy to get close enough, and when he does, I kick out my heel and scoop the boy's legs out from under him. He crumples to the ground, his hair falling over his creased forehead, but he doesn't cry out in pain. I seize the opportunity and drop down, placing the crook of my elbow around the boy's neck, and I hold it secure, squeezing and squeezing. His legs flail, and his fingers claw at my arms and face, but I keep my face neutral. *I'm just doing what I'm supposed to do*, I tell myself.

Behind me, a Red hollers, "Enough!"

I release the boy's neck and stand back up. A faint line of blood trickles from his nose, and guilt crashes into me harder than any punch could have. I did that to him, but I didn't need to. I want to extend my hand to help the boy off the floor, but I can't. I can't reveal myself. The boy wipes his nose with the back of his hand, and his expression remains mild. Behind me, a Red chuckles.

"Playing cat and mouse with him, huh, August? Didn't think you kids were capable of having fun while you fight... You'd have killed him if I hadn't stopped you. Good job," he says and slaps me on the back.

I can't stop myself from wincing, but it's not the slap that causes it. I didn't remember until now that it was a kill-hold. I thought it would simply knock him out. And I hadn't intended to "play" with my opponent... I just hadn't wanted to hurt him anymore than necessary. My stomach churns, but I'm not given the chance to think about anything for too long before we're reassigned to different partners for the next sparring match. And so it continues for another hour — one fight after another. For the rest of the time, I avoid anything that could be miscon-strued as cruelty and end the fights quickly with a knock-out punch to my opponent's head. With every body that slumps to the ground, my guilt grows until I have to fight for air.

When twenty minutes of class remain, the Reds direct us outside to an obstacle course that weaves through the Compound. I've run the two-mile obstacle-laden track around the Compound countless times, climbing over various barriers and making multiple twenty-foot leaps onto the roofs of several buildings. One of the lead Reds tells us we have fifteen minutes to complete it. From a distance, I watch the younger students move at an unnatural speed, bounding over obstacles and climbing with such grace that it looks as though they float over the ropes.

When it's my turn, I test my ability to match the perfor-mances of the other boys and discover not only can I do the same things as them, but I can also do them better and faster, and I pass many of them within minutes after I begin. I suppress the grin that longs to form across my face as I take three firm steps and propel myself on to the gritty black shingles of a rooftop and then leap across the streets below. Fear does not exist in the face of physical obstacles for me. I am a machine, trained with skills beyond normalcy, and the thought both delights me and horrifies me.

4

After dinner, I attend the evening ceremony in the Compound's courtyard. We stand at attention in rigid formations, grouped by age and skill, and I am in the front line nearest the flag. Speakers overhead blare the dramatic national anthem while a few Young Ones lower Belstrana's flag, a white-and-red-striped rising sun set on a black backdrop. This is my first real opportunity to see the magnitude and makeup of the Compound. The students to my immediate left and right seem intimidating and formidable, and I know they must be some of the best students on the Compound. This must mean I'm one of the best students on the Compound, which makes me even more confused about why they haven't revaccinated me yet. I wonder if the triangle has anything to do with that. Of all the things I *can* remember, why not that?

When we retire to our barracks, I shower and dress for bed. At the same time as every other boy, I lie down on my cot and pull the wool blanket up to my chin, leaving just enough space for me to breathe. My eyes wander up to stare at the rafters overhead, illuminated by a patch of moonlight that creeps across the floor. I replay the events of the day in my head, and my hatred of the Compound continues to fester and grow, even if I'm some-what thankful for the skills they've taught me.

I feel used, betrayed. Nobody asked me if this was the life I wanted. They — the Foundation — forced me into it, and what's worse is that I had no clue it was happening, which means none of the other Young Ones know what they're doing either. It *has* to be the vaccine. It makes us forget who we are and what we want. It transforms us into machines, willing to obey whatever orders we're given. And it ticks me off. I try to channel my rage to keep me awake, but eventually, my pulse slows and breaths deepen. Despite my attempts to stay awake for my meeting with the girl, my eyes drift shut.

———

WITHIN MOMENTS, I FIND MYSELF STANDING IN THE MIDDLE of a small, tidy garden. A warm breeze rustles across my bare arms, and my thumbs are hooked around the straps of a worn pair of denim overalls. A curious bee flits amongst the springy tops of carrots until it disappears behind the flowing layers of a faded yellow dress, worn by a young woman.

She kneels between rows of leafy, green vegetables and tugs at a carrot until, with a small spray of dirt, it releases from the ground. She drops it into a brown wicker basket, and it lands with a soft pat. With her right hand, she pushes her long, thick, black braid back over her shoulder. A faint smear of earth lingers on her sun-kissed cheek. I'm mesmerized by the site of her simple, yet undeniable beauty. She is an angel, and I dig my toes deeper into the warm, damp soil as if I could hide the blatant adoration on my face like the dirt hides my small feet.

"What are you doing, August, you silly little thing?" she chimes as she rises from the ground. I twist my fingers behind my back and giggle in response, tucking my chin down to hide my

amusement. She claps her hands together, and a thin cloud of dust catches the sunlight and glitters around her. After wiping her hands on her dress, she turns her attention back to me, and she waves the friendly bee away from her shoulder. A sly grin creeps across her face, and I giggle even more as she lowers into a crouch with her hands raised in front of her face like claws. Though her fingers are truly too delicate to intimidate anyone, my eyes widen at the game, and I let out a yelp. She stifles an amused laugh, and sensing her mistake, she contorts her face in an attempt to prevent any others from escaping.

"I'm going to get you!" she squeals as she runs towards me with her arms still extended in front of her. I throw my head back in laughter and sprint as fast as my small legs can carry me between the rows of vegetation. But rather than running away from her, I run towards her. She is my mother, and my heart swells under the pressure of my love for her. We reach one another, and I throw myself into her outstretched arms. Surrounded by a chorus of giggles, she twirls us around in circles, making her dress flow out like a buttery yellow flower.

"You're getting so big! I can barely lift you," she says as I wrap my legs around her slim waist. I lean my head against her shoulder, and she brushes some of the dirt off my cheek and then follows the movement with a soft peck on my nose.

"I'm not that big, Momma. I'm only three!" I reply, extending my fingers to show my age.

"Silly, you have four fingers up," she replies and taps my pinky finger. I clench it back into my fist, and she laughs.

"Three!" I reply. She squeezes me in approval and then sets me back down into the garden.

———

WITH A START, I JERK UPRIGHT IN MY COT. AROUND ME,

the other boys sleep soundlessly, and I scan the room in a panic to see if anyone saw my sudden movement. When I decide no one else is awake, I relax onto my side and wipe the sweat from face. The dream lingers in my head, and I focus on the fading image of my mother. A surge of love explodes in my chest, flooding my body like water released from a dam. It's an unfamiliar emotion, and it overwhelms me and sends my pulse racing. I have a mother somewhere, and a father, too. It's a comforting thought, but it lasts a mere moment.

The relief erodes as I remember where I am. A swirling series of questions settle into an uneasy lump in my chest, and I dig my fingers into my mattress to suppress the moisture that pools in my eyes. How long have I been here? And why would she send me here? Is she alive? And if so, doesn't she realize what takes place on the Compound?

I rest my head back on my thin pillow and cross my arms, hugging my chest. A scream builds in my lungs, but I swallow it down. The last thing I need to do is wake up the whole barrack and alert the Reds. With that thought, I remember the meeting I had scheduled with the brunette girl. I curse under my breath. There's no telling how long I was asleep. I hope she's still there waiting on me.

I slip out of my cot, shove my bare feet into my boots, and creep between rows of sleeping boys towards the exit. The doors are unlocked — I guess locks are not necessary when you have some sort of mind control over everyone inside — and I check the street for guards before sneaking out into the night. I'm met with a blast of crisp, autumn air, and the light of the waxing moon pierces through the thin, silvery cloud cover, providing just enough illumination for me to find my way back to the storage building.

As I hurry through the alleys, my nerves build with anticipation. I'm not sure if it's because I might get some answers or because I'll be seeing the beautiful girl again. Most likely, it's both. With a quick exhale, I pull open the door and step inside, greeted by darkness and the faint smell of mildew. The door clicks as I push it shut, and I squint into the blackness to search for the girl. A female voice startles me before I can get too far into the room.

"Is that you?" she whispers from several yards away, hidden in the shadows.

"Yeah," I say. "Where are you?" A flash of flickering light erupts to my right as she strikes up a match.

"Right here," she replies, and I detect her faint smile beyond the tiny flame. My breath hitches in my throat at the site of her, and I shuffle forward to join her on the floor. We sit beneath a window that flanks the right side of the door, and I try to figure out what to say to her as the flame dies out and darkness surrounds us again. It's almost easier not seeing her, I realize, and I roll the tension from my shoulders.

"I'm August," I say as my eyes adjust and her features become visible under the soft, ambient glow of lamps several yards down the road.

"Elisa," she whispers.

"Sorry I'm late."

"It's okay. I'm glad you came," she says. Pleased, the corners of my mouth turn up.

"So, what do you know?" I ask, and she proceeds to tell me her version of the last twenty-four hours. It's similar to mine, filled with confusion and anger, but there's something else in her voice. She's sad, I realize. Distraught. But I don't know how to comfort her or even if I should.

"Do you think whatever is in the shots is what keeps everyone so vacant?" she asks.

"It's the one thing that makes sense. We didn't get them, and we're the only ones who have any bloody clue what's going on around here," I reply. A vision of the black-haired boy flashes through my mind, and I remember that there are two more of us. I don't mention it, though, not yet.

"True," she confirms. "And we don't know why they haven't caught us yet?"

"No. But we can't wait around for answers. I think we need to leave this place before they change their minds," I say.

"What do you mean? Aren't we pretty much stuck here? You've seen the gates. We might be able to jump high, but there's no way we can get over the walls surrounding the Compound," she says. I understand where she's coming from, but we at least have to try. Why not take the training the Reds gave us and use it against them?

"You saw what we can do today. We're unstoppable. What good are our skills to us if we can't use them to escape? First chance I get, I'm out of here," I say. "And you should come with me. It's a matter of time until they revaccinate us." Heat floods my cheeks at my own brazenness, and I'm thankful she can't see it.

She's quiet for several moments, and I lean my head back against the cool wall while waiting for her response. The pale moonlight has crept close enough to her through the window that I can see her chewing on her fingernails with a distant expression on her face. After several minutes, she looks up and locks eyes with me, and I feel myself get pulled into her.

"We can't leave them. It wouldn't be right," she says. And just like that, I jump back out. My mouth drops open in disbelief, and I study her face to see if she's joking.

"Are you serious? We're prisoners here. They're holding us against our will," I spit, annoyed by her hesitancy.

"I'm not talking about leaving the Men in Red," she hastens to say while shaking her head. "I'm talking about the rest of *us* — the Young Ones. We can't abandon them to a lifetime of drug-induced fighting. We don't even know the whole story behind why they use us to do their fighting. We can't leave them until we know they aren't going to be harmed."

"Then you won't be going anywhere for a long time," a female voice chimes in from across the room. I jump up into a protective crouch, edging myself in front of Elisa.

"Who's there?" I ask, cursing myself for not having brought my sling or knife with me. I can't see anyone through the darkness, and my fists curl in front of my face, ready to strike if necessary.

"Oh, calm down. It's just me," the voice says. A girl saunters out of the shadows, illuminated by the faint, golden glow that streams through the window. I recognize her instantly as the other girl who had been at the gate with us. Her light blond hair is brushed back into a long, braided ponytail. She's far more petite than Elisa, and there's a menacing quality to her face that doesn't seem to match her size.

"Who are...?" Elisa begins to ask.

"The name's Nikola, first of all. Secondly, I've been watching you all day, Elisa. You should pay more attention to your surroundings, by the way. I slipped in here right after you did and you didn't even notice. Anyways," she continues, crossing her arms over her chest, "I think I can help."

"You're the fourth one," I say, and Elisa cocks her head to the side as Nikola smirks.

"Wait... who's the third? You know already?" Elisa asks.

"A boy. He sleeps in the same bunk as me," I reply and then turn my attention back to Nikola. "Now, what are you talking about?" I say, lowering my fists a few inches. She's wearing the telltale white uniform pajamas that Elisa and I both have on, and her sharp features have a definite youthful quality.

"We're their soldiers. They're not going to let us get away," she states.

"But why would they use children? What's wrong with the Men in Red?" Elisa asks, leaning in towards Nikola with interest.

"Isn't it obvious? Nobody's going to fight against their own child," she says. "Using children gives the Foundation the ultimate upper-hand. You know how this place works — nonstop training and lessons on how great President Karlmann is and how the 'citizens' have to be controlled and how it's all for our own good. It's total garbage. Or is that just me?" she asks.

"No, it's us, too," I say, relaxing back on my heels. "So what do you suggest?"

"Leave, of course," Nikola replies, looking bored.

"Seriously?" Elisa asks. I can tell by the edge in her tone that her patience is beginning to wane.

"We'll do it together. Leaving this prison will be safer if we all go at the same time," Nikola replies.

Elisa waves her hands back and forth and says, "No way. I'm not leaving them. I already told August."

"And what would you rather do?" Nikola asks. "Stay here and wait until they tire of watching us run around like idiots and then let them revaccinate us? No thanks. You can do that if you want, but I'm out of here the first chance I get, and I'm not coming back."

Elisa takes a deep breath and rubs her temples. "Okay. Say your plans work and you *do* escape. Where are you going to go? We don't have a clue what's outside of the Compound. It could be even worse out there than in here. You're stupid if you think you've got it all figured out. We're all confused here. None of us knows enough to make any sort of call right now, especially one that involves leaving a bunch of little kids," Elisa says. Nikola sneers in response, and I suppress a groan.

"Well, let me ask: isn't the fact alone that they're using children to fight their battles for them enough of an argument for us to get out of here while we still can? Whatever twisted game they're playing, they're using *us* as their weapons, and it isn't right, regardless of the dribble they teach us in class about how great Belstrana is," Nikola says.

"Which is all the more reason for us to protect the rest of the children," Elisa urges, pointing her finger at the window in the direction of the barracks.

"Do you honestly think the best way to do that is by staying trapped in the Compound? You said it yourself — it's a matter of time until they catch up to us and our opportunity is over," Nikola says. She has a valid point, and I can tell by the softening of Elisa's expression that she realizes it, too.

"No. When you put it like that, you're right. We'll have to get help from the outside," Elisa replies.

"Or we could just leave," Nikola quips with a toothy smile and a wink. She looks at me and asks, "What about you, quiet boy? Are you in or out?" I'm torn between the two options, but Elisa's soft expression pulls at me. I sigh.

"I'm with Elisa. We should help them," I say, though I'm not sure how committed I am. Elisa beams with gratitude, and my heart skips a beat. It's a good look on her, and I hope to see it again.

"Okay. Well, at least we all agree to leave," Nikola says. "What you guys do when you get out of here is your own business."

"Fair enough," Elisa replies.

"So what's next?" Nikola asks.

"Well, let's wait a couple of days and see what else we can find out, and then we'll meet again and plan our escape," Elisa suggests.

I shake my head. "We don't have time to wait a couple of days before we start planning," I say. "If we're going to leave, we need to *do* it in a couple of days at the latest. Let's meet back here in two nights. Gather as much information as you can, and be prepared to leave."

"Sounds good. I mean, what do we have to lose, anyways?" Nikola asks. "See you then," she adds as she slips out of the door, closing it softly behind her. I give Elisa what I hope is a supportive, confident smile and crack the door back open to scan the alley. There's no trace of Nikola, and I wave Elisa forward and then follow her out. As I close the door behind me, I see a faint, glowing red dot in the far corner of the room. It must have been obscured from our view by the shelves full of boxes when we sat down. Nobody stormed the room while we were tucked away in there, so I assume it's nothing sinister, but I can't help but peek over my shoulder numerous times as I head back to my barrack.

5

"They're going to try to leave, sir," the Colonel says. For the first time in months, he's thankful to have the warmth of the fire caressing his red, wind-burned face after walking through the freezing rainstorm outside. "Shall we act now?"

"Whatever for?" the Man replies. "Do you already know who the rebellious Men in Red are?"

"No, sir."

"Colonel, just because they leave doesn't mean you should stop watching them. I mean, where are they going to go? The borders are sealed, and winter's coming soon. Do whatever you have to do and use whatever resources you have to track them," he says. "They *will* lead us to the rebels. I promise."

"But, sir..."

"Let them leave the Compound," he says with a dismissive wave. "But don't let them get out of the village, and don't let it get out of hand. I trust you can supervise this... or should I give the responsibility to someone more willing? Colonel?"

"I'll take care of it, sir. You have my word."

"And Colonel?" the Man adds.

"Yes, sir?"

"Don't. Lose. Them." The carefulness with which the words exit the Man's mouth send a chill down the Colonel's back, and he nods and leaves the room.

———

I MAKE SURE TO PAY BETTER ATTENTION TO MY ROUTINE this morning and become a perfect clone of the other students. The conversation with Nikola and Elisa is on constant repeat in my mind as I try to figure out more of the puzzle, but nothing clicks. The same Red knocks over my water again at breakfast, but I anticipate it and hold out my right hand for the replacement cup. His behavior confounds me, and if Elisa hadn't mentioned someone was doing the same thing to her every mealtime, I would be concerned that the Red might not be as friendly as I hoped. But by this point, it's part of my bizarre routine, and I'm not dumb enough to question him.

I'm surprised to find a different instructor at the head of my literature class. The replacement is a pudgy, balding Red with a slight lisp and red cheeks. Stern's belongings are still on the desk, including his satchel. I don't bother asking what happened to him. I'm probably the lone student in the room who realizes we have a different teacher, and I'm not about to point it out. I keep my mouth shut, a feat made more difficult by the bumbling, uneducated nonsense that spills out of Baldy. I'm more than relieved when the class is dismissed, especially knowing Elisa is in my next class.

I spy her as I walk into the combat room, but she doesn't notice me or at least pretends not to. My stomach flutters at the sight of her, but I don't have a chance to explore those feelings. Instead, I unclasp the sling from my belt and run my fingers over the smooth leather. As I do, an image of me as a little boy, holding this same sling, flashes through my mind. It startles me so much I forget what I'm doing and pause with what I'm sure is a profound expression of stupidity on my face.

"What are you waiting for?" a Red barks over my shoulder.

I flinch and retrieve a handful of stones from my pocket and then load the first one into the loose pouch of the sling. I twist the thongs through my fingers and twirl it over my head, gaining momentum until it reaches the correct speed, and then I release one of the straps and hurl the stone forward. It strikes a small metal can with a clang, and I load the next round while the Red moves on to watch the girl with the black braid beside me.

For the rest of the day, I cling to the two new memories like a jeweler would to a rare gem. I listen in on every possible conversation between Reds and the nurses, but none of them speak of anything relevant. They mostly laugh at one of the kids or make comments on the weather. My frustration continues to grow, and it wears on my patience to have to play the part of the mindless student. I try over and over to picture my mother again or to remember anything about my father, but only blurry, veiled outlines swarm in and out of focus. Where are they? Are they even alive? Am I an orphan, and that's why I'm at this school? My stomach sinks at the idea, and I have to force myself to eat the bland bar of food issued to us for dinner.

That night, I fidget in bed, thinking about the escape we're going to attempt tomorrow night. It might be the worst escape plan in the history of the world, but I'm hoping we'll be able to take them by surprise since I doubt anyone else has ever tried to sneak out of the Compound before. The towering fence is too high to jump, especially not knowing what's on the other side, but we can just climb over it, and then we'll be free, and I'll be able find my parents, assuming they're still around.

I get so wrapped up in my daydream that I almost forget to tell the black-haired boy who spoke to me yesterday morning.

I'm almost certain he was the other boy at the gate with us, but there's only one way to find out, and he should know about the plan.

I push myself up on to my elbows and glance around the room. Everyone appears to be asleep, so I slide out of bed, cross the floor in silence, and find the boy in the last row of bunks near a door that leads to the Reds' sleeping quarters. I can hear the deep, hearty laughter of male voices through the barrier, and I hesitate before kneeling and tapping the boy's shoulder.

He opens one eye and peers at me with a crooked grin. "I wondered when you were going to speak to me again," he whispers. The muffled roar of laughter grows louder, and I duck down. Unsure of if and when the Reds make their rounds through the barrack, I skip the formalities.

"We're leaving tomorrow night," I say, watching the light that creeps through the cracks around the door for shadowy signs of movement.

The boy opens his other eye and sits up. "What? You're sure?" Another round of laughter slips through the air, and I flinch while nodding.

"This time tomorrow night. Be ready to go if you want to come with us," I whisper before hurrying back to my cot.

Just as I relax into the blankets, the Reds' door opens and the glow of electric lights spills into the room. Several guards bumble through the entrance, leaning on one another for support. I pretend to be asleep, but my eyes stay open enough to see the outlines of their figures through my lashes.

"Look at these poor saps," one of the Reds slurs. "Karlmann got his crap together for this whole operation."

"I know, right?" says another Red with a deep rumble.

"Hey, check this out," says a third, and he picks up the arm of a sleeping boy and waves it around. The boy doesn't stir, which only makes their laughter increase. The Red uses the boy's hand to slap his own face. "Quit hitting yourself, kid!" he says with a snort and then drops the boy's hand. It lands with a fleshy smack against his face, and the Reds let out another round of drunken laughter.

"Get back in here," a fourth voice orders from the doorway. His tall stature blocks most of the light, but I think his arms are crossed over his chest. He's not intoxicated like the others, or he at least holds his alcohol better. "These boys could kick your tails while blindfolded. Leave them alone. Their lives are pathetic enough as it is without you messing with them."

The voice sounds familiar to me, but it isn't until the man moves and the light falls on his face that I recognize him. It's the same guard who's been kicking over my water at every meal. *Who is he?* I wonder. The drunken guards grumble and release a line of annoyed profanity, but they obey the dark-skinned Red and stumble past him, closing the door behind them, and the light around the doorway clicks off after a few minutes. Somehow, though I'm not sure how, I manage to fall asleep despite the hordes of questions building inside of me.

———

THE NEXT TWENTY-FOUR HOURS PLAY OUT MUCH LIKE THE previous two days. Externally, I try to be the perfect conformist, but on the inside, my hatred continues to grow. Being forced to sit through my classes is like having venom dripped into my ears, and I rebel internally against the constant stream of manipulation that surrounds me. I try instead to focus on my growing anticipation for tonight's escape. I know I told Elisa I'd help her free the other students, but I remain torn over my decision. Part of me wants to get as far away from Belstrana as possible, but the other part feels obligated to help. Wouldn't I want someone to help me? Better yet, would I realize I needed to be helped if I was still vaccinated?

Around midnight, I sneak out of my cot, change into the warmest clothes in my trunk (including my coat) clip my pocket knife and sling onto my belt, and then pad over to get the other boy. He's already dressed when I reach him, and with a silent motion of my hand, we snake through rows of sleeping boys and exit the building.

The air feels particularly chilly, and the brisk wind carries an endless blanket of ominous clouds overhead, eclipsing the moon. I lead the way through the Compound's dark alleys towards the storage building where I had met with Elisa and Nikola. A faint golden glow fights its way through the layers of dust on the window panes on either side of the door. Alarmed but not repelled by the presence of light, I kneel down and push the door open. Before I have a chance to survey the room, a hand grabs my coat collar and yanks me inside so that I fall on my back with a thud.

"Are you insane?" a deep, male voice whispers harshly. With a surprised grunt, the black-haired boy lands beside me in a heap. The dark-skinned Red who has been replacing my water and who ushered the drunken guards from our barrack towers over us. He looks different tonight, though, with his red shirt hidden beneath a heavy, faded black coat.

"What do you think you're doing, August?" the Red scolds. Even through his clothing, I can see how muscular his chest is as it heaves with deep breaths. The boy glares at me, but neither of us speak.

"Infants..." the Red mutters as he takes a few steps away and rubs his chin. The realization we've been caught crashes over me, and I tremble from both cold and fear.

"I've been trying to keep you guys safe, and here you go prancing around the Compound at midnight like a bunch of villains," he continues as he wraps his thick arms over his chest. "Well?" he asks, and his eyebrows rise with expectation.

"I... We..." I stammer, unsure whether or not to tell the truth. He raises a hand and directs me to stop.

"I know *what* you're doing, or at least what you *want* to do," he snips. "What I don't understand is your method of doing it. You think they're just gonna let you walk out of here like you're a delivery man? Why don't we stick you in a cardboard box and try to ship you out like a crate of toilet paper?" He shakes his head and continues, "*I* can't even walk out of the Compound, so you definitely can't." His sarcastic tone begins to annoy me, and I work up the courage to defend our decision.

"It's not like we were going to go up and ask them to let us out of the gate," I reply, but the words crack as they slip between my lips.

"Oh? You had another idea?" he asks with a smirk that reveals a perfect set of white teeth against his warm skin.

"We were going to climb the fence," I say with as much confidence as I can muster, which isn't much considering I feel like a scolded child.

"You... you mean the electric fence? The one that'd turn you into a big crispy pile of ash as soon as you place the tip of your finger on it? Try again, son," he says and chortles under his breath.

The black-haired boy rolls his eyes towards me and says, "THAT was your great plan? Are you kidding me?"

"I didn't know it was electrified," I say as my blood begins to simmer, angered by the condescension in the room. I decide I've had enough of the Red's unhelpful commentary, so I jump up and crouch in preparation to attack him. The guard sees my fingers curl into fists, though, and without batting an eye he pulls a pistol from his belt and aims it at my chest. I freeze in place, unable to finish exhaling.

"This gun is loaded with darts that have enough tranquilizers in them to knock you off your tail and make you forget how to wipe your chin. Now you listen to me. I've been running interference for you guys every day since the explosion, giving you clean water instead of the Crystal-tainted stuff and trying to make sure the other guards believe your newfound awareness is a temporary kink that'll work itself out." He closes the distance between us, and I suck in a deep breath. "Who do you think set off the explosion that day, anyways? Huh?" he asks, and I think I might melt under the intensity of his stare.

"You did that?" the other boy asks as he pushes himself upright and dusts the grime from the floor off of his clothes.

"Yeah. I did that," the Red replies. He backs away from me and returns his gun to the holster on his belt.

"Why?" I ask. "Won't you get into trouble?" I feel like an idiot for having cowered so much during the tongue lashing I received, so I straighten my back and square my shoulders in a feeble attempt to regain some sort of manhood. My effort feels futile however, because although I'm at least six foot one, the Red towers over me and makes me feel like a child.

"Because we need a change, and because I'm tired of brainwashing children and turning them into soldiers. I didn't ask for this when I enlisted. They lied to me... to all of us," he answers. The corners of his brown eyes drop down in regret, and he rolls his neck back and forth.

"It's the vaccine, isn't it? What did you call it — Crystal?" the other boy asks. "That's the reason why I can't remember much about life before the Compound and why I've been doing whatever I'm told for who knows how long. I don't even know how old I am..."

"You're fifteen, Alek, two years younger than August," the Red says. "And yes, it's the vaccine. They've been giving you a steady stream of Crystal through the water supply every day since you first got here so that you remain compliant. If you leave the Compound for any reason, you're given a heavier dose of it when you get back in case you met anyone who might tell you something that could turn you against Karlmann. It makes you an empty canvas, ready to receive and accept whatever garbage the Foundation wants you to believe. When you're laced on that stuff, you'd cut your own throat if they told you to. Add that on top of the food you receive that gives you your amazing strength, and you're a force to be reckoned with. That's why it's important for you to get out of here before they correct their mistake and shoot you up with it again. You can't be their pawn any longer." He taps the veins inside of his arm for emphasis, and a chill rolls through my body as my mouth goes dry. I exchange nervous glances with Alek.

"You're going to help us? Why? What does any of this matter to you?" I ask out of sheer curiosity.

"It matters because it's simple human decency, something the Foundation dismissed years ago and something the rest of Belstrana is too scared to believe in anymore for fear they'll be struck down," he replies coolly. "I want you four," he says while looking over my shoulder, "to help put an end to it." Elisa and Nikola approach from around the corner of a tall shelf.

Well, this is unexpected. A part of me is aware this whole thing could be a trap, and I glance to where I thought I saw the red light last time, but it isn't there. That's strange... Turning my attention back to the man, I'm still not quite convinced.

"Why don't you just eat some of the bars of food that we eat so you're strong like us? Then you can just take care of every-thing yourself. It seems like an easier method. Plus, you wouldn't have us as liabilities," I say.

"We're not allowed to eat them, and they give us blood screenings weekly to make sure we haven't had any."

"And if they find out you have?" I ask.

He doesn't speak for a moment.

"The Foundation controls us, and we control you. Or at least that's how it's supposed to work. If we're stronger than them, they can't control us, and their system breaks down. They won't allow their system to break down," he replies, and the dryness of his tone gives me all the information I need about potential consequences for him.

Even still, how do I know he isn't lying? I don't, I realize. Now *he's* the liability. I scan the lines of his face, and his impatient gaze meets mine. Hidden beneath the strong, hardened persona he projects, there's desperation. It's barely visible in the few white hairs around his temple and the darkness under his eyes that could otherwise be attributed to age or fatigue, but it's there. I don't know why, but something tells me I can trust him. I agree to help with a simple nod of my head, especially since I know Elisa's watching me. I look at her and find amusement dancing behind her eyes. She's been here the whole time. My cheeks burn as I recall the Red's scolding.

"Excellent," the Red says. "I'm Joseph, by the way." He leans close to me and grabs my shoulders so that he's looking straight into my eyes and then whispers in my ear, "That's no ordinary symbol on your arm. Keep it hidden or you'll have the whole country hunting you." My mouth gapes at his warning as I recall the black triangle inked onto the inside of my wrist. He returns my gaze and his eyes mirror the seriousness of his tone.

"Wha—" I begin to say, but he cuts me off with a single, stern shake of his head.

I back away from him and face the girls, who stand with large packs strapped to their backs. Two more sit by their feet, equally bulging with what I hope is a lot of supplies. Joseph must know more than I realized, and he must be serious about helping us to have gone through the trouble of preparing packs for us. I'm relieved we have provisions for the near future, since

I don't know where we're going or how we're going to get there. Before I can move to grab my pack, Joseph shoves a folded, white piece of paper into my hand.

"Read this and do everything it says when you get out to the forest. You won't be able to stay in the village. I hope you realized that already. You'll have to live in the woods like the drifters, and you'll probably run across some of them while you're out there if you're lucky," he says. One of my brows rises at the mention of drifters, and he continues, "Don't worry. They're pretty rough people, but they're harmless... mostly. They might help you if you can humble yourself enough to ask for it. You understand?"

"Yes sir," I say, as do the others. He nods, and a bit of warmth returns to his expression.

"You'll be fine, and you'll figure out what you need to do. Just read the letter, okay?" He blows out the lone candle, and the door opens to a deluge of rain. Perfect. Just perfect.

6

I pull up my coat collar once we're out in the alley, and Joseph directs us to jump up to the rooftops so we're less noticeable. I take three firm steps and launch myself onto the slippery shingles, and the others follow me up. Joseph remains on the ground and leads the way to one of the four Compound gates from below as we leap from one rooftop to another. The rain falls harder the closer we got to the fence, and by the time we're near the gate, our visibility has diminished. Joseph calls to us from the ground, and we drop down into the mud and duck behind the corner of a building.

"Hear the buzzing of the fence?" he asks, and I strain to hear it above the rush of the wind and rain, but it's there, a faint hum. "Give me five minutes and I'll have it shut off. Wait here until you hear the buzzing stop and then get yourselves out of here. The lock should slide right off once the electricity is shut down."

"Sounds good," I say as I pull the collar of my coat up around my chin and then stuff my hands into my pockets. Joseph studies us for a moment and runs a hand over his face, trying in vain to wipe it dry.

"I doubt you'll see me again, but good luck, kids. And thank you. You have no idea what this means to Belstrana." He nods once and has just begun to walk away when I remember something.

"Hey, Joseph," I say. "What happened to Stern?" A darkness falls over Joseph's expression.

"He was... re-appropriated," Joseph replies before ducking his head and slipping out of sight beyond the rain. I squint after him, unsure what he meant. Surely he and Stern aren't alone in their resistance to the Foundation.

I shake away the thoughts and pat my pocket to make sure the letter is still inside. The rain splatters and splashes around us from a black sky, and the lamp posts staggered between buildings provide enough illumination that we can watch the drops come in sideways from the wind. Even though it has the worst possible timing, it's still mesmerizing to me, as if I have never seen rain before.

A sudden absence of noise in my ears snaps me from my daze right before the shouts of men erupt from deeper within the Compound. Floodlights scream into the night and swing wildly through the alleys before settling on one building several blocks away. Our best chance to go is now while the Reds are distracted by something.

"Go!" I cry to the others, and we all race across the opening to the gate. I grab the latch and fling it open. Ahead of me, Elisa and Alek hop onto the rooftops of the first line of buildings in the village. The pecking sounds of gunfire ring out as I propel myself forward to join them, and Nikola swears several steps in front of me. I'm tempted to turn back to see if we're being followed, but I resist the urge. Only containment and mind-numbing Crystal await us back there.

We trek towards the eastern side of the village, careful not to slip on the shingles. Below us, the buildings are painted in the same scheme as the Compound — grey and red and void of personality. Mailboxes and storefront windows frame the sidewalks, though I don't take the time to study them. We have to get out of the village before they know we're gone.

Up ahead lies the final edge of the buildings, and beyond that is an endless dark field. I know the forest is out there somewhere, but the storm prevents us from seeing it. We come to a halt, and despite the miles we've covered, none of us are out of breath. Thank you, Foundation.

My companions stare out over the vacant space with wide eyes and soggy hair. There's enough glow from the street light that I can see Elisa's wet cheeks are extra pink, as is her petite nose. I blush at my own imagination of how I could warm her up. Thoughts like these are new to me... I think. She looks at me right as I crouch in preparation of my descent back to the ground.

"No!" she croaks somewhere between a scream and a whisper. I pause, and my legs are still tense with unreleased energy. "We can't go that way. Joseph said there are Shepherds out there who wait for people to escape from the village. They'll catch us before we reach the trees."

Well that's new information, and it would have been handy to know it before we ran all the way over here. "Then what else are we supposed to do?" I ask, trying not to let my irritation leak into my voice.

"Follow me," she says and then leaps across another street to our left, heading north. I exchange a glance with Alek, whose eyebrows are pinched, and he shrugs. We follow Elisa's lead for several minutes until she stops on top of the last building and leans over the edge.

"This is it," she whispers and then drops down without an explanation. I'm confused, but I trust Elisa. And as long as I can get out of here, I don't care how we do it or where we go. I throw my legs over the side and push off, landing with a splash. We stand in front of the back entrance to an old bakery. A net of glistening cobwebs guards the casing around the doorway. Elisa twists the iron knob, and the door groans open.

"What are you doing?" I ask, startled by her apparent boldness.

"This is where Joseph told me to take you," she replies with one wet foot in the building, motioning us forward.

"When?" I say. I had been under the impression that I was the leader of this... whatever we're doing, but apparently Joseph didn't think so if he'd been consulting Elisa without me.

"Before you got to the storage room and got your butt handed to you," Nikola says with a smirk.

"I did no—" I huff, but Alek interrupts me with a pat on the back as he pushes forward into the bakery.

"Yeah, you kinda did," he says, smiling. "But then again, so did I. I would hold that against you, but we'll call it even." He winks, and I clamp my mouth shut while everyone else goes inside. Just because you can't remember much of your life from the last twelve years doesn't mean you don't have the capacity to dole out sass.

I cast one final cautious glance down the street and follow the others, closing the door behind me. Clumped together in a tangle of soggy, cautious limbs, we shuffle past a series of grimy display counters. I try to picture them full of sweets and breads, but the idea of any food beyond the packaged bars seems so foreign that I can't see it. Elisa leads us through a swinging red door into a kitchen. A thick film of old grease and dust coats the floors and counters. Our shoes leave visible tracks on the ground. That's not good, but there's nothing we can do about it.

Elisa crosses the room and yanks open a narrow pantry door. She kneels, and I peer over her shoulder as she removes several floorboards and stacks them to the side.

"You're up," she says, smiling at me. I stare down into the dark void below.

"You're kidding, right?" I reply. I know I'm super strong and fast, but there's something sketchy about leading the way through a long, dark tunnel that leads to who knows where. Elisa's smile broadens.

"With you? Never. Joseph said it'll take us into the forest," she says as she scoots to the side.

"I'll go first," Nikola chimes from behind. Oh, no. There's no way I'm letting someone else lead me... not that I have anything against girls. An image of Elisa in the training room flashes through my mind.

"No, I'm good," I say and then crouch down. With my hands braced on either side of the opening, I lower my legs into the darkness until my boots hit the bottom. I have to hunch over to shuffle forward so Elisa can follow me down. The tunnel is narrow, as dark as dark can get, and smells of wet earth and mildew. I guide myself forward with my hands on the walls. I'm embarrassed to admit it, but my breaths speed into quick gasps as I contemplate going further into the damp, musky darkness ahead of me. I could shut my eyes, and it wouldn't make a difference. Alek and Nikola join us, and once she has replaced the floorboards, I resign myself to an uneasy truce with the tunnel and press forward.

All of the sudden, a beam of light screams past me, illuminating a seemingly endless passage with a harsh electric glow. "What is that?" I shriek, trying to shield my unprepared eyes from the blinding light.

"It's a flashlight, August. Joseph thought we could use it, and now I know why," Nikola responds. "Here, pass this up, Alek."

"Well, hoity-toity. You guys are just best friends, aren't you?" I say under my breath. I don't know where the ridiculous phrase came from, but I can picture my mom saying it with a mocking sneer as she stares at the television. Random. Light bounces off of the tunnel walls as the flashlight makes its way forward, and I clench the cool metal. If darkness is my opponent, then this light is my new weapon. My shoulders relax and my breaths come easier.

"So what's the plan?" Alek says. Nikola stifles a laugh.

"Hate to break it to you, friend, but we don't have a plan other than getting out of here," she says.

"You can't be serious," Alek replies. "That's suicide."

"And staying back there isn't? I'd rather die a thousand deaths out where I can fight for myself than to live another minute as a mindless rat," Nikola spits.

"So you plan on killing anyone who gets in your way?" he asks.

"Pretty much, so don't mess with me, pretty boy." Man, I knew Nikola was intense, but that borders on the edge of insanity. Regardless, I can relate.

"Don't worry yourself about that, Nikola," Alek says. "I'm not a violent guy."

"How do you know you're not violent?" she asks. "You get put in the right situation, and I bet you could rip someone to shreds. I can promise you that one wrong glance from anyone, and I'll beat the life out of him. I might be little, but I'm not afraid. I can do a lot of damage with my bow staff."

"Bow staff?" Alek says.

"Yeah. What's your weapon, pretty boy?" she asks.

"Five feet of chain," he replies. "I can also, to quote you, 'do a lot of damage,' but only as a last resort," he says. Nikola scoffs.

"What about you, August?" she says. I feel everyone's eyes on me as I lead them forward, ducking beneath the occasional ridge above my head. I think for a moment about my place on the spectrum.

"A sling. Though I'm pretty good with a knife, too. As for style, I guess I'm more on Alek's level," I say, and Nikola groans. "I was the best in all of my classes on the Compound, but once I figured out what I was doing, I didn't enjoy any of it. It seems wrong."

"I agree," says Elisa. Thank God for that. "I know Nikola plans to thrash her way to safety somewhere, Alek, but I want to stay close and see what we can do to help the rest of the Young Ones. We could use your help. August has already agreed, unless he's changed his mind." I trip over my own foot and stumble forward.

"You sure you were the best in your class?" Nikola quips. I roll my eyes and mull over Elisa's request.

"I already said I would, Elisa," I reply. "I don't go back on my promises."

"How do you plan on helping them?" Alek asks.

"Well, I don't know yet. But I refuse to leave them behind. It's horrible what the Reds are doing," she says.

"Let me put it this way: how far are you willing to go?" he asks. Elisa is quiet for a moment.

"I can't be positive how I'll react if the situation came up, but I think I'm willing to go until death," she says. It rolls out of her mouth with such nonchalance that my jaw drops.

"Whoa! You'd sacrifice yourself for them?" Nikola screeches. I also want to know the answer to that question. I didn't think self-sacrifice was part of the bargain.

"Yeah, I think I would. How could I live the rest of my life knowing I didn't do anything to help thousands of children who are stuck in camps? I would always feel regret and guilt." I can practically hear Nikola's eyes roll through her head, but the rest of us stay silent. When she puts it that way, I understand her need to do something. But part of my heart longs to do the same as Nikola and run away from it all.

"Well then I'm in, too," Alek says after several minutes. "You're right. We can't forget about the others."

"Aw, geez," Nikola mutters. "Fine. Have it your way, princess, but promise me we'll see some action."

"You are insane," Elisa says. "I'll promise you no such thing, but if you ever feel like you're not getting enough time in combat, I give you full permission to attack August."

"What the—" I begin to say.

"Great!" Nikola says. I have half a mind to jab Elisa with my elbow, but I can tell from her tone that she was teasing, maybe even flirting. Chances are Nikola didn't pick up on those cues.

"Thanks for that," I say, and Elisa and Alek laugh.

After a few more minutes of stooped walking, I begin to feel the damp chill of the storm on my face. I suck in a deep breath as we near the exit, which I discover is hidden beneath a pile of soggy ferns at the edge of a small clearing. The ground is slick with rain, and it shows no sign of lessening anytime soon. The wind bites at my cheeks and nose as I pull myself up to the surface. Turning, I grab Elisa's soft hand with my cold fingers and help her out of the hole. Alek offers to help Nikola, but she shoves past him into the forest. Around us, the limbs of pine trees hang low with the weight of wet needles.

"What now?" I yell over the howl of the storm.

"We should keep going and find shelter," Nikola hollers, motioning towards the line of trees with fingers that are already red and stiff.

"I don't think that's a good idea. We aren't ready for this kind of weather," Alek replies, and I know he's right. They're shivering, as am I, and I wipe my nose with the back of my hand.

"Let's stay in the tunnel overnight," I yell. It hadn't been particularly warm in there, but it also wasn't freezing cold.

Starting our mission by spending the night in puddles of mud wouldn't help anything.

"Aaagh!" Nikola groans, but her hunched shoulders indicate she doesn't want to spend the night in the middle of a storm. She might be suicidal, but where's the fun in freezing or drowning to death?

She drops back down into the tunnel, followed by Alek and Elisa, whose hair hangs heavy with the weight of water. I'm the last one in, and I pull the shaggy fern branches over the opening as much as possible to try to stop the wind. It doesn't help, but at least I tried, right?

We move away from the mud at the entrance, and I sit and lean my head back against the earthen walls, folding my limbs into my body. I try to retain as much body heat as possible, but it's difficult since my clothes are soaking wet. For the first time, I think this escape may not be as easy as I had imagined. We might be able to fight, but other than that, we are woefully unprepared. I hope the rain will stop soon and everything will dry out tomorrow so we can keep moving. I think of the different possibilities that lay ahead of us as I drift to sleep, listening to the soft breathing of my companions in the dark.

7

"Where are they, Colonel?" the Man asks. He watches his secretary heave another log on to the fire and wiggles his toes out of his slippers so he can prop his feet up on the ottoman in front of his chair. The heavy aroma of fresh coffee wafts from his mug, and he takes a sip and swishes it between his teeth while waiting for a response.

"They, uh... they left the Compound last night, but we're not sure where they went. An electrical failure allowed them to get through the gate, but our surveillance system lost track of them when they jumped to the rooftops. I'm sure they're still in the village. Shepherds would have spotted them on the roads or in the field if they had tried to leave," the Colonel says. Outside, the light from the sunrise reflects off of the surrounding glass buildings and streams through the windows to his left, brilliantly illuminating the room around him.

"And you don't know where they are?" the Man asks as he watches the steam swirl off the top of his coffee and dissipate into the room.

"I'm not sure, sir. Like I said, we lost them last night, but they've got to still be in the village or we would have seen them leave."

"Are you forgetting something, Colonel?

"Sir?"

"Anyone who was around during the war knows about the emergency tunnel that leads out into the forest... well, except *you*, apparently. I told you not to lose them, Colonel, and I told you not to let them out of the village. You have twelve hours to track them down or there will be consequences. Do you understand?"

The Colonel's eyes widen at the revelation, and he stammers to get out a quick "Yes, sir," before running out of the door.

———

I SPRAWL ACROSS A WORN AREA RUG IN THE LIVING ROOM with my chin in my hands and my feet in the air behind me. A giggle slips through my lips as one of my favorite cartoon characters cracks a joke, and I can't wipe the glee from my face. My mother shuffles past me, through the doorway and into our small kitchen. Over the roar of my program, the steady chop of vegetables and the warm aroma of stew wafts through the air.

As the show ends, a faint jingling sounds from down the hall, and I leap to my feet and then tear down through the house towards the front door. Our foyer is sparsely decorated, adorned with a plain wooden table against one wall and an electric chandelier that hangs crooked from the ceiling. It's simple and unassuming, and I like it.

A tall, lean man with light skin, dark brown hair and a short, stubbly beard steps through the front door and closes it behind himself. He's dressed in his usual attire: khaki pants, a starched, blue button-up shirt (sealed at the collar with a navy tie), a brown leather belt, and matching shoes. A few shadows of gray flirt with the edges of his hairline, but his blue eyes sparkle with youth on either side of his straight nose. He bends over and scoops me into his strong arms. I laugh and squirm as he places a scratchy kiss against my forehead.

"I'm glad you're home, Daddy," I whisper as he places me back on to the hardwood floor, just in case he's forgotten it since this morning.

"Me too, son," he replies with a broad smile. He ruffles my hair with his long fingers and takes my hand as we walk down the hall and into the kitchen. My mother greets him with a kiss.

"Big news, Rose," he says as he leans against the counter by the sink. He pulls a folded newspaper from his back pocket and hands it to her. I scoot close to him and wrap my arms around his leg, burying my face into the stiff fabric. He usually won't allow me to stay like this for long, so I'm pleased when he places a hand on my back.

"Isaac Karlmann won the election," he continues. My mother's eyebrows rise as she studies the newspaper in her hands.

"Are you sure?" she asks.

"Pretty positive. There was a major turnout at the polls for him today. He's pretty much a shoo-in at this point." He claps his hands together as he adds, "We should celebrate tonight!" My mother folds the paper, slipping the pages through her fingers slowly.

"Celebrate, yes... but also hope he keeps his promises. 'Efficiency Leads to Prosperity' is a great slogan, but it means nothing without a solid force behind it. There has to be change, Jon," she says. Her mouth is drawn into an unsure frown, which puzzles me.

"I know, dear. At this point, there's nothing we can do now but trust him."

My mother sets the newspaper on the counter and tugs at a political button that hangs from the collar of her sage-green dress.

She drops it with a soft thud on top of the paper. I stand on my tiptoes to see the image. White and red lines surround a portrait of a middle-aged, round-faced man. Black hair has been combed over his broad forehead, and his dark, beady eyes make me shiver. I don't know who he is or why my parents have worn buttons like this for the last several months, but I trust them with my life. They are my parents, so they must know what's best for me.

————

I'm vaguely aware that I'm still asleep as the dream fades. I've somehow ended up curled on my side, and my hands are shoved so far up my coat sleeves that I struggle for a moment to free them as I sit up. Stretching, my eyes flutter open. The air is silent, and everyone else still sleeps. Our breaths form small puffs of fog in the faint traces of dawn that fight their way into the tunnel, and I catch myself staring at Elisa. At some point, she had scooted to within inches of me, and I wonder what it would be like to sleep with her head on my chest and my arms around her narrow waist. I reach forward to stroke a spiral of curl that trails along the ground behind her back. She wouldn't notice, would she?

A twig snaps outside of the tunnel, and I jerk to my feet, withdrawing my knife and flicking it open. My eyes strain to focus as I make my way towards the slices of morning sun that sneak through the fern-covered opening. With the dull side of the blade placed between my teeth, I brace my hands on the walls and creep forward until only an inch stands between me and the outside. My shoulders tense as I weigh the possibility that we've already been surrounded, and the lingering image of the beady-eyed man from my dream does nothing to ease my worries. I consider warning the others, but a protective desire surges through my body as I glance back at Elisa. I can handle whatever is out there.

Before I can psych myself out, I crouch low and then spring from the hole. A shower of water droplets flies through the air as I land with a soft squish on the ground. A few yards away from me, a buck rears back with wide eyes as a scream bellows from its wet snout. It bounds off through the trees, and I turn in circles to survey the small clearing. Cold air burns my nostrils, but I don't care. We're free. We did it. I close the knife and whoop with excitement.

Elisa rushes from the tunnel and almost crashes into me. Her curls hang in disarray, and her rosy face holds a hint of wildness. "What's going on? What's happening?" she stammers, twirling the handle of her uncoiled whip. I chuckle at how cute she is and then shoot forward to grab her into a hug before I can stop myself. She sucks in a breath and stiffens between my arms. I don't know why I did that. And worse, I don't know what to do now.

"Um, August?" she mumbles into my shoulder. "Are you okay?" I panic and try to pry my arms from her, but I'm frozen, mortified by my own behavior.

"Whoa! What's going on here?" Nikola screams with mock scandal. That's the push I need to snap me out of my stupor. I jump back and cross my arms over my chest. Elisa stands there with her arms tucked by her sides and one eyebrow cocked.

"Uh, sorry. I don't know what came over me." I turn away, hoping they think the redness in my cheeks is from the cold.

"Pretty sure I do..." Nikola mutters as she adjusts the straps on her pack. I want to smack her. Beyond her, Alek chuckles.

"Anyways," Elisa says, and I'm grateful she let it drop. "We're out of the village and in the forest... so what now?"

"We've got to get away from here," I say. The Reds have

noticed our absence by now. It's only a matter of time before they come looking.

"Well, duh," Nikola says. "But where are we supposed to go?" The tunnel deposited us at the base of a mountain range, and the further we get into the woods, the safer we'll be. A gentle chorus of tapping rings out as water drips from the trees, and a breeze speeds up the tempo as branches sway overhead.

"Up the mountain," I say, "away from the village."

"I second that," Alek says, and I toss him a grateful half-smile. He returns it and holds his hand beneath a limb, catching a droplet of water before it can reach the ground.

"Then up the mountain we go. You want to lead the way, lover boy?" Nikola asks, looking at me with a raised eyebrow. Alek and Elisa stifle their laughter. If Nikola hadn't agreed to help us, I would have no problem hurling her back over the fence into the Compound. As it is, we can use her skills.

I slide my arms through the straps of my pack, which Alek was gracious enough to retrieve for me, and begin walking uphill towards the north. After a few feeble attempts by Elisa to get the rest of us to talk some more, we all fall silent, which is fine with me. I don't remember the last time I was outdoors like this, so I spend my time searching for chirping birds hidden deep in the canopy of trees. The air grows warmer the longer we walk, and I soon shed my coat and stuff it in my pack as we step over puddles and streams.

For several hours, we walk, and the deeper we go into the mountainside, the more alive the forest becomes. There's an amazing serenity that comes from the damp, earthy smells and the swishing whisper of the wind. How long has it been since I've noticed it all? Elisa makes us stop every once in a while so she can inspect different types of ferns and trees, but Alek and I don't mind. Only Nikola seems annoyed at our pace, but as far as I'm concerned, she can shove it.

We scramble up a small rock face, and once we get to the top, Alek launches himself into a tree. He leaps from branch to branch like an oversized squirrel, and several nervous birds squawk their disapproval at him. I can't stop myself from laughing, and it dawns on me then: I am happy. Who knows how long it's been since I've felt that way?

After several hours of weaving uphill, we come across a small meadow. Surrounded by trees on three sides and the steep, rocky face of the mountain on the fourth, it makes an ideal campsite. Moving at a much slower pace than this morning, I push through the tangled hedge of shrubbery and plop down on a small, mossy boulder. My eyes feel heavy and my muscles feel tight. I'm exhausted, and I know if I stay still for long enough, I could fall asleep. This worries me. I didn't think I could get tired like this.

My stomach growls just as a brown paper package lands on the ground beside me. I glance up in time to see Elisa rip open her own wrapper and take a bite of the stale bar of food within it. It dawns on me then — for the first time I can recall, I'm hungry. It's no wonder I can't think straight. I snatch the bar from a pile of soggy fern leaves.

"Where did you get these?" I ask just before I sink my teeth into the food. The flavor is as lacking as ever, but I scarf it down immediately. Within seconds, my energy and mental clarity begin to return.

"Joseph gave them to us," Elisa replies, wiping a crumb from her lip.

"I love that guy," says Nikola, "especially when he's making the two of you want to wet your pants." She smirks and winks at Alek and me. I roll my eyes, unamused.

"Anyways," Elisa continues, "we should have enough of these for a couple of months, or at least that's what Joseph told us before you got there." She kneels down and unzips the main compartment of her pack, revealing a plastic bag full of bars. "There's supposed to be around eighty in each of our bags. At three a day, this should get us through almost three months."

"That's amazing," I say, but my excitement doesn't stay for long. The bar has left a dryness in my throat, and it's made worse when I watch Elisa retrieve a metal canteen from her bag. I have a sudden urge to lunge forward and steal it from her, which I shake from my head. But my expression must have given me away before I could correct myself.

"You have your own canteen, August," Nikola says with razor eyes that scan my posture. She perches on a fallen log, using her extended bow staff for support while she takes a sip from her own supply. There's a glimmer of challenge in her stance, like she is daring me to follow through on my initial desire to take Elisa's canteen from her.

I force a smile and say, "Oh. Yeah. Thanks." I retrieve my bag, grab the canteen, unscrew its lid, and proceed to drain the majority of water into my eager mouth. The burning disappears, and I gasp for breath as I lower the container from my lips. Nikola smirks at me, but Elisa seems oblivious, though I doubt that's the case. I know better than to doubt her in any way.

On a whim, I decide to climb the rock face at the edge of the clearing in hope of figuring out how far we are away from the village. The sunlight has helped dry the rocks somewhat, but there are still many slick patches of rock above my head. Ignoring the faint warning deep within my mind, I begin climbing, choosing my hand and foot placements with caution. Being in a deserted area while running from the Reds? Good. Being there while injured with a broken back? Not so good. I keep this in mind as I simultaneously shove the toe of my boot into an open crevice in the rock and launch myself upwards while pulling with stiffened fingers.

It doesn't take long before I have an audience below. Elisa

and Alek watch, occasionally guiding my movements when I come to a difficult passage. There's no telling where Nikola is, but I imagine she's waiting at the top of the ledge with a boulder for me to catch. I get about halfway up the wall before I find a deep enough shelf for me to sit on. Twisting my body with stifled breaths, I manage to contort myself so I can survey over the feathery tops of the pines and down into the valley.

The village sits in the middle of an expansive clearing, surrounded on all sides by an electric fence and a perimeter of open fields. The Foundation spared no cost or angle to keep residents from fleeing their homes. Squinting, I notice small figures moving around the edge of the field to the west. They're the Shepherds Elisa warned us about last night, traitors who hunt rebels for profit and the main reason why we had to take the tunnel last night. I'm not sure if they would try to kill us or capture us, but I could go the rest of my life without finding out.

Sighing, I refocus my attention on the landscape below. My best guess is that approximately fifteen miles of forest stand between us and the village. We could circumnavigate the route within one day as long as we run, but it could take the Reds several days to find us. They may be trained enough in combat to teach us how to fight, but they aren't as strong as we are and are nowhere near as fast. I doubt the Foundation will let them eat any of the students' food for fear that their main security force could become too powerful. Regardless, a group of Reds has probably already been dispatched to find us, so we won't be here long anyways.

With a grunt, I decide to return to the others below, twisting in place as I lower my legs over the ledge. Getting down is much harder than getting up, I soon learn. I'm not growing tired, but annoyance is starting to prick the edge of my mind as I scale down the rock wall. I drop one of my legs and set my foot on a narrow lip, but it crumbles under my weight, and my arms go taut as I dangle twenty feet above the ground below. It may be springy with ferns and moss, but a drop from this height would still hurt.

I glance over my shoulder, hoping Elisa and Alek are still around to offer help, but they're on the other side, sitting side by side and speaking with one another. My chest contracts as though I'd been punched, and I turn back, grazing my cheek on a jagged piece of rock. Oh, screw this.

I pull my legs up between my torso and the wall and plant my feet so my knees are tucked beneath my chin, and then I launch off backwards, flipping through the air. I try to keep track of the ground as I tumble over myself, praying I'll land without a problem, but that thought is shattered as I land flat on my back, and the wind is knocked out of me. Pain shoots through my body, clouding the edges of my vision as I struggle to inhale. It feels like my lungs have been squeezed shut, and I know they must think I'm an idiot as my limbs flop around on the ground. Elisa's face comes in to focus above mine, floating in front of the blue sky beyond. She gasps and places a hand over her open mouth. Somewhere in the background, I hear the irritating cackles that can only mean Nikola is doubled over with laughter after watching my fall.

"Are you okay?" Alek asks, nudging my arm with the toe of his boot. Nice. I manage to suck in a shallow breath and cough.

"Yep," I squeeze out between hacks as I prop myself up with my arms. "Never... better." Nikola's laughter grows louder, and Alek stifles his own. Even Elisa has a wry smirk on her lips. I try to ignore it as I push myself up so my arms are slumped over my bent knees. That did not go as planned.

"What were you trying to do?" Elisa asks. "Are we such terrible company that you had to fling yourself off the mountain?" She giggles and tucks a curl behind her ear. My cheeks grow warm at her question.

"What? Of course not..." and then Nikola's piercing laugher breaks through my concentration again. "Well, maybe she is." A small stone smacks the back of my shoulder.

"Shut it," Nikola snips. I roll my eyes.

"Think anything's broken?" Elisa inquires, placing her hand on my shoulder. I stare at it for a second and then shake my head.

"No, nothing's broken," I mumble.

"Except his pride," Nikola adds as she saunters past us, a mischievous grin planted on her face. Elisa makes an effort to frown, but it doesn't do much to conceal the amusement in her green eyes.

"You know, I wish I could say she's wrong, but..." I say, and Elisa squeezes my shoulder gently.

"Well, lesson learned. Just because you *can* jump like that doesn't mean you *should*," she whispers. She leaves then, and I fold my hands over my face. At least I made her smile, right? And at least she cared enough to check on me... At the moment, I decide to take what I can get and brush off the embarrassment, along with a bunch of dirt and leaves from my shirt.

8

We spend the majority of the afternoon setting up our poor excuse for a camp. Alek and I manage to find a few dry twigs to use for a small fire while Elisa and Nikola create a makeshift tent from a couple of plastic tarps they found in the bottom of their packs. After I'm sure the fire will hold, I use the last few minutes of sunlight to take inventory of my own supplies. At least a hundred bars of food have been placed in the largest compartment of my pack, and nestled on top of them are two clear, plastic bags containing matches, candles, a utility knife, twine, bandages, and tiny packets of antibiotic ointment. A side pocket contains extra pairs of wool socks, and a water-proof blanket is clipped to the bottom of the pack. The front-most pocket holds another small knife, a compass, a pair of thick weather-proof gloves, and a pad of paper with a pen clipped within its spiral binding.

The sight of the paper awakens something in me, and I throw it down and reach inside of my coat pocket, retrieving the letter Joseph had given me. It had been urgent, and I had forgotten. One of many more failures, I'm sure. The sun has fallen behind the tree-line by this point, but enough of an evening glow hangs in the air that when I squint, I can make out the slanted writing on the page.

You need to go back into the village — alone — and visit a friend of mine. His name is Luca, and he lives at 1733 4th Street, east of the square, near the courthouse. He'll give you instructions and help you with whatever you need. Remember — this is about more than you. It's about everyone, about Belstrana. Take care, and keep your head down. Best, Joseph.

I read the letter to myself three times before reading it aloud to my companions. Why would he address me alone if he knew three others would be with me? I trace the mark on my wrist, barely aware of the conversation between Elisa and Alek about the letter. How am I supposed to help the entire country? I'm just a teenager. The sole thing I can do is fight, but one person against a country, against a government with as much control as the Foundation? It's impossible. It's suicidal.

I'm not the only one who questions Joseph's unspoken appointment of me as leader of this mission. Nikola sulks off to the side, and the bouncing light from the fire reveals her down-turned lips and narrowed eyes. I'm caught up in my own thoughts and fears but notice when she slips away into the forest. Moments later, a violent crash erupts from her direction. Out of instinct, I leap to my feet and unclip my sling from my belt, worried the Reds have found us. Nikola emerges from the forest, dusting her hands off on her pants, and lets out a cathartic sigh. From my side, Alek chuckles before turning to me.

"So when will you go?" he asks. It hasn't occurred to him that I wouldn't do what Joseph wants me to do.

"Who says I'm going?" I reply. Elisa, who had been

unfolding a blanket, stops with her hands in midair and stares at me. Surprise illuminates her features.

"Why wouldn't you?" she asks as she drops the blanket and approaches me. I don't want to quarrel with anyone, much less her, but something snaps inside of me.

"What can I do to help the Young Ones? Look at me! I don't know who I am or where I come from or anything about myself except the fact that I can fight. What could I possibly offer? I can't do it. I won't do it," I reply. I crumple the letter and throw it to the ground, where it sinks into a lingering puddle. Elisa bends down and retrieves it. She does her best to un-crinkle the paper and fans it through the heat from the fire to dry it.

"I understand what you're saying. I don't know why he asked you to do this instead of any one of the rest of us," Alek says, "but there has to be a good reason for it. I can't explain it, but I think we can trust Joseph. And besides — he's not actually asking you to do anything other than go talk to some guy."

"Yeah, August," Elisa chimes in. "At least go and see what the man has to say before you decide you can't do it. What could it hurt?"

"Hey, if you don't want to do it, I will," Nikola says with wide, hopeful eyes. I'd lie if I said I didn't consider her offer for a moment. It would be easier to sit back and let someone else lead. I remember Joseph's words to me before we left, his warning about the mark. Maybe Alek's right. It's not like I've been asked to sacrifice myself or kill Karlmann on my own. All Joseph asked is that I meet a friend of his. Joseph. Thinking of him makes my mouth dry. What had happened to him after we left last night? What had caused all of the gunfire last night while we ran? Had he... had he died? For us? I hope not, but it feels like a stone has taken residence in my stomach. I owe it to him, don't I? After a few moments of internal conflict, I clear my throat.

"I'll go," I mumble. Nikola groans and walks away, which

makes me feel somewhat better about my decision. "But it'll have to wait until morning."

"Of course," Elisa replies as a smile lights up her face and crinkles her eyes, which dance in the firelight. That makes me feel better, too. She continues, "I doubt one day will make a difference. Besides, it's dark now and you'd get lost." Alek pats me on the shoulder and tosses another branch onto the struggling fire, which perks up after a few seconds.

"Do you think we should keep it burning all night?" he asks, his gaze bouncing between me and Elisa. "What if someone sees the light and comes for us?"

"I don't know how else we'll stay warm. We'll freeze if we don't. It's worth it to me if everyone else agrees," Elisa replies, wrapping her arms tighter around her chest as if the mere suggestion of losing the fire has made her colder.

"Oh, relax already," Nikola says, and I almost jump from her proximity. I thought she had left us, but apparently she's much quieter than I'd given her credit for. "What could they do to us if they found us?" she says, patting the folded bow-staff on her hip. Alek casts her an anxious glance and turns his attention back to the fire, adding a couple of more sticks. While he works, the girls and I unroll our blankets and wrap ourselves up like large, chilly caterpillars. By the time Alek nestles into his, the fire has surged, casting heat and light throughout the clearing.

The fire cracks and pops beside me, and I stare up through the canopy of foliage overhead. There's enough of a breeze that the tops of the shaggy pine trees sway lazily, creating occasional gaps in the limbs that allow me to see more stars than I could ever remember seeing before. I focus on their glittering dance, trying to relax, but something about them reminds me of the exploding vials of Crystal. A renewed surge of anger swells inside of me like a churning, violent sea, threatening to suck me down. So many lies and needles and fights. So many stolen months and days and moments and memories.

Before I know what's happening, tears flood my eyes and spill down the sides of my face, dripping onto the blanket. Grief. This is grief. I let it wash over me, fueled by the life that was taken from me, the life I can't remember. I grieve for the few memories I do have and for my parents, wherever they are. I get it all out, every last tear, and resolve to myself that I will not do this again. I have to be strong, and as far as I know, strong men don't cry.

I don't know how much time has passed when exhaustion settles into my bones and blood, making my bleary eyes heavy. I don't feel grief anymore. I feel anger. Even in my tired state, it courses through my veins and reassures me that I made the right choice to meet Luca. I don't dread it anymore. I want answers, and he'd better give them to me.

9

"What now, Colonel?" the Man asks as he stands near one of the three floor-length windows that adorn the outer wall of his otherwise claustrophobic office. He doesn't care to see the man to whom he had addressed the question, and instead peers out over the expanse of country before him. Belstrana is beautiful, and it belongs to him.

"We've sent in some cameras, sir, to monitor the group," the Colonel replies, feeling confident in the swiftness of his obedience.

"And where are they?"

"North of the village, sir. They're in a clearing about fifteen miles up. They left the building through the old security tunnel, like you said." He watches as the Man stands relaxed by the window, his pale face illuminated by the morning sun that crept into the room between thick, dusty black drapes that framed the view. The view of Belstrana's mountainous landscape to the south is exceptionally lovely, even when looking at it through such a grimy portal.

"What cameras are you using?" the Man asks.

"We thought it would be a good opportunity to test the Sparrow, sir. Our first prototype seems to be doing well." The Man raises an eyebrow but his face doesn't turn from the window.

"Very good. If they're going to be in the forest, then it's best to keep a camera on them at all times, Colonel. But, don't think this gets you off the hook. Keep up with them."

———

I START MY MORNING FROM THE TOP OF A STURDY PINE. I choose this one in particular since its large branches open up from the trunk like worshipping arms, welcoming the sun as it peeks over the horizon. It's peaceful, and I need peaceful. I eat my breakfast in silence while I process the myriad of emotions I went through last night. All are gone now except the last one. I'm still angry, but the gentle swaying of the tree and the breeze on my face helps to assuage it.

"August?" Elisa says from below. "You up there?" I shove the empty food wrapper into my pocket and begin to ease my way down through the branches.

"Yeah. Coming," I reply. I let go of the tree when I'm ten feet up and drop to the ground. Elisa greets me with a crooked, concerned grin that doesn't reach her eyes. I force myself to return the expression. Alek and Nikola stare quizzically at me. Nobody questions why I had disappeared for so long. Chances are I wasn't as quiet last night as I had hoped. I rub my eyes with my fingertips. They're still puffy. Great. I don't want to talk to anyone about it — not that they would ask — so I gather my things together and prepare for my trip back to the village. I force myself to mumble a goodbye to everyone, and I promise to return as soon as possible.

I don't want to waste any time, so I run the route, thankful that Alek had thought to mark a few branches along the way yesterday to help us retrace our steps. My legs pump, bounding over fallen branches and stones, and beyond the sound of my heartbeat and steady breaths, songbirds fill the air with a sweet melody. I follow their rhythm all the way down the mountain, arriving at the tunnel within an hour.

I retrieve my flashlight from my back pocket and flick it on before dropping into the tunnel. I force myself forward, and the sudden silence pushes its way into my head. I distract myself by trying to predict what the meeting with Luca will be like. What will he be like? What will he say? And how will I respond? Why had Joseph insisted I meet with Luca instead of telling me the information himself? What does the triangle mean? Would Luca know, or should I mention it? Joseph's warning echoes in my head.

I reach the bakery soon enough and push the floorboards up. I set them to the side and pull myself through the opening before replacing them. I then slip through the building, sling in hand, expecting an ambush, but nobody is here. I reach the front door and stick my head out first, scanning the street for life. When I find it empty, I exit the bakery and bound up on to the roof.

From there, I head south, careful to keep away from the edges of the buildings to avoid detection by the Reds and Young Ones who patrol the streets below. I'm not surprised to see a small number of people moving about below. I now remember enough from our classes to know the Foundation only allows people to leave their homes at certain times of the day, and the residents who work are required to carry a travel permit. Those who disobey are sent to labor camps near Apex as punishment, where I assume they are controlled with the same Crystal serum as the Young Ones. I hold my breath each time I leap over a street, unsure if I'll be spotted.

The sound of children's voices resonate from below, and I come to a stop and drop to my stomach. I pull myself forward across the gritty shingles and peer down. Pairs of Young Ones patrol the streets below. One of the pairs, two adolescent boys, stands in the street, watching one house in particular.

Without warning, they dart to its front door and yank a shoe-less elderly man, dressed in tattered pants and a faded blue shirt, into the street and onto his knees. He looks as though he could have been a banker or teacher or accountant at one point in time, but the tangled, white hair that hangs limply around his thin face indicates his life has not been easy in recent years.

"Please!" he cries, holding his hands together in front of his chest. "Please! I have to get some medicine for my wife. She's dying! Please let me go!"

One of the boys reaches out and places a set of handcuffs on the man's narrow wrists while the other grabs the whistle from around his neck and raises it to his lips. A foul screech cuts through the air. The man cries, and tears streak his reddened face and drip from his nose onto his khaki pants, creating darks splotches. He pleads with the boys to release him, but they don't acknowledge him.

A large, rumbling, black, van with tinted windows rounds a corner, and its brakes screech as it halts in front of the scene. Two Men in Red exit the vehicle, one of whom lumbers to the back of the truck and yanks open a set of doors to the cab. The other Red grabs the desperate man by the collar and flings him inside without a word. The cab doors are slammed shut, but the muted sound of the man's cries hang in the air still. They climb back in the cab and the truck disappears around another corner. The two Young Ones who started the altercation don't seem phased and walk away, continuing their patrol.

It takes me several moments to gather myself before I can continue south to the address Joseph had written in the letter.

After a few more minutes, I peer over the side of a building across from Luca's house and survey the street for any signs of life. Finding it empty, I drop to the ground and jog to the crimson front door. I lift my right hand and tap on it, glancing at the white "1733" painted beneath the peep hole to double check that I had the correct place.

The door flies open, causing me to jump. A man, whose build is similar to Alek (though a bit softer), stares back at me. A shallow network of creases frame his deep-set eyes, and his forehead is covered by long, wavy black hair. A matching, unkempt beard surrounds his broad mouth, the lips of which are pursed into an unflinching line. I hesitate before speaking, unsure of how the man will react upon seeing a Young One at his door. He gives me a once-over, and then his narrow eyes meet mine. I clear my throat before speaking.

"Are you Luca?" I ask. I clasp my hands together in front of my stomach, feeling nervous and unsure of myself.

"Who wants to know?" he replies, continuing to stare into my eyes. I feel locked in place, unable to break eye contact with him until he makes the first move, craning his neck out of the door and peeking down the street. I assume he's making sure I'm alone.

"I'm August. Joseph sent me," I say, and it comes out more as a question than a statement. I, too, scan the street, anxious to get past the awkward introductions and inside to relative safety.

The man's lips stretch into a grin, accentuating the lines around his eyes and displaying a set of crooked teeth. I let myself breathe again, relieved. Luca reaches forward and grabs my left upper-arm, dragging me inside. The door closes with a forced thump behind us, and I stumble into what appears to be a living room. The walls are a neutral beige, of course, and a long, black table stands against the far wall. It holds a few kerosene lamps and a couple of framed photographs of a smiling, bald baby and a beautiful, blonde woman. An empty fireplace occupies the middle of the wall to my left, encased on either side by eight straight-backed, wooden chairs. Across the room, to my right, sits a single, faded blue couch. Dark curtains conceal the thin windows behind me, making the room feel stifling and gloomy.

Luca motions for me to sit on the couch while he retrieves a chair from beside the fireplace. He sits down and crosses his right leg over his left knee, relaxing his shoulders and folding his hands in his lap. I keep my feet on the floor and tuck my sweaty hands under my legs. I know I'm making a terrible impression right now. Nikola should have come. Not me. I'm going to screw this up.

"Joseph told me a lot about you," Luca begins. "I'm glad you all were able to escape the Compound." He watches me closely, like he can read me to my very core. He's going to be disappointed, I know it.

"Thanks," I reply. "We couldn't have done it without his help." I pause for a moment and wriggle my hands out from under my legs and place them on my lap. "Have you... have you heard from him since we escaped? Things sounded pretty rough when we were leaving, like a fight broke out or something."

Luca's dark brows furrow, and he rakes a hand through his hair, brushing it from his forehead only to have it fall right back in place. "I don't think Joseph is around anymore," he says after a moment. My body stiffens, frozen.

"What do you mean?" I ask.

"I haven't seen him or heard from him in a couple of days," he replies. My heart races, and panic claws at my chest.

"What does that mean? Where could he be?" I demand, leaning forward in my seat.

"It's not your concern, August. Let it go and focus on why he sent you here. We have to talk about what needs to be done," he says. I can tell he's uncomfortable and doesn't want to discuss Joseph's fate, but I can't let it drop.

"But..."

Luca interrupts me. "Look, I know you're concerned, but don't be. I'm sure he's fine." I give him my most incredulous look, trying to figure out whether he is pranking me or testing my character. My fuse is growing short now, and I ball my hands into fists, popping my knuckles against my taut thighs. I feel like a coiled spring, ready to explode under pressure. Joseph was the only friend I had, and I need to know what happened to him.

"I can't let it go," I say.

Luca waves his hand dismissively. "You're not here to be Joseph's mama," he says. "Let it go."

"So what am I here for?" I ask, poised to walk out if I don't get any answers. I won't be played with.

"How much do you know about Belstrana?" Luca asks. The question takes me by surprise.

"I'm not sure what you mean. I mean, I remember new stuff every day, like from my childhood. I know they're using Crystal on the Young Ones in the Compound and that we're used as a police force against our own people, but I don't know why," I reply. "What can you tell me?"

"Well, I guess the best place to start is at the beginning," Luca says, settling back into his chair. For the next hour, I listen in disbelief as Luca describes life inside Belstrana. Not only has Karlmann passed a series of edicts that limit travel and communication, but he has also banned all media apart from that which comes straight from the Foundation. The news programs do not question diplomatic or social policies, nor do they criticize Belstrana's politicians, namely Karlmann. The blame for any arrests is placed onto the citizens, who are labeled rebels and outlaws and are shipped to work camps to serve as examples for other would-be criminals. According to Luca, most people threw out their televisions years ago, choosing to live in ignorance than to have the Foundation's propaganda circulate through their homes.

"There's an underground movement to remove Karlmann from office, but most people are too scared to speak out. The elections are rigged by the Reds, not that it matters since any opponents are handpicked by the Foundation itself and destined to lose from the beginning. Everything you see has been organized and orchestrated to ensure Karlmann retains his rule, and any attempts at rebellion have resulted in catastrophe," Luca says. "But of all of that, none of which is acceptable on any level, the worst part of it is that people continue to have children, despite knowing what's going on in the compounds." He rubs his forehead and presses his eyes with his fingertips.

"Why would they do that if they know what's going to happen to them, that they'll be drugged and trained to fight?" I ask, trying to comprehend such a screwed up system.

"Well, it's complicated. Many families lost everything when Karlmann came into power, even those people who voted for him. Early on, there was a major push towards abstinence or birth control among married couples after many of them had their older children taken from them. But then the Foundation abolished birth control and began to offer... incentives... for any healthy babies born within a marriage," he says.

"Incentives?" I ask.

"The Foundation began offering financial rewards, which many people need in order to just survive," Luca replies. His face is pale, and his neck stretches as he swallows hard.

"So wait. They... sell their children?" I ask, connecting the dots. The blood retreats from my face, and I have to wipe my palms on my pants to clear them of sweat.

"I guess that's one way to look at it. It's mostly the bottom class. The children of the wealthiest citizens are too valuable to be shipped off as soldiers," Luca mumbles.

"Well, why doesn't anyone do something about it? Why not fight back?" I ask, and it's hard not to feel betrayed by my own people.

"Don't think people haven't already tried to overthrow him. Several rebellions took place early on, but most of the people involved in them would disappear overnight. After a while, the protests stopped. Occasionally, someone will try to make a point and rile everyone else up into action, but if they aren't shot immediately, then they're sent to a labor camp and never heard from again." Luca's lips sink into a deep frown, and his eyes glaze over as if caught in a dark memory. I lean forward and rest my elbows on my knees, pressing on my temples as if that will help me comprehend the multiple layers of unbelievable crap I've learned today.

"Where are the labor camps?" I ask. "I didn't see any in the village or on the mountain."

"They're in Apex. That's where most of the Young Ones go when they turn eighteen. The Foundation doesn't let them back onto the streets. Their strength is too valuable, so they're kept on the Crystal and forced to work on plantations or in factories for a few years until they're a suitable age for reproduction. Then they're taken off the Crystal and are given regular food instead of the bars, so that they lose their strength and pretty much return to normal, aside from the terrible memories, of course. After that, there isn't anything they can do to go against the Foundation, so they're released back into society," Luca says.

"To make more babies..." I say, catching on.

"Yes."

I feel sick.

"There's more," Luca says, and I groan. "I didn't tell you everything I should have earlier..."

"Which is..." I say, leading him on.

"The biggest reason why there aren't any insurgencies anymore is because of how the Foundation dealt with them." I lock eyes with Luca.

"I know they use us to do that. We're the ones who make them disappear," I say. Luca nods. "I remember doing it. I actually saw some Young Ones arrest someone for being on the street. They threw him in a truck and took him away." Luca jerks forward, eyes wide.

"What did you say? Who was it? Did you hear a name?" he asks, rushing to get the words out. "Tell me!" he yells.

"I didn't hear a name. But it was an older man with white hair. He was pretty thin," I stammer, trying to recall as many details as I could. "He said he had a wife and that she was dying and needed medicine. But they still wouldn't let him go."

Luca's expression softened, and he let out a sigh, relaxing back into his chair. "Ah," he says. "Don't worry about him."

"Are you serious? What about his wife?" I cry, shocked by his callous attitude. My energy levels plummet. I don't know how much more of this conversation I can take. It's too much. I feel like I'm caught up in a game without knowing the rules, which doesn't seem fair since the stakes are so high.

"She'll be fine, son," Luca clips, ending the discussion. I stare at him, debating whether I should leave, but decide to stay. I close my eyes, shaking my head.

"Well if he's fine and she's fine and nobody is doing anything about Karlmann, and you seem okay with it, then why in the world am I here?" I ask, careful to keep my voice steady as I articulate each word through my teeth.

"You tell me, August," he says. My eyes fly open. "You came here for a reason. What is it?"

"I did it as a favor to Joseph. I owed it to him for helping us get out," I answer. Elisa's face flashes in my mind.

"No you didn't. Maybe on the surface, that's what you want to use as your excuse, but that's not why you're here."

"What are you saying?"

"You're here because you want to be here, because you've been without Crystal for less than a week and already despise everything you see. You hate the Foundation for what they've done to you, don't you?" he asks. He jumps up and paces around the room.

"Of course I hate them. I have every reason to hate them. They took my life from me!" I bellow, pushing up from the couch. "What do you want me to do about it? Nobody can give me back what they stole!" Luca crosses the room in four large strides and shoves his face inches from mine. I can smell the faint hint of stale alcohol on his breath.

"You're not the only one, kid," he spits. I open my mouth to speak, but he cuts me off again. "Everyone in Belstrana has the same story as you, even if they weren't on the compounds. You guys, the Young Ones, you have a right to be mad and a right to want to leave, but you *have* to stay here and deal with it. You may believe that nobody has tried to defend you, but they have, and they've lost their lives because of it, and sometimes it was by your hand..." I gawk, dumbfounded at his accusation.

"That was NOT my hand!" I yell, although I don't truly believe it. "I didn't do that." But then, memories of me giving orders and rounding up people on the streets of the village flash through my mind. I shove them away, locking them up deep inside.

"Not by your own will, you didn't," Luca says, backing away slowly. "Don't you see? If you don't help us do something about this, then it will continue. More children will end up lost to the Foundation, more lives will be lost for stupid reasons." I know he's right. In truth, I do want to help free the Young Ones and remove Karlmann from office, but I don't know what to do. I don't know where to start. It feels like such a huge problem, and I feel infinitesimal.

"What difference could I make?" I ask.

"The four of you have more strength and skill than fifty civilians. We need you to spread the word. We're going to make a move against Karlmann." My brows raise in question.

"What kind of move?" I ask, curious.

"It's not that complicated. There's an election in a little over two months. We need everyone to make sure that people vote for Simon Fletcher this year. He's one of us, a rebel, but Karlmann doesn't know it." I can't help but snort at the idea.

"You *just* said the elections are rigged," I say, trying not to crack.

"They are, or at least they have been up until now. The Reds are changing their alliances. I think enough of them will help us, which means people will have security when they vote. But they have to believe it's safe first before they'll ever consider voting for anyone besides Karlmann," Luca replies. I can tell he feels confident about his plan, but it sounds too simple and, well, dumb.

"Tell me the truth, Luca. Do you honestly think a simple election will make Karlmann hand over his rule like it's no big deal?" I ask. It feels like I am now the responsible adult in the room, questioning the blind faith of a child.

"No, I don't. But it's a step in the right direction," he says.

"So what's your backup plan when it fails?" I ask.

"That's something I can't tell you right now. You'll have to trust me."

"Trust you? I don't know you, and the other three with me haven't even met you," I say. "You're asking for a lot."

"Well, you can trust me and listen to me, and I'll help you, or you can leave here and forget this conversation ever happened and go about your merry business for however long until the Foundation picks you up again. Go ahead. You choose," Luca snips. I scowl under the pressure of his challenge. But I think he's right.

"Fine. I'll help," I mumble, shoving my hands in my pockets.

"What was that?" Luca asks. I can tell he's messing with me now.

"I said I'll help."

"Okay then. Good choice." He slaps me on the back of my shoulder, and I grit my teeth to keep from slamming my fist in his presumptuous face. "As for your role, it's like I said. You four will go around to the outskirts of the different villages in Belstrana and tell the drifters about Fletcher. See if you can maybe get inside some of the villages to tell the mainstreamers. I've got a list of names for you of people who you should go see. Give me a second," he mutters and walks through the door to the back of the house.

I take the opportunity alone to walk over to the table and pick up one of the framed photographs, studying the smiling baby inside. Luca returns, and I set it down with an unceremonious thump. He hands me a piece of paper and a map, which I place in my pocket.

"Is this your kid?" I ask, seeing a resemblance between the two. Luca's fingers slide over the frame, straightening it in its spot.

"Yes, that's Frederick... Freddy. And that," he says, pointing to the other framed photo, "is my wife, June."

"Freddy's on a Compound somewhere, isn't he?" I ask as the pieces click together.

"Yes. So is June, actually. She was lonely after he was taken, so she volunteered as a nurse. She couldn't cope. And now she can't come back. It's been ten years since I last saw her," Luca rambles on to himself. We stand in silence for a moment until he takes a sudden breath and claps his hands together, ushering away his grief.

"You'd better go. It's a little after midday, and you don't want to get caught with that list," he says, forcing a chipper edge into his tone. But it's just that — an edge. It's not natural, and it doesn't fool me. But I let it go. He walks to one of the windows by the front door and peeks out of it. "You're clear to go. Come see me when you've finished. I'll be here waiting," he says. I shake his hand, noting how soft his skin feels against my calloused hands, and then sneak out of the door and back towards the mountain.

I run, mulling over the information Luca shared. The meeting hadn't gone the way I'd expected, but I'm anxious to share the info with the others. When I reach the camp, I don't bother slowing down and leap through the trees into the clearing. Nikola shrieks in surprise, raising her staff in the air, ready to strike.

"Gah, August! I could've killed you! Why would you scare me like that?" she cries. I can't help but smirk as I walk past her towards Alek.

"I'm not joking, August," she continues, lowing her staff a few inches. "You missed our little visitor earlier." I stop in my tracks and turn towards her, waiting for an explanation.

"Visitor?" I ask.

"It wasn't a big deal," Alek says, cutting his eyes at Nikola as Elisa approaches from her spot beside the fire. "It was one guy, an old man actually, and he looked pretty deranged. Innocent, but deranged. He was covered in dirt and was missing a bunch of teeth... pretty much exactly what I figured a drifter would look like." Alek grimaces and points to his teeth, which are straight and white.

"Well, what did he want?" I ask.

"He said he was wandering through the area towards a

camp of drifters about five miles northwest of here. He'd seen our campfire, and I guess he was curious about who we are," says Elisa, joining the conversation. Her lack of alarm helps me relax.

"And he didn't say anything else?" I ask.

"Didn't seem that way. We didn't even get his name," Alek says. I decide to let it drop and head towards the fire.

"So, what did you find out, great leader?" Nikola asks. I sit and pull the papers from my pocket.

"This is a list of people who Luca wants us to contact," I say as I unfold the first page. "And this is a map of Belstrana."

"Why does he want us to contact them?" Elisa asks, peering over my shoulder at the list.

"It's a long story, but there's an election in a couple of months, and there's a rebel movement to vote in a new president other than Karlmann. These people are going to help us spread the word," I say, aware that the plan sounds ludicrous.

"An election? That's the plan?" Nikola snorts.

"I know. Luca didn't seem confident in it, but he said there's another part of the plan that he would tell us about later on," I say.

"That doesn't make much sense," Nikola says. Elisa and Alek wait for my response with concern etched on their faces.

"I know. But that's the best we've got for now," I say.

"Let's do it," Elisa says. "Even if it is a suicide mission, I'd rather go out and help in some way than to sit here while everyone else suffers." I'm torn between wanting to hug her and yell at her to get away while she can. I do neither.

"What about you two?" she asks, looking at Nikola and Alek.

Alek shrugs his shoulders. "Sure," he says nonchalantly. A wicked sneer creeps over Nikola's face, and she twirls her staff off to the side, whipping it through the air.

"Anything for a little bit of action," she says. I think. But she'll be useful on the trip, regardless of her bloodlust.

"Then it's settled. We'll leave in the morning," I say, spreading out the map on my lap. Elisa retrieves a pencil from her pack, and we spend the remainder of the day mapping out our route.

10

"One of the boys has been to see someone in the village, sir. They're getting ready to leave the area," the Colonel says.

"How did he get back inside?"

"Through the tunnel, sir."

"You mean the one I told you about? The one you should have placed guards at already? You have to be kidding me. Who did he go see?" For the first time, the Man looks straight at the Colonel as he paces the room with his arms wrapped around his chest, and the officer shrinks back from the impact of his gaze.

"Luca, sir." He gulps, unsure how the news would be received.

"Luca Karlmann? Whatever for?"

"We don't know, sir. We couldn't get sound on the inside of his house. Should I have Luca arrested?" The Man pauses for a moment before continuing.

"No. Just have a Red stationed outside of his house at all times from now on. If he so much as peeks out of the window, I want to know about it."

"Yes, sir. And what about the students?"

"If they're leaving, then you'd better follow them. Alert the Men in Red countrywide, but don't let the Young Ones know they're being monitored. I'm curious to see what they're up to. There have been rumblings of a possible rebellion among the villages. They might lead us to the fools."

"As you wish, sir."

———

Elisa glides between the trees, seemingly weightless despite the large pack strapped across her back. I watch her when I can, impressed by her strength and speed. Only the risk of running into a tree forces my gaze to leave her figure. The last thing I want to do is knock myself out on our first day, hours after leaving to visit the first of the fourteen townships on the list, Village G. We talk occasionally about nothing in particular — the plants or the weather or some other superficial subject. Our conversation had lasted deep into the night last night as we feuded and conferred about our plans. I think we are all exhausted of talking by this point.

It takes us one day to reach Village G, which lies about twenty-five miles to the southwest of our original campsite. I've been instructed to find a drifter named Ivan but have no clue where to start, so I help find a suitable site for us to rest. We settle on a small clearing next to a bubbling spring, perfect for drinking water. Nikola and Alek gather brush for a fire while Elisa and I string up the tarps among a few young pines. I focus on my work to get my mind off of the monumental task before us, but the feel of twine between my fingers evokes a memory.

I see him — my father — building a makeshift tent from patchwork quilts and worn, thin sheets. We're inside of our living room. When it's finished, he crawls inside on all fours, smiling at me. I beam back at him, proud of our work. We lay on our backs with our hands crossed under our heads. I bounce my foot to the side, mimicking his movement. He tells me stories about dragons, white knights, and evil sorcerers. And then the memory fades, and all I'm left with is the scratchy bit of twine, which I've wound around my own fingers. It takes a few seconds to come back to reality, but I force myself to move, uncurl the twine, and use it to secure a corner of a tarp to a low limb.

"Hey, Elisa. I was wondering... Do you ever wonder where your parents are?" I ask, moving to another corner of the tarp and avoiding eye contact with her. She looks up from her own knot, and her hands stop in mid-twist for a moment before resuming their task.

"Of course I do," she replies, looking away again. A sudden breeze breaks through the trees, lifting her curls so that they slide across her cheeks and block my view of her. "Why do you ask?"

"Well, do you remember anything about them?" I ask, ignoring her question.

"Kind of... more of it comes back to me every day. I remember some things, like birthdays and Christmases." She pauses to tuck her hair behind her ears and then releases a breathy laugh. "I keep thinking about a song my mother used to sing to me." Her smile fades, and she turns her attention back to the tarps.

"What is it?" I say.

"Nothing." She sighs, glancing at me. I tilt my head to the side, questioning her in silence. "I... I don't remember the words."

"Oh." We work in silence for a few more moments. "Do you think they wonder where you are?"

"Of course they do. I'm their daughter. They love me," she says while she uses a spare bit of twine to tie her hair behind her neck, laying the curls over her left shoulder. Nikola, who I thought was out of earshot, releases a sarcastic snort.

"Why is that funny?" Elisa asks, whipping around to face Nikola. Nikola folds her hands in front of her waist and sighs, full of false pity for her companion.

"Because they don't love you," she says, poking out her bottom lip. A low growl fills my throat as Elisa's eyes widen, full of hurt and anger.

"How would you know?" she asks, placing her hands on her hips. Nikola snorts again, and I step closer to her, unable to stay back any further.

"Please. Look where you've been for the past however long. If our parents loved us, they wouldn't have dumped us off at the Compound," Nikola says.

"They didn't do that because they didn't love her," Alek chimes in. "You heard what August said last night. They didn't have a choice... nobody did." He still holds a pile of broken branches in his arms, watching the scene with caution etched on his usually calm features.

"Of course they did! They could have become drifters and taken us out to live in the forest. They could have and should have fought back. If they had cared for us at all, then they would have protected us," she says, and the tension slips from her shoulders as her arrogance wanes. Her voice quivers. "It doesn't matter anyways. They ditched us, and now, here we are!" She holds her arms out to her side, motioning to the forest, and then lets them drop with a clap against her narrow hips.

"Don't you think we might have been more protected on the compounds? Think about what all August told us about life in the villages. It's brutal," Elisa says.

"Don't. Don't try to defend the compounds to me," Nikola spits. "They use us Young Ones like animals, bred to do their bidding, bred for the slaughter."

"I'm not trying to defend them. I just... never mind." Elisa closes her mouth, sensing the futility in her argument.

"So you don't care anything about finding them?" Alek asks, facing Nikola.

"I couldn't care less where they are," she answers, but the moisture pooling in her eyes reveal her lie. She wipes her face. "But I do want to find my brother."

"You have a brother?" asks Elisa. Nikola dismisses her query with a wave, but Elisa continues to question her, searching for more information.

"Fine," Nikola says, turning her attention to the arrangement of branches for the campfire. "His name is Stephan. He's three years older than me, which makes him nineteen, I think."

"That means he's too old to be on the Compound anymore," I say. I feel bad for Nikola, and I wonder if maybe I have a sibling somewhere, one bought by the Foundation from my desperate parents. I shake the thought from my mind. I can't picture them doing that.

"Exactly," she says, pulling out a match. She strikes it against the box and ignites a pile of leaves nestled among the wood. She blows on the tender flame, fanning it until it grows and crackles with strength.

"Maybe he's already been released back into Belstrana," I say, searching for a thread of hope.

"Maybe..." she replies, staring into the fire. "I told you I'd help you with this, but when we're done, I want to find him."

"How?" Elisa asks, sitting beside Nikola with her legs crossed. "Where would you start?"

"I don't know, but I have to try. As far as I'm concerned, he's all I have." The hurt in her voice is palpable. We don't bother to correct her or reason with her, because we don't know if her parents are alive. Besides, I've only known her a few days, and I can already tell that her stubborn mind is set. Nikola will do and believe what she wants, and we have no authority to stop her, even if we don't think it's the right choice.

The rest of the night is quiet, sober. I don't know for sure, but I get the feeling everyone has been sucked into their own childhood memories. I think of my own parents, trying to remember the details of their faces and the sound of their voices. But everything is faded and distorted, like I'm underwater while assorted images and scenes flow past my blurred vision. I'm not sure when I fall asleep, because the memories follow me, pulling me down and weighing on my chest. I don't sleep well that night.

11

I 've just drifted off when a twig snaps nearby. My eyes fly open, and I listen for signs of movement but hear nothing else. It's probably a deer, I think, and relax back on my blanket. Just as I am about to close my eyes, the fiery reflection of a silver knife blade flashes as it presses against my throat. An arm presses against my shoulder, pinning me to the ground while a set of knees land on my chest. The edge of the blade is cool and sharp on my skin, a sensation I barely notice while straining for air. From somewhere close, Elisa gasps. That's all it takes to force me into action, and I sit up, hurling a body off my chest.

The man flies back and slams into a thin tree that snaps from the force, crashing to the ground. A loud crack fills the air, and Elisa disarms a dark figure with one lash of her whip, knocking his knife to the side. At the same time, Nikola unfurls her staff and begins a series of lashes against the legs of a short, stumpy woman who yelps and falls to her knees. Her thick braid slings behind her as she moves. Alek uses his chain as a bola, wrapping it around his assailant's feet so that he slams into the ground with a pained grunt. I wonder how many more will attack us but don't have time to count.

A knife whizzes past my head, landing with a clunk deep in the woods. I turn back to the man who had attacked me and hurl myself on top of him. I wrestle with him, trying to gather his arms in my hands to pin him, but am not fast enough to stop him before a finger gouges into my right eye, trying to force my eyeball out of socket. I scream and slam my fist into the man's face, feeling the crunch of bone as I make impact, and his hand leaves my eye. The man cries out in pain and tries to push me off of his chest, but I gain control of his hands and overpower him. I use my legs to roll him on his stomach, yanking his arms behind him and pressing his face into the ground with my knee.

"Who are you?" I bellow, pulling the man's wrists further up his back so that his shoulders threaten to dislocate. He yelps in pain but doesn't answer, so I press a little harder. The crunching of dead leaves and pine cones alerts me someone is approaching from behind. I jerk my head around and see Alek. Elisa and Nikola stand guard over the others. It looks like Nikola's attacker is unconscious. I'm not surprised.

"I said who are you?" I continue, and he grunts.

"I'm Erik," the man sputters into the ground. "Who are you?"

"Why did you attack us?" I ask, moving his arms up another fraction of an inch.

"We thought you might be looking for us. We don't want your type around here. We know what you people do," he says through pained gasps, but he quits struggling.

"What who does?" Alek asks from over my shoulder.

"You! The Young Ones, soldiers for the Foundation," another deep, male voice answers. It's from the man Alek had fought, now chained to a tree.

"We can tell by your uniforms," the first man adds.

"We don't belong to the Foundation," I say, glancing down at my brown shirt. "We left the Compound a week ago. You had no right to attack us." I release the man's — Erik's — wrists and stand up, towering over him and daring him to move. I can see him better now that he's illuminated by the dying fire. It's an older man, probably in his sixties, with a ponytail full of stringy, grey hair and a mouthful of crooked, yellow teeth. A long, pink scar streaks beneath his right eye, ending beside his wide nose, and he wears a faded pair of denim jeans and a tattered, green jacket. He pushes himself up, rolling his shoulders to relieve the discomfort I had caused him.

Elisa and Alek follow my lead and release their captives, but Nikola's continues to lie limply beside a clump of ferns. A faint snore emits from her direction, and Nikola stifles a laugh as she leans on her bow staff with a smug smirk. Between her pride and prowess, she manages to take the time to send a stifling glare at Erik.

"So if you're not here to arrest us, what are you doing in the forest?" Erik asks, turning to face each one of us. I nod towards Alek, who nods back, assuming the role of our group's diplomat.

"We're looking for somebody," he says and holds his palm out in my direction. I hand him the list of names, which I had stored in my front pocket. Alek unfolds it and shows it to Erik. "His name's Ivan. Do you know him?" Erik casts a sideways glance at the other men but doesn't speak.

"Well?" I ask, stepping forward, aware he might receive my advancement as a threat.

"Why?" asks Erik. He's not moving anymore, just watching us and waiting for our response.

"It's..." Alek begins but stops himself. "Tell us where to find him. I can tell that you know him." One of the other men gives Erik a nod so small I might have missed it had I not been looking straight at him at the exact moment.

"He's at our camp," Erik says. "Get your stuff. You can stay with us tonight and speak with him." Alek and Elisa both shrug. Nikola grips her staff tighter.

"Okay," I say. Alek and I rush to disassemble the tarps and roll up the blankets while Elisa kicks dirt onto the fire, trying to smother the already-dying flames. Nikola doesn't move but continues to stand over the stocky woman like a lioness over her prey. The woman jerks awake and gingerly touches her temple with her stumpy fingers. She glares at Nikola but doesn't speak, taking her cues from her male companions.

Within ten minutes, we leave the smoldering fire and trek towards the camp of drifters. By the glow from my flashlight, I see Elisa chewing on her bottom lip as she pushes further into the trees. She is quiet now, too quiet. I speed up, matching her stride, and before I know what I'm doing, I reach out and squeeze her cool, smooth hand once, before letting go. She glances at me and shoves her hand into her pocket. I know I had no right to touch her, but I still feel slighted and confused. I drop back from her again, floundering in my own incompetency. What was that about? Does she despise me? I suppose so.

After what seems like several hours, the familiar aroma of burned earth begins circulating through the air. We push through a break in the trees and enter a meadow. Several tents are strung up throughout the area, and laundry ripples on taut lines at the edge of the forest. Sleeping, blanketed figures cover the ground in almost every available spot, and a group of men sit on several fallen logs that surround a sizable campfire. As soon as they see us, they jump up, raising an array of crude weapons. I reach for the sling on my belt, placing my fingers around the smooth strands of leather.

"What's going on? Who's there?" one of the men asks. Several of the sleeping bodies sit up, looking back and forth between our two groups, and scuffle to their feet. The light emanating from the fire behind the man prevents me from seeing any of his features, only that he is thin and walks with a slight limp, favoring his left hip.

"They were camping nearby and wanted to speak with you," Erik says, shuffling his way across the opening towards the fire. It doesn't go unnoticed that he omits the part of the story where he and his friends had attacked us. I suppress an annoyed scoff.

"What for?" the man asks. "Are those Young Ones?"

Erik points a crooked finger at me. "Let him speak."

I clear my throat and step forward. "My name's August. My friends and I were sent here by a man named Luca, from Village K. Do you know him?" I ask. I'm a few feet away from the fire now and better able to see the man to whom I'm speaking. He's much older than I had anticipated, and his scraggly, white beard reminds me of Luca.

"Luca?" he asks, raising an eyebrow. "Yeah, I know him. What's this all about?" He motions to the logs, and the others and I sit down with him, grateful for the warmth. I proceed to inform him about our escape from the Compound and the meeting with Luca, though I leave out details about the election until I'm sure he can be trusted. As it turns out, if anyone despises Karlmann more than me, it's Ivan.

"I knew Karlmann during the war, and I never liked him. Didn't trust him neither. As soon as I saw his name on the ballot years ago... knew it was trouble. I left the Village within the month. We called him Parochni, if that tells you anything," he says with a raspy chortle, echoed by several other drifters.

"I'm afraid it doesn't. What does it mean?" asks Alek, resting his elbows on his knees and waving his hands in the warmth of the fire.

"It's derived from the old language of Belstrana. Means 'vicious'," Ivan says. A chorus of agreement emanates from around the camp upon hearing the word. "He was harsh with his own soldiers and even worse with his captives. Parochni isn't an exaggeration. He earned it with every foul word that came out of his mouth. Always wanted to go to the extreme..." he trails off, and his eyes become unfocused.

"Why stay in Belstrana?" I ask. "Why not seek refuge with a neighboring country?" His attention snaps back on me.

"Don't think we haven't thought about it, but this is our country, and we won't run away from it," he says.

"Not to mention that our neighbors don't take too kindly to us barging into their country," adds another man who sits to Ivan's left. "They'll lock us up for being illegal immigrants, maybe ship us back across the border to Apex."

"Don't they understand what it's like here?" Alek asks. "Why wouldn't they help us?"

"Who knows, kid," Ivan replies. "Politics are a fickle beast. And anyways, you still haven't told me why you're here. Why did Luca send you to find me?"

"Well," I begin, "this is what I've gathered from talking to Luca. He says the rebels are planning to vote against Karlmann this year in the election." Silence fills the air and then is shattered by the eruption of bellowing laughter. I can't help but cringe. Nikola rolls her eyes and shrugs. Elisa drops her head over her bent knees, letting her hair conceal her face, but Alek's calm expression doesn't change. I know what they're all thinking, the drifters in particular, and I feel dumb mentioning it, but I had promised Luca.

"Listen," I say, cutting off the laughter as eyes focus back on me. "Luca said that if we can get enough people to vote for some guy named Fletcher, then we might have a chance."

"Are you insane?" Ivan asks, crossing his arms over his chest. "We'll be slaughtered for trying it. You should know. After all, the Young Ones are the ones who do the slaughtering." My stomach clenches, feeling the sting from his words. "And besides, we," he says, motioning around the camp, "can't even vote. We'd have to go to the village to do it, and once you go through the gate and show yourself to the Reds, you don't come back out. It's not worth it. Not to mention that Karlmann won't hand over his reign. Luca knows that, I know that, and you should know that. So what gives?"

"I know what you're saying. I get it. But regardless if you can't vote, there are tons of people inside who can, and they're the ones we're trying to reach right now. Luca said many of the Reds have changed alliances. There might be some in your own village who will help you. See if you can get in there and find them. They can't help you if they don't know about what's going on," I say.

To my surprise, Nikola joins in. "This is the best we've got right now. If you don't want to use this approach, then you'll have to either figure out another way to un-rig the election yourselves or deal with Karlmann for another three years."

Ivan frowns. "He's going to retaliate. You know that, don't you?" I don't answer, not so much because I'm embarrassed or ashamed, but because I don't know what to say.

"Tell them about the other part, August," Elisa says, nudging my shoulder.

"What other part?" Ivan asks. "Bending over?" A roar of laughter echoes through the clearing.

"Well, I'm not sure what Luca has planned, but I guess you can do that if that's what you feel led to do," I say, knowing I'm on shaky ground already but not caring anymore. Nikola chokes back an amused snort, and Elisa drops her head again. I think the corner of her mouth turns up. The laughter fades.

"Just spread the word. Go vote for Fletcher. It'll be safe this year," I say, dismissing Elisa's suggestion. I can't bring myself to tell them that I think there might be another part of the plan, especially since I don't know what it is.

"This will fail, boy," Ivan mutters. All signs of amusement have faded from his face. He looks around the clearing at his family of drifters. "But we'll do it. We'll spread the word. But hear me now. When this thing explodes in your face — which it will — don't say we didn't warn you." It's like a weight has been lifted from my shoulders. I sigh in relief and stand up, smiling. I shake his outstretched hand.

"Thank you. Seriously," I say, meaning it.

"Whatever," Ivan says, dropping my hand and walking away. I'm joined by Nikola, Elisa, and Alek, and the release of tension is palpable among us. I glance at Elisa and find her smiling at me. It's nice. I think for a moment about speaking to her, but something catches my attention. Over her shoulder, a tiny bird with brown wings and a white belly flies down and lands on one of the fallen tree trunks. It bounces across the graying wood, closer and closer, until its dark eyes lock with my own. I start to raise my hand to point to it, but it flits away into the dark of the forest. I want to ask the others if they saw it, but they're enveloped in their own conversation, so I drop it, letting its boldness sink away in my mind.

12

"They're on the move, sir. We've followed them all over Belstrana," the Colonel says, feeling confident in his delivery but unsure how the news will be taken.

"Whatever for?" the Man asks.

"Unfortunately... You're not going to like this." He shifts to his left foot, realizes his mistake, and straightens back up.

The Man looks up from a thick, tattered book that sprawls across his lap. "Spit it out."

"They definitely are planning a coup, sir, by way of the election."

The Man freezes for a moment and then throws his head back in laughter. "That... that's ridiculous! They think they can change presidents so easily?" he jokes between giggles.

The Colonel's eyes widen at the response, and he continues. "There's more, sir."

The man's laughter dies down, and he closes the book and drops it onto the floor beside his chair with a thud. "What else? They're writing a letter to say 'please'?"

"No, sir. They're telling drifters that they have help on the inside, that some of the Men in Red have changed alliances and will help them," the Colonel responds.

The change in atmosphere in the room is abrupt. The Man stands up, walks to the nearest window, and runs his hand along the velvet curtain that hangs by its side. He squeezes his fingers around it and yanks it across the opening, blocking out the view.

"I want names, Colonel. All of them. Who are they? Where are they? And do they have a family?" he demands as he walks around the room and closes the other curtains until all natural light has been eclipsed. The fire illuminates the office, and the glow bounces off of the walls and rests on the Man's face, which is twisted in anger.

"We don't know their identities yet, sir. They haven't mentioned anyone in particular," the Colonel says meekly. A bead of sweat rolls from his forehead down to the tip of his nose and drips onto his lips so that he tastes the salt mixed with fear.

"FIND OUT WHO THEY ARE AND BRING THEM TO ME!" the Man bellows, and he knocks over a stack of papers, sending a furious cascade of white through the room.

———

THE NEXT MORNING, THE OTHERS AND I SET OUT southwestwards again towards the next village on the list. The rush from our success last night leaves us more energized than usual, and we split our time between racing and walking. As we move, we talk, learning more about one another. It seems strange to me that we had lived our entire lives together on the same Compound but know pretty much nothing about one another. I guess it makes sense considering we don't even know much about ourselves.

I find myself staring at Elisa more often than I would like to admit, watching her move with grace through the forest. She reminds me of a fairy from one of the bedtime stories my mother told me when I was a child. I wonder if we would have ever spoken back on the Compound while drugged on Crystal. No, probably not.

Late that evening, well past sunset, we reach the outskirts of the village and decide to rest for the night. We go about our usual chores. Alek builds the fire while Elisa and I string up tarps to shield us from the crisp winds rolling off of the mountains to our north.

"What do you think this group will be like?" Alek asks us as he tucks himself beneath his blanket once we've all settled down, nestled close to the fire. He rests the back of his head in his hands, which lace through his hair, and closes his eyes.

"Hopefully they won't be as combative as the last bunch," Elisa mumbles. "Don't get me wrong — they were nice and all, but I'd rather not get attacked in my sleep tonight." She, too, had folded her blanket around her body and stares dreamily into the flames that dance between us. I watch the firelight reflect off of her eyes and feel myself drifting.

I think I hear Nikola ask a question, but by the lazy tone of her voice, it doesn't seem important or urgent, so I don't respond. Alek can answer. Or Elisa, at whom I haven't stopped staring. It's like I'm in a trance.

"Uh, August?" Alek says, and I glance at him for a second and then my gaze wanders back to Elisa.

"Huh?" I mumble. Alek chuckles.

"August!" Nikola yells, and the volume of her cry jerks me to my feet. I grab my knife and flick open the blade, turning in circles to find the threat. She bursts out laughing and rolls to her side, beating the ground with her open hand as she fights to catch her breath.

"What's going on?" I ask, feeling embarrassed as my cheeks become warm.

"I think you have the answer to your question, Nikola," Alek says, smiling at her. He turns his head towards me. "She was wondering if we need a lookout. And from your reaction, I'd say you're still a little paranoid from last night, like the rest of us." My momentary burst of adrenaline crashes, and I drop back to the ground.

"Uh, yeah. A lookout sounds good," I say, folding my knife shut. I slide it back in my pocket and throw a sheepish glance at Elisa, who has pulled up her blanket in a pathetic attempt to hide her grin. Her amusement shows in her crinkled eyes, though, which shine. I plop back on my blanket, folding the outer half over my body.

"I'll take first watch, if you'd like," Nikola offers. "I'm not big on sleep anyways."

"Thanks, Nikola," I reply, and my voice is muted beneath the blanket. "Wake me when you get tired, and I'll take over."

"Will do, jumpy," she smirks. "Just try not to cut my head off when I do, m'kay?"

"Hardy-har, Nikola," I mutter. Even with my eyes closed, I can still picture Elisa asleep beside the fire, blanketed in her dark curls.

————

WE SPEND THE NEXT MONTH TRAVELING THROUGHOUT Belstrana in search of drifters outside of each of the villages on the list. We wade across bubbling rivers, trek up and down the green foothills of the northern mountains, and swim in clear, unpolluted lakes. As we travel, the oak and maple trees that intertwine amongst the evergreens begin to change hues with the coming of winter, sparking into brilliant reds, oranges, and yellows. I particularly like when a gust of wind breaks through the canopy overhead and sends a cascade of multicolored leaves twirling around us. It seems hard to believe that a country so beautiful could have a capital city, Apex, which emanates so much darkness.

The majority of our encounters with drifters are similar to the first and often end with a hesitant agreement to help. I learn more about Belstrana's people and its history. Their lives have been so different than ours, but they share our deep-seated hatred of the Foundation. It's hard to convince them to abandon their resignation and work with us, but the vast majority of people are friendly, and they're tired enough of their circumstances that they're willing to at least try to change them through this plan. Each camp has at least one bitter challenger, though, who insists on pointing out the inevitable failure of the mission and dangerous ramifications it could bring upon the country. When they ask us why they should help, I try to shift the choice back on them, insisting that they decide together if removing Karlmann is worth risking their safety. Three of the groups refuse immediately.

"We're doing fine out here on our own," one woman tells me between mouthfuls of dried berries. "We're not gonna go stickin' our heads out for nobody but ourselves. If the villagers don't like what Karlmann's doing, then they should've left when we did. Now they're stuck with their choice, and it's too bad for them." The juice stains what few teeth she has left, and I can't help but cringe as I watch her. I don't bother spending more time here and instead thank her for her time and move forward.

Others groups have major doubts and conspiracy theories about the Reds coming to help the rebellion. "They get paid three times as much as I did as a grocer, they do," one malnourished man mutters as he displays his collection of hats, none of which are clean or suitable by the standards of most modern societies. He vacillates between four different hats, some of which appear centuries old and are caked with dirt.

"No, they don't, Harold," another man says as he whittles a javelin from a fallen branch. "They're as scared as the rest of us. They're only doin' it to keep Karlmann from goin' after their own families."

"That's the most idiotic thing you've ever said," replies Harold. He tips his ascot cap to the side, revealing a dusting of red hair on an otherwise balding forehead. "Those idiots believe everything that comes out of that man's mouth. Accordin' to him, we're all ravin' lunatics out here waitin' for death to come and fetch us from the torment of being excluded from his perfect little society or whatever he'd like to call his nation-wide prison. And they believe him!"

"Aren't we? Waitin' for death, I mean," mumbles a middle-aged petite woman whose braided red hair signals her sibling relation to Harold. "I can't remember the last time I saw someone other than you two gits, which is why I'm so happy you're here," she says to Elisa and Nikola. The woman, whose name is Joanne, shakes with excitement to have other females around her. She doesn't mind the weapons attached to their sides or the brute strength and skill that they carry with them.

"You're very kind," Elisa replies, smiling and shaking the woman's frail hand. Even Nikola forces out a brief grin, though she keeps her hand resting on her folded staff while the two men continue to quarrel. Alek and I exchange glances but don't interrupt.

"Who are you callin' a git?" the other man replies. "It's the truth, I tell ya. They're caught up in their own nightmare. That could've been us if we hadn't gotten out before they put the gates up. Desperation will cause men to do horrible, unimaginable things — things like what goes on in those villages."

"Amos, you've gone off the deep end now. Those men

would slit your throat in a heartbeat if you showed your face in the village. Better yet, they'd get one of the young 'uns to do it for them, the bleedin' cowards," Harold says, concluding his sentiments by spitting on the ground.

"Believe what you will, Harold. They might slit my throat or they might do as this boy has suggested and help us out when the time comes," Amos answers, unaffected by Harold's rant. He continues to shave down the wooden tip of the javelin into a sharp point.

"I feel bad for ya if that's what ya really think," Harold replies with narrowed eyes. "You keep my sister out of this mess, ya hear? Get your own self killed or whatever, just don't get her in the middle of it." Joanne slinks over to him and points her finger in his face.

"Let me make up my own mind, would ya?" she says. "I trust my husband and have for fifteen years now." Her eyes soften as she peers over at Amos, whose back leans against a tree. He winks at her, and I steal a glance at Elisa.

"I'll help you," he says, locking eyes with me. "Even if my lousy brother-in-law thinks it's a suicide mission, I think anything's better than 'waiting for death' as he put it." He sneers at Harold, whose eyes and mouth turn down.

"Thank you, Amos," I say, closing the distance between us to shake his hand. "It means the world to us and to others like us that you would risk everything to help."

"Look around, son. He ain't got much, and this plan of yours will only serve to rip away what little he has left," Harold says with a forlorn glance at Joanne before stomping off into the trees.

"We don't want to put you into any danger, Elisa says, stepping forward. "We know we're asking a lot from you. If you can't help us, then we'll understand."

"Child, we'll help you regardless of the cost," Joanne replies.

She cups Elisa's face in her weathered hands. "God will be with us, and we will manage as we always have." A small tear slides down Elisa's cheek, and in that moment, I know I've fallen over the edge of the cliff, reaching towards whatever future I might be able to have with her, even if she doesn't see me yet in the way I see her.

13

After several weeks of traveling, we return to our original campsite just as the season of frost and snow begins to settle in around us. Our supplies have dwindled, and the weather continues to deteriorate, each night colder than the last. The incoming cold front brings occasional thunderstorms that fill up the sky with webs of lightning and rain. Thankfully, it hasn't snowed yet.

"I guess I should go see Luca soon," I say that night after we fortify ourselves as much as possible against the cold wind. The sky is clear, but we've learned from experience that storms can sneak up quickly. I slip beneath my blankets, which are now closer than ever to the fire, thankful to be in a familiar place. Elisa nods drowsily, but Nikola does not respond. I can't tell if she's asleep or still bitter about not being chosen by Joseph to be the one who visits Luca. Surely not...

"Need me to go with you?" asks Alek before stifling a yawn.

"Nah, I'll go alone," I reply, thankful for the offer.

I'm not sure when the others fall asleep. My body is exhausted, but I can't stop my mind. I stare up through the trees, watching the familiar parade of stars. I hold my right arm up over my face and pull back my sleeve, exposing the triangle, and run my finger over its lines. I still don't know what it means, so I cover it back up and put my arms back under the blanket. Each exhale clouds over my vision, and I begin to shiver. I'm cold, but also scared. For the first time, though, it's not my safety I worry about, but that the plan will fail.

Traveling through the country had exposed us to the troubling conditions our fellow citizens deal with on a daily basis. Their stories weave together in my mind, forming as complete of an illustration of Belstrana as ever. It's not just about me anymore, or even the Young Ones trapped on the compounds. It's now about reuniting families, providing basic provisions and security, finding something worthy of trust, and protecting everything worthy of love. The warnings from the drifters ring in my ears, and I force myself to believe that whatever Luca has planned after the election will save us. Only then can I shut down my thoughts and fall away.

———

As I run down to the village the next morning, a familiar, small bird flits between the trees nearby. I'd seen birds like this all over Belstrana — brown with white bellies — each of them bolder than the last. It follows me to the tunnel, and I imagine it to be some sort of guardian, watching my back. I'm almost sad to leave its company, but I drop down into the tunnel anyway. I pull out my flashlight and flick it on, but to my surprise, I find the darkness doesn't scare me as much as it used to, so I turn it back off and invite the blindness in as I press forward, proud of myself.

When I reach the other side, I exit through the cupboard

inside of the old bakery, hurry to the living room, and peek through the grimy window panes. Two brown figures stand a few yards away, and I drop to my stomach and slide so my back is against the wall beside the window. I wait a few minutes and sneak another look. They're gone. After another minute or two (for good measure), I run out of the door and throw myself onto the roof across the street. I sprint across the maze of buildings, stopping when necessary to check for clear streets below.

It's during one of these surveillances that I recognize a familiar face. It's Alek. His picture is pinned to a wall, and the words "DESERTER: $200 REWARD IF RETURNED TO THE COMPOUND" have been typed beneath his face in bold, red ink. I wonder if there are similar posters of me or Elisa or Nikola. I find my answer as I continue my route to Luca's house, spying at least one poster of each of us, labeling us deserters and offering rewards. I'm surprised to see the reward for my capture is significantly higher than that for the others. I wonder if it has to do with the triangle on my wrist.

I arrive at Luca's house, drop down to the empty street, and knock on the door. It swings open at my touch, but there's nobody on the other side. Holding my breath, I step in, placing one foot in front of the other as quietly as possible. The chairs that had once stood on either side of the fireplace are strewn around the room. Some are toppled over while others appear shattered into chunks of splintered wood. The picture frames on the table had been knocked over, and the kerosene lamps are missing. I unhook the sling from my belt and pull out a stone from my pocket, resting it in the leather pouch, ready to defend myself if necessary.

I continue through the door leading to the hallway, and the smell of rotten food stings my nostrils. I head upstairs first and find it covered in a motley collection of scattered clothes. Even the bathroom cupboard has been ransacked. With every step, my heart sinks, and by the time I return to the staircase, I'm positive Luca must have been arrested for plotting against Karlmann. I shouldn't be surprised, but I am.

As I descend, a metallic clatter rings out from the kitchen, which happens to be the last room I have to search. Startled by the noise, I almost lose my footing but manage to regain composure and avoid falling down the stairs. With my breath stifled by caution, I head down, pressing my back into the wall and watching the kitchen doorway. A series of thumps and thuds and clangs emanate from the room, and a man's voice mutters a series of profanity-ridden complaints. I hesitate, unsure how many men are inside and I try to decide if I should run while I have the chance or approach the intruder and demand information about Luca's whereabouts.

I decide it isn't worth the risk and turn down the hall towards the living room just as the kitchen door flies open. My training kicks in, and I lower myself into a defensive crouch with my sling twirling at my side, ready for use. A black boot protrudes around the corner, followed by a pair of dark denim pants and a black t-shirt.

"AAAAAAAAH!" a voice screams, sounding more feminine than masculine, and a pile of papers scatters to the floor. "Who's there?" the man cries, jumping back against the door frame. I brace myself for a struggle until I realize who the man is.

"Luca?" I say, lowering my sling. Luca stands with his fists raised, and his chest heaves with adrenaline. Papers continue to flutter down to the ground as he stares wildly at me.

"August? When did you get here? And why'd you scare me like that? Haven't you ever heard of knocking?" he scolds, placing his hand on his chest to catch his breath. He bends over and begins gathering the papers into a messy pile. I stare, unsure if I should help until I see my own face on one of the papers. I bend over and pick it up.

"Uh, Luca? What's this?" I ask, holding out for him to see. "Why do you have a picture of me? And where'd you get it?" Luca stops moving for a second and glances up at me before returning to his task.

"Irony of ironies," he mutters, snatching the paper from my hand. I recoil, feeling betrayed. "I, of all people, have been appointed to a committee of citizens that's supposed to be looking for you and your friends. These," he says as he holds up a stack of photographs, "are your fliers. Congratulations. You're famous." His voice is dry and bitter.

"What? Why you?" I ask, aware that I could be in danger. I squat down and pick up one of Elisa's pictures, studying it for a second before handing it to Luca.

"Because it's the Foundation, and I'm sure they're suspicious of me. There's usually a Red posted outside my door, and I'm supposed to report you whenever I see you," he replies, patting the edges of the stack of papers on the ground to even them out before standing up. My breath gets caught in my throat, and I go rigid.

"I'm not going to do it, of course," he says, rolling his eyes. "I'm leaving." Luca peers over my shoulders towards the dingy window at the end of the hall, where a brown bird perches motionless on the sill. He pushes his way past me and pounds his fist against the window, but his visitor doesn't flinch. "Stupid birds," he mumbles to himself and trudges to the living room. Curious, I think, taking one last glance at the bird before joining him.

"Leave?" I say, picking our conversation back up.

"Yeah, to join you guys in the forest. I assume that's okay with you." He strides across the room and dumps the papers into the open fireplace. After retrieving a thin pack of matches from his pocket, he strikes one and flicks it onto the stack of fliers. Within seconds, the flames burst forth and the edges of the stack blacken and curl inward. I watch as a photo of Elisa shrivels into a charred heap like a dying rose and frown. A heavy pat on the back of my shoulder snaps me to reality. I turn around and see the straps of a bulging, brown pack loaded on Luca's shoulders.

"What happened here?" I ask, motioning around the room.

"What does it look like? They searched my house." He pulls the photographs out of the frames and tucks them in his back pocket.

"What for?"

"How should I know? Probably to see if I had any information about the rebels. Doesn't matter, anyways. They didn't find anything. They did, however, leave me that heap of garbage and a kind note informing me of my job," he says, motioning with his head towards the fire. "Screw 'em," he adds.

I take a moment to study Luca. He's aged since our last encounter. The gray in his hair has pushed deeper into his hairline, and his wrinkles appear wider and darker within his paled skin. Even his beard is sprinkled with white and has grown unkempt. He walks towards the door and swings it open, allowing in a sudden breeze of cold air. It catches in the fireplace and sends a swirl of papery ash through the room.

"Aren't you forgetting something, Luca?" I ask, stepping towards the door and wondering if he's got a sudden suicidal wish. "You'll be arrested if you go out there. You can't hide from them like I can."

Luca reaches into his pocket and pulls out a brown package. It's one of the bars of food like what we eat. He must have gotten a supply of them somehow, which means he could potentially be as strong as us now. Luca smirks, replaces the food in the pocket, strides out of the door, and disappears above the roof line. I scan the room one final time and shut the front door before jumping up to meet Luca. I don't have time to ask him any more questions before he sprints off towards the bakery. I follow, aware of the brown bird that flies off to my side, keeping pace with us.

14

For the first time in months, the Colonel enjoys stepping into the dark office if only for the heat produced by the eternally roaring fire across the room. He sees the slumped outline of his superior in one of the winged chairs near the window, and he approaches it slowly, allowing his red-cheeked face to relish the warmth after walking through the cold.

"Who's there?" the Man asks.

"It's me, sir, Colonel Pervak," he replies as he comes to a stop several feet away from the chair.

"And?" His voice sounds groggy, almost wistful as though caught in a dream.

"An update, sir. Luca joined them in the forest. They're continuing with this plan of theirs even though they're aware that we know about it."

"Why did he leave the village? Or better yet, *how* did he leave the village?"

"We're not sure how it happened, sir, but he got some of the bars. He's going with two of the Young Ones to see his wife. The other two stayed behind."

"He got some of the bars? *How did he do that, Colonel?* You were supposed to have the traitors arrested!" the man bellowed. "Do you know what could happen if someone's leaking out a supply of those bars? *Do you?*" He throws his glass across the room, and it shatters with an alcohol-fed roar of flames in the fireplace. The Colonel begins to feel too warm, like he's suffocating again, and he inches away from the fire and away from the Man.

"Yes... yes, sir," he stammers. "I told them to arrest any suspicious people. Apparently they missed one."

"*One* is all it takes. One crack in the foundation, and the whole house can fall in on itself. Is that what you want, Colonel? Would you like *your* house to fall in on itself? You have children, right? Four and two, isn't that right? How would you feel if your house caved in on them?" he says.

"Terrible, sir." The Colonel fights back the urge to comment on the Man's subtle threat towards his family, and anger stirs in the pit of his stomach. "What should I have them do?"

"Have Luca and the two with him followed. Arrest the others who stayed behind. It's getting too dangerous. You have not been doing your job well, Colonel. I have to say, I'm more than a little disappointed in you. See what you can do about that, will you?"

"Yes, sir," he replies. He lingers in the room, unsure if the conversation has ended.

"Leave, Colonel," the Man advises, and the Colonel shuffles through the door and back into the hall.

———

WE EMPLOY OUR TIME OVER THE NEXT WEEK BY TRAINING and exploring the forest. The weather continues to cool, but the snow remains at bay, chased away by clear skies and the bright sun. We take turns in mock fights, practicing with our weapons and teaching Luca what we can. Nikola seems to have suppressed the majority of her sullenness, though her sass still comes out in bountiful quantity. She even cracks a few jokes here and there, though she usually follows them up with some sort of dismissive scowl. Alek, on the other hand, remains quiet but continues to carry an air of collected optimism. He spends his free time perched in trees, trying his best to remember the words to songs his parents used to sing to him. His smooth voice blends with the rustling leaves and fills the meadow.

To my pleasure, Elisa spends every afternoon with me, sitting at the edge of the meadow and watching animals wander in and out of their hiding places as they forage in preparation for winter. It had never occurred to me that we were surrounded by so much wildlife, and the woods are full of fawn-colored rabbits, chattering squirrels, and graceful deer. Each day, Elisa scoots closer, becoming less and less timid around me. By the end of the week, things are different between us, lighter than they'd ever been. We sit side-by-side, laughing between intervals of silence, and stealing soft touches between our arms or crossed legs. The air around her feels electric, and I feel warmer when she's nearby. I want so badly to at least hold her hand, to feel her skin against mine again, but I refrain.

We spend tonight reviewing our plans for tomorrow, which is when we'll leave for Village B. Everyone is calm and rested, and we begin to wrap things up when the peace is shattered. A familiar female drifter comes into our clearing. Her thick, brown hair hangs in frazzled braids down to her thin waist, framing her hollow eyes and concealing her tattered clothes.

"You don't remember me, do you?" she asks as we encircle her, stealing glances at the woods in search for other drifters. "I'm Ana. You came by our camp several weeks ago, outside Village E? Do you remember? You spoke with my brother,

Timothy." The memory clicks into place at the mention of his name.

"Of course, Ana," I say, lifting my hand from my sling. I shake her bony hand and smile. "How are you? Is everything okay?" She sniffs.

"I'm okay, but I'm afraid I have some bad news. I'm sorry, but the elders have decided not to help you in the election. They say it's too dangerous." My heart drops. "They believe that they've made a workable life for themselves out in the forest and that nobody is in any real danger in the villages. All the villagers want is more freedom, and Timothy and the others don't think it's a valid enough reason to risk their lives. So they won't." I can tell she's uncomfortable, but I'm grateful to at least have word back from one of the villages. I glance at Luca, who frowns.

"I'm sorry to hear that," I say.

"You can't be serious," Luca growls at her. "It's not that the villagers want freedom to watch television or eat ice cream. They're prisoners in their own homes. They can't go outside without being shoved in the back of a truck and shipped off to a labor camp!" His face turns red as he paces back and forth, jaw clenched. The girl's eyes widen, and she wraps her arms around her frail body.

"What does it matter what their logic is, Luca?" Alek asks. "This isn't the first village to say no. Why are you so upset about this one?" It's a valid question, and we all wait for his answer.

"It's just a stupid reason," Luca says, stopping his stiff strides. "Does nobody understand what goes on beyond those walls?"

"Probably not," Elisa says, trying to reason with him. "They left before the walls went up. Nobody but the Reds go in or out, so why would they know what life is like?" Luca grunts and turns back towards the girl.

"Do they have any other grand ideas?" he asks sarcastically.

"No, not really. They think people need to stick it out, and that if they don't like life in the village, then they should escape and become drifters like us." Her eyes shift around at us, waiting for our reaction. Nikola's knuckles turn white around her staff, and Alek rubs his face with his hand, sighing.

"But you do realize you can't just stroll out of the villages, right?" I ask. She nods and shrugs her shoulders. Arguing with her is pointless.

"Thank you for letting us know," Elisa says, forcing a half-hearted smile.

"I am so sorry. A few of us tried to stick up for you, but we were outnumbered and outvoted," she says, and Elisa nods. "Anyways, I'd better be going. It's a long way back, and I'm not exactly the world's fastest traveler."

"Here," says Elisa, rummaging through her bag. She hands the girl three brown-wrapped bars of food. "You can use this more than me, I think." The woman beams and tucks the food into her pockets. Without another word, she disappears into the night. I watch her go, staring into the woods long after she's vanished.

"I can't believe it... I mean, I can, but I can't," Luca says, kicking a small stone across the clearing.

"Let it go, Luca. There's no point, and you know it. The plan's already exposed anyways. They probably made the right call by keeping themselves and the rest of the village off of the Foundation's radar," Alek says. I find myself in agreement.

"There are plenty of other villages who have sided with us. I understand why they don't want to take the risk," I say.

"You're right. I know you're right. I'm just frustrated. There are plenty of people out there who will vote for Fletcher. We'll get our point across," Luca says.

Nikola watches him carefully, and I wish I knew her

thoughts. I don't think she trusts Luca, and I'm beginning to question my trust of him as well due to the mixed signals and vague explanations he keeps giving. The elections are only three weeks away, and I have yet to feel any form of confidence going in to them. Something doesn't make sense. Why does Luca insist on carrying out this busted plan when he knows it'll fail and that the Foundation will strike back? And why is he so secretive about the rest of the plan? Why does it need to be concealed?

These questions carry over through the night, and I continue mulling them over while I eat my breakfast. I chase the dry food down with a lengthy gulp of water from my canteen and scan through my supplies, taking inventory. Most of it's still there and relatively untouched, and Luca had restored our food supplies, so I'm pretty much ready to go whenever. I clip my sling and knife onto my belt and gather a few small stones to place into my pocket. Nearby, Elisa coils her whip and secures it to her waist and then slides a thin, folded knife down the outside of her boot. I know I shouldn't worry about her coming with us. She's as strong and smart as the rest of us, after all. We strap our packs onto our backs and say goodbye to Alek and Nikola.

"Good luck," Alek says, shaking our hands. "Be careful and hurry back."

"Yeah, what he said," Nikola adds, thumbing at Alek. She crosses her arms, and I can tell she wishes it was her going instead of Elisa.

"Thanks, I think," Luca replies, not bothering to try to shake her concealed hand. He checks his compass and walks away. Once his back is turned, Nikola's eyes narrow on me.

"Don't trust him," she mouths. I shake my head, and Elisa and I follow him out of the clearing, heading to the south. This is the coldest morning yet, and my breath clouds in front of my face, but the longer we move, the warmer I feel. We spend the majority of the time running since there's no reason not to make the trip any longer than necessary. After a few hours of a steady pace, we take a break. Elisa excuses herself into the forest, and while she's gone, Luca speaks for the first time since we'd left.

"So how long have you loved her?" he asks, motioning towards the woods where she had disappeared.

"What? Who, Elisa?" I reply, startled by his sudden boldness.

"Well, yeah. Who else?" he says. I lean my back against a young fir tree and wonder how much I should say.

"I don't know her that well. We've known each other for just a few months," I answer.

"But you love her..." Luca prompts, leaning against his own tree. "I can tell by the way you look at her. I thought you were going to freak out when she said she was coming with us." He smirks, amused by my embarrassment.

"I... I guess so," I say softly. "I don't know..." I run my fingers over the cuff of my coat sleeve. "It doesn't matter. I'm pretty sure that's the last thing on her mind. She's too focused on rescuing the Young Ones to notice me."

"Doesn't seem that way to me," he replies. He takes a swig from his canteen and screws the lid back on. "You two remind me of my wife and me when we were teens. We married when I was only eighteen, and she was seventeen. We had Freddy a year later." The reminder that Luca is a father and husband snaps me back to reality. How can I think of a relationship with someone in the midst of all of this chaos? I take the opportunity to at least learn more about Luca.

"Did you know when you met her that you loved her?" I ask. It's as good a place as any to start, I suppose.

"Lord, no," Luca says, chuckling. "We met when we were both little kids. Our parents were good friends. I actually thought she was a snob, and she informed me many years later that she thought I was an idiot." I can't help but laugh. Luca plucks a crinkled, brown leaf from a branch and twists it between his fingers as he continues talking. "It wasn't until after we got to know each other in high school that we realized we had feelings for one another, and she learned I was not, in fact, an idiot." He smiles at his own memory.

"What about you?" he asks, flicking the leaf to the ground.

"What about me?" I ask, confused.

"Did you know the first time you saw her?"

"I... I don't know. The first time I remember seeing her was in class, right before we left the Compound. I looked over, and... there she was." Leaves crunch in the distance, and I jump up, brushing the dirt from my pants and trying to hide my blushing cheeks. Elisa grins sheepishly when she returns to us and grabs her pack.

"Ready?" she asks, but she won't make eye contact with me. I think I see her face flush, but it's hard to tell in the shadows of the trees.

"As ever," Luca answers, and we set off without another word.

15

We run at a brutal pace over the next two days, only stopping to sleep or eat, until we reach the outskirts of the village. We circle around to the north side and make camp out of eyesight of the road that cuts through the forest and heads into the village. As a precaution, Luca and I change into our uniforms even though the truck isn't supposed to come for another day. We're too close to light a fire tonight, so the evening is restless and cold.

We wake the next morning and rush to eat and get in place before the truck comes by. According to Luca, it should pass by here a few minutes before nine o'clock, so we wait in the trees, poised for action. Right on time, the faint rumble of the engine cuts through the quiet, steadily growing louder. Luca nods at me, and together, we emerge from the trees and stand in the middle of the road with as much authority as possible. When the driver sees us from inside of the cab, he glances at his companion and slams on his brakes, stopping a few yards in front of us. Luca walks to the driver's side, and the Red rolls down his window. I stay in front of the truck, close enough to notice they're not wearing any seatbelts. Good.

"What's this all about?" the driver asks. "Who are you?"

"There's been some suspicious activity on this road, and I'm afraid we're going to need to see your credentials before we let you get any closer to the village," Luca replies, playing his roll well.

"What? Who authorized this?" the man says, but he reaches for the white identification card in his breast pocket. I glance to the woods at my left and make eye contact with Elisa while Luca distracts the guards. She darts out of the forest, leaps on to the passenger's side of the cab, wrenches it open, and drags the man from his seat so that he falls to the dirt road below. I move to help her but stop. She can handle this. He reaches for his pistol, but Elisa doesn't seem phased. She smacks it away with a slash of her whip, and the gun skids into the brush along the road. The man cries out as she rolls him on to his stomach and ties his hands together with several yards of heavy twine. She hasn't even broken a sweat.

The driver, who had watched the scene unfold, looks through the windshield at me expectantly, waiting for me to defend the Red. I shrug, and he moves for his own gun right as Luca yanks him from his seat. The Red falls to the ground but scurries back to his feet. He pulls the gun from his holster and points it at Luca. Before he can pull the trigger, I've already loaded a stone in my sling and now fire it across the road. It hits the guard on his temple, and he yelps and drops his gun to shield his face with his hands. Luca retrieves it while I run over and grab the man's arms, roping them together in front of his stomach with twine before shoving him into the forest, where Elisa has secured the other guard. I dump the Red beside his companion, and she coils more twine around their feet. Luca retrieves the guards' identification cards.

"You good here?" I ask Elisa, who is supposed to stay behind and watch the Reds. She nods and waves us away.

"Yeah. Be careful, okay?" she says, looking at me.

"Will do," I say, unable to hide my smile. Luca and I run back to the truck and jump into the cab. Luca drives, and we take the road a little faster than we probably should to make up for lost time. After a few minutes, the tree line opens out, and we drive through the grassy perimeter of field before we reach the gate. Two Reds stand guard, and Luca hands one of them the white card he had taken from the driver moments ago. The guard swipes it through a small, black box secured to the fence and hands it back to Luca without a word. Beads of sweat form on my face, and I try to wipe my face without drawing any attention. The Red waves us through, and I feel myself relax slightly.

This village is laid out in almost identical fashion to ours, so we have no problem navigating through the empty, narrow streets. We arrive at the entrance to the Compound right on schedule and are greeted by six nurses, all dressed in white and all wearing little expression on their faces. Luca parks the truck, and I scan the faces of the women, wondering which one is Luca's wife. A few Reds stand at attention on either side of the gate, and I hope they don't ask any questions. To my relief, they don't seem to notice that anything's amiss, so we open our doors and slide out, welcoming the skeptical nurses who approach the truck.

"Where are the usual drivers?" asks the lead nurse. She's tight-lipped and graying, and her brown eyes study my face. She's suspicious already, and although my beard has grown considerably over the past several weeks, it doesn't seem to hide my age as well as I had hoped.

"They've been reassigned. Do you want the parcels or not?" Luca barks, snatching her attention from me. Astonished by his tone, her lips part and her eyebrows rise, but she doesn't say anything else. Luca and I walk to the back of the truck, and I open the sliding door to reveal the cargo. The nurses push in around me and retrieve the supplies. While they're distracted, one of the nurses — a blonde woman with slim hips and a slimmer waist — lets a gasp slip out when she sees Luca's face. They stare at one another for a moment before Luca makes the first move.

"Ma'am," he says, addressing her, "I'll need you to sign for this delivery." She nods and steps forward but stops as the lead nurse protests.

"That's my job!" the woman says, shoving her way in front of Luca's wife.

"I didn't ask you! I asked her! Don't question me again, or I'll have you reported," Luca growls. "Now, you. Come here." He points towards his wife, who lowers her head and walks to him, avoiding eye contact with her superior, whose face is as red as her lipstick by this point. His wife follows him to the other side of the cab, out of our sight, while I stand guard of the cargo and the nurses. The women steal glances at me, and I notice Luca's performance has also gained the attention of the Reds at the gate. Luca and his wife reemerge a moment later, and she falls in line to help the others with the shipment. When everything has been unloaded and rests in the back of two small utility trucks, I slide the door shut, hop back into the truck's cab with Luca, and we leave the gate.

Luca turns to me and cautions, "Don't be surprised if we run into some trouble on the way out. June warned me that the head nurse would report us to headquarters."

"Yeah, I saw the Reds checking us out, too," I say, feeling tension slip up my back and into my shoulders, turning them into rigid knots. My heart pounds, and sweat pours down my face and back, wetting my shirt and causing it to stick against the cheap leather seat.

"We'll probably have to do some evasive maneuvers," Luca

mumbles, but his body language seems relaxed, which irritates me.

"Evasive maneuvers, Luca? In this truck? We don't stand a chance," I reply, staring wide-eyed into the long side mirror on the other side of my window.

"Good news, though, is that I told her about the election, and she's in. Let's hope that one, she doesn't get into any trouble and two, she can get some Reds over to our side. She's smart. Real smart. But also too trusting." A goofy, inappropriate grin spreads across his face, and I can't help but gawk.

"She kissed me and told me she loved me," Luca adds with a chuckle. "I didn't think I'd ever hear those words again."

I resist slapping him. "You've got to be kidding me. Snap out of it, Luca! You need to focus on getting us out of here. We'll throw a party for you later to celebrate your thirty second reunion, but if they do decide to chase us down, you're going to have to get us out of here. Now think!" I yell at him. Part of me feels bad about squashing his moment, but we're in way too deep right now for him to focus on anything but getting us back to safety.

Luca's eyebrows furrow in thought and he replies, "Right." We arrive at the gate to leave the village, and he hands the guard the same stolen card from before. I hold my breath as the Red swipes it, only exhaling once we've passed through the gate and entered the field.

"Maybe we got away with it," I say as we reenter the forest. Too soon. At that exact moment, the rumbling, gravel-grinding sound of another engine rises up behind us. A boxy, tan, off-road vehicle containing four Reds speeds up behind us. My heart stops when they motion for Luca to pull over. He sighs, annoyed.

"What should I do?" he asks between glances in his rear-view mirror. I jerk my head over and shove his arm.

"Are you stupid? Pull over!" I say, "Before they start shooting at us!" My imagination takes over, and I envision at least a dozen different scenarios of what's about to take place, and none of them end well. Not that I want Elisa in jeopardy, but we could definitely use her help now, and I hope she's watching from somewhere close.

We approach a bend in the road, and Luca pulls off on the shoulder and stops the truck. We're out of sight of the village, isolated on the empty road, and surrounded by acres of thick, sound-consuming forest. Two of the Reds exit their vehicle and walk towards us. I wipe the sweat from my forehead and sit up in my seat, trying to appear calm and casual. Luca rolls down his window.

"What can I help you with?" he asks the Red who now stands by his door. The other one continues around to my side, eying me warily.

"Are you two okay?" the Red on Luca's side responds, looking at me. I'm sure I'm a mess, but I can't help it.

"You talking about Kristov here?" Luca says, pointing his thumb at me. "He's fine. He's new, a little green still." Luca tries to force out a chuckle, but it sounds more like he's choking. Both guards continue to stare at me, and I try to slow my heartbeat.

"Well, we followed you because you forgot to pick up the package to go back to Apex. Hold on a minute, and I'll get it. Open your cargo space if you don't mind." My breath slips out with a *whoosh* as Luca concedes and exits the cab. The truck door slides up, only to be interrupted by the scuffling sounds of a struggle from behind me. I move to grab my door handle when the other Red jerks it open and reaches for me. I turn in my seat and kick the Red with my right foot. He flies back across the road and lands in a broken pile, face down. Out of the truck in one, swift leap, I pull the sling from my belt, load it, and wait for his next move.

The Red staggers up, blood trickling from his nose, and charges me. I leap straight up over him, striking his head with a stone while in midair before landing on my feet. He stumbles to his knees with a grunt, and I fling out another stone, knocking the man unconscious. He flops to the ground, and I run to the back of the truck to help Luca. Another guard lies motionless on the road, and a third guard manages to wrap his arms around Luca's upper body, placing him in a headlock. The Red reaches for the handcuffs on his belt, but before I can load another stone into my pouch, Elisa flies through the air and lands a solid blow with the handle of her whip on the man's head. Both he and Luca tumble forward, and a fourth Red rushes forward, drawing his gun. He raises it and points it at Luca. I can't move fast enough, and a shot rings out. I duck from the noise, suppressing a scream, but it isn't Luca who collapses. It's the Red. I stare in disbelief at the pool of blood that forms around the Red's head on the dusty road. An old woman, whose pistol is still aimed at the dead guard, stands on the other side of the road.

Based on her clothing and general lack of hygiene, I can tell she's a drifter. How did she know Luca and I were the ones worth saving? We're dressed like the other Reds. I look back to the body on the road and feel a wave of nausea. A man is dead. Suddenly everything seems far more real and far more dangerous than ever before.

"Why'd you kill him?" I demand, stepping forward and pointing at the body. I feel sick, and I'm angry that I'd played a part in the death of a man. Killing as a first line of defense is unacceptable to me, and I intend to let her know it.

"You know why I killed him," she replies coldly, lowering the gun to her side. Her voice is deep and hoarse, and her wrinkled face looks hard, like stone carved over time by wind and sand. I hadn't noticed it before now, but in her other hand, she holds a thick, curved limb, which I assume she uses as a makeshift cane. Her short, silver hair sticks out in curls from her head, and her thin lips press into a scowl.

"He was going to kill you, and I decided I wasn't gonna let that happen. I know who you are, August."

Elisa and I exchange confused glances, while Luca drags the unconscious men down the embankment beside the road. He ties their hands loosely, more as a deterrent than as permanent bondage. They'll be able to escape when they wake up, and by that time we should be far away.

"How do you know who I am? And who are you? Better yet, how could you have been sure he was going to kill us?" I ask, feeling like gravity is gripping me tighter and tighter in its hold as the adrenaline leaves my body. I'm crashing, but I want answers while I have the chance.

"I'm not gonna talk here. We need to get off the road and into the forest, fast. I can guarantee there's gonna be a massive manhunt when the other three guards wake up and find their buddy in a pool of his blood. They'll think it was you," she replies with a shrug. "Now, come on. I'll tell you more when it's safe."

I appeal to Elisa and Luca for approval, both of whom wait for me to make the first move. I step forward and nod my head, motioning for her to lead the way. We walk for several miles without stopping before we come across a small, gray tent. A scorched, black spot mars the ground nearby, indicating where she builds her fires, and a few pieces of shabby laundry blow in the breeze, suspended from a rope that stretches between trees.

"Home sweet home," she mutters as she plops down against a large boulder, resting her back against its cold, jagged surface. She lays her cane across her lap like a seatbelt and claps her rough hands around its middle. We slide through her site — her home — as I try to decide if we should stay.

"Sit down, already, will you? You're making me tired just

from watching you." She rests her head back against the stone and closes her eyes. "I know what you're thinking, and I'll answer your questions. Now sit down." She opens one eye, which lands on me, and then closes it again. I decide to give her a chance and sit down on the forest floor, several yards away from the woman. Elisa and Luca take their cues from me and join me, sizing her up.

"I'd heard that some kids from one of the compounds were going around to the different villages and were speaking to the drifters," she says, leaving her eyes closed.

"How'd you know it was us?" I reply.

"For one, you are far too young to be a guard. And then when I saw you two leaping like frogs over the Reds, I knew it had to be you. No normal person can leap eight feet into the air, and certainly not myself. Plus, you look like a baby compared to most Reds, despite that mess of a beard you're growing," she says with a raspy chortle. "I don't know what to think of your older friend here, though. He got family in there or something?" She opens the opposite eye this time to peer at Luca, who nods once with a blank expression. "Thought so."

"You're a dangerous one, you are," she continues, looking this time at Elisa, whose mouth drops at the accusation. "You may look all demure and gentle, but inside of you seethes fire and anger. You'd better be careful that you don't hold it all in, or it'll boil over on someone you love, and I promise you'll be worse off than before," she warns. "And as for you," she says, turning her attention to me, "your compassion is warm and fuzzy and all, but it's a bit too idealistic. This isn't a game, and your hesitancy will get you killed. You're going to have to overcome your aversion to violence if you plan on getting out of this alive. Seems like you'd be okay with taking a Red out, but I guess looks can be deceiving."

I open my mouth to defend myself but stop. Who does she

think he is, acting like she knows more about us than we do? I suppress a growl and roll my eyes towards Elisa, whose face is red. The woman sits up and pulls a thin leaf of white paper from her pocket, along with a small, canvas bag from which she withdraws a sprinkling of dried, brown leaves. She's rolling a cigarette for herself, I realize. I've never seen one before. Cigarettes were banned years ago along with most other personal liberties.

"I'd heard you all were out petitioning the villages to vote for Fletcher in the election. It's a good plan in theory, but it won't work. You know that already. There are too many cowards in Belstrana. They'll never speak up the way you want them to," she declares as she finishes rolling the cigarette with a lick of the paper. She pulls a match out of a booklet and swipes it on the back, sending a tiny flame up in front of her face.

"What makes you so confident we'll fail?" Luca asks, and the tip of the woman's cigarette catches fire. He seems offended by her candidness and no wonder why. Luca had mentioned to me on the way down here that the drifters in the South aren't supportive of any form of coup, and this woman fits that description. He hadn't overestimated their apathy if she is any indication.

"What do you mean? You already know you're going to fail. I can see it in your eyes. It's not the failure that's going to ruin you. It's what comes after the failure. You don't know what you're getting into," she retorts, taking a long drag from her cigarette. She exhales a stream of thick smoke, and I cringe. It smells as bad as it looks.

"Well, that's your prerogative," Luca snips. "At least we're doing something other than hiding out in the forest."

The woman raises her eyebrows and releases a slow stream of smoke as she sizes up Luca. "Young man, this person hiding out in the forest just saved your hide."

Elisa huffs. "Actually *I* saved his hide," she reminds the woman. "You shot someone who hadn't even attacked any of us." I could hug her right now.

"Technicality..." She rolls the cigarette between her fingers. "He would have tried to shoot you. You're fast, but you're not faster than a bullet. So, I ended it before it started." Smoke billows from her mouth as she talks, filling the space between us. Elisa turns her head, searching for fresh air. Luca seems unfazed by her performance.

"You don't know that for sure," he says. I'm surprised he's as angry about the murder as I am. I figured he'd be more okay with it. The woman shrugs her shoulders in response.

"We should keep moving," I say, standing up to leave. She closes her eyes and shrugs again.

"Okay. Just don't be surprised when your brilliant plan fails and you end up starting a civil war," she mutters with a dismissive wave. Luca grabs his pack off of the ground, shaking his head.

He must think he's out of earshot of me, because I hear him whisper, "Maybe that's what we want..." I stop in midstride but decide not to say anything, at least not in front of the woman. Luca and I change out of our red shirts, check the compass, and the three of us set off to the northeast without saying goodbye to the woman. The trip is a quiet one. Luca's words are on repeat in my mind, and I try my best to figure out what he meant by them. It can't be good, whatever it is.

16

"We captured two of them, sir. One named Alek and the other named Nikola, a girl. What should we do with them?" The Colonel hopes the capture of two of the five fugitives will be enough to appease the Man for now, but it becomes apparent that his naïve wish won't be granted. The Man slams a book shut and drops it on to his desk with a dusty thud.

"Only *two*? Where are the others?" the Man asks. He grabs a bottle of brandy and yanks the stopper from its opening. Brown liquor splashes onto the desk as he overfills a dingy snifter that's smudged with several days' worth of oily fingerprints.

"They're moving north, sir, back towards K. We have an ambush awaiting them at their campsite. We should have them all by tonight, sir," he boasts. "Would you like to bring them here for questioning or send them back to their Compound?"

"Bring Luca and the two with him to me. Send the others back. Make sure they're isolated until they've received plenty of Crystal. We don't want them pulling any stunts under our nose, now, do we, Colonel?" He slurps a mouthful of brandy and swishes it before swallowing with a wheezy, choking cough. The Colonel watches the Man dab at his mouth with a yellowed handkerchief before answering.

"No, sir. We don't."

———

WE'RE A FEW HOURS AWAY FROM THE CAMPSITE WHEN Elisa asks us to stop for a short break. We agree, and she drops down onto a fallen log, unlaces her boots, and pulls them off to reveal a pair of tragically worn, threadbare socks. I grimace and grab one of my extra pairs of socks for her, though mine aren't in much better shape after all of the running we've been doing.

"Here," I say, handing them to her. "They're too big for you, but they're better than what you've been wearing." Her eyes light up as she looks from me to her feet, which are scarred by large, red blisters. She rinses them with water from her canteen and scowls, but she doesn't complain.

"Why didn't you tell us?" I ask while I search through my pack for the small first-aid kit that's fallen to the bottom by now.

"Didn't want to worry you. It's not that bad," she insists, but I know better than to believe her. My fingers graze a package of fresh gauze, and I pull it out with a grunt and rip it open. Elisa holds out her hand, but I push it away and bend down by her feet.

"Let me," I murmur, lifting her right foot to rest on my knee. I wrap it as gently as I can and place a fresh sock on it before moving on to the left one. She leans back on her hands, watching me.

"I can't figure you out," she says as I dress her left foot in the other sock. I lift my gaze but don't speak, intrigued by what she has to say. "When we met, you were so bitter and angry. But you seem different now. Why is that?" she asks, cocking her head to the side so that her hair hangs loose in cascading curls behind her back. Smudges of dirt streak her face, and even though her eyes are dark and tired, they still somehow shine. I look away from her again.

"I don't know. I'm still angry, but I guess I want to make it right," I reply. I lean my back against the log on which she's sitting and fold my hands in my lap with my legs outstretched in front of me.

"How so? How can we make it right?" She sounds stressed. "We're just five people against thousands."

"Aren't you the one who begged me to stay so that you could help free the rest of the Young Ones?" I ask. "Seems like you'd be glad we're doing this."

She sighs. "Don't get me wrong. I am glad, or at least as glad as I guess I can be given the circumstances. I just don't get why you stayed." She slips her feet back into her boots with a pained flinch and laces them back up. I stare, dumbfounded, into the forest. What more does she want from me? As I think of how to respond, a brown bird floats down from limb to limb several yards away. To my side, Elisa stands up and then gasps.

Kneeling behind a pile of brush, watching us, is a little girl. Her skin is barely visible beneath a thick layer of dirt, and her tattered clothing hangs around her narrow shoulders. She holds a small, brown bundle of fabric in her right hand, which she drops upon locking eyes with Elisa.

"Papa!" she screams with a wild look in her eyes. "They're here!" Luca jumps up from his nap, spinning wildly to find the source of the yelling, and I unclip my sling. Elisa remains calm as she watches the little girl. A man, a drifter by his scruffy face and holey clothes, comes running up through the trees and stops behind the girl. He kneels down and swings her up into his arms.

"Good job, Emily," he says and kisses her forehead. She

nuzzles her head into his neck, never taking her eyes off of us. The man turns to us. "You need to come with me. You can't stay here," he says. Elisa's timid smile drops.

"Who are you?" I ask, slipping my hand in my pocket so my fingertips rest on the smooth surface of a stone.

"Don't have time for that right now. The Reds took your friends. If you don't believe me, go to your campsite. They're swarming the place, waiting on you," he says. His daughter squeezes her legs tighter around his waist.

"How... how do we know we can trust you?" I ask, unsure if this is a trap. The man reaches into his back pocket and pulls out a slender, black object and tosses it to me. It's Nikola's bow staff.

"It got left behind," he says. I stare at the object in my hands, and Elisa takes it from me and tucks it behind her back, inside of her belt.

"Hurry!" the man urges, motioning westward towards the sun-lit horizon. "We can talk later. The longer you wait here, the better chance they have of sniffing you out."

Luca, who has been silent this whole time, nods at me, so we gather our packs and follow the man. We've traveled less than half a mile before the drifter stops and sets his daughter down.

"What in the...?" the man mumbles, staring into a large, shabby fern. He slides up to it without making a sound and then lunges forward with his hands extended. Elisa and Luca watch him with caution. The man emerges with something clasped between his hands. He transfers it to his left hand and moves his right one out of the way.

"You see this?" he asks, beckoning us forward. He holds one of the small, brown birds in his hand, the same type that I've seen all over Belstrana.

"It's beautiful," Elisa whispers, leaning in closer. "We've seen these ever since we left the Compound." The bird behaves calmly, not trying to fight or flee, and allows us to study it care-fully. The drifter scoffs.

"Do you know what this is?" he asks.

"I mean, yeah... it's a bird," Elisa replies, looking up at the man, whose forehead is creased with concern.

"No, actually, it's not. This is how your friends were taken." He clenches his fist, and Elisa yelps as the bird crunches and pops. When he opens his hand again, there's no blood or bone. Metal pieces protrude from its artificial skin and feathers.

"What is that?" I ask. Luca runs his hands over his face, bending over.

"Son of a..." he starts to say, but he bites his knuckle to stop the profanity from spilling out in front of the little girl.

"It's a camera," the drifter says. We exchange glances, unsure what he means. "It's been following you and recording your every move and everything you say. It sends all of this information back to Apex. They've been watching you." I don't know what to think, much less how to respond. It seems so foreign. A memory fires from the recesses of my mind, and I remember lying in front of a moving-picture box as a small child. It retreats again, and a feeling of vulnerability washes over me.

"How do you know this?" I ask.

"I used to do audio/visual work for a news station, but of course that fell apart when Karlmann was elected. There were rumors about this type of technology when I was in school, but I didn't think they were true until a few months ago when I tried to kill one for food since we were so hungry. Didn't you notice that no other birds are in the forest right now? They've gone south for the winter. It's too cold for them here. This is why your friends were ambushed," he says, tossing the bird to the ground. He steps on it for good measure, and it crunches under the twisting heel of his boot.

"How many of these things are there?" Luca asks. "Could there be more around?"

"There's no telling. But, if you see anything like this around the forest right now, I can pretty much guarantee you it's not what you think it is. You're being tracked." His words hang heavily in my mind. This is not good.

"That's how they found out about the election," I mumble, turning to Luca. "They know everything."

"Not everything," he responds. He turns to the drifter and says, "Thank you for your help. We owe you one."

"No, you don't. My name's Dominick, by the way. This here is Emily," he says, squeezing his daughter's shoulders as she stands in front of him. She forces out a weak grin and lowers her head so that her messy, dark hair conceals her face. "We need to keep going. You can stay with my family tonight while you figure everything out." We thank him and follow his lead. Luca and Dominick chat together as we walk, and Elisa befriends the little girl.

I drop back to the rear of the group and follow the others. Anger boils up again, but this time it's directed at myself. I've seen those birds everywhere we've gone. And how much have we said to one another? Or done? I should have known we wouldn't be free out here. The Foundation is everywhere and in everything. Even nature isn't safe, I realize, and I scan the trees above my head for signs of motion. When I'd been stuck on the Compound, I hadn't felt this enclosed and encaged. It fuels my determination to end the Foundation, and by the time we reach the family's campsite, I've resolved to go back to the Compound and retrieve Alek and Nikola. I can't allow them to stay prisoner.

The relative warmth of a small fire greets us when we break into the tiny clearing. A young woman, who appears to be Emily's mother, stands up and crosses the clearing to greet her husband. A large band of fabric is strapped around her chest and neck, and inside, nestled close to her heart, sleeps an infant. Elisa squeals when she sees the baby, and she and the woman connect at once. They sit around the fire, discussing their lives as drifters, but I can't bring myself to talk. After a while, the woman moves to sit beside me.

"You know, you remind me of my little brother," she says, slowly unwrapping the bundled infant from her chest so she lays snuggled in her lap, swaddled in cloth. The woman continues to talk, but I don't listen. I can't take my eyes off of the baby, and I reach out gingerly to touch the one, tiny hand that's exposed to the cold air. Without waking, the infant claps her perfect hand around my finger. A shiver slides down my back. I'd never seen an infant before, and I study her little fingers, comparing the untouched, unblemished perfection of her smooth skin against my own. My hands are calloused and dirty, and they have committed violent acts and unthinkable sins, but hers are innocent... pure. The contrast tears at my heart, and I withdraw my hand, unworthy of touching such a sweet little person.

"...and we're going to leave tomorrow. Word will have gotten back to the Reds soon that Dominick led you out here. We've been here for six years now," the woman continues. I nod, aware that she's speaking, but can't stay focused. My mind drifts to Nikola and Alek, who must have been revaccinated by now, and my heart sinks further. Despair claws and fights against any reasonable approach to rescuing them. It's my fault they were captured. I should have told Luca to go find his wife on his own, but I didn't, and now my friends have been taken. Responsibility sits like a boulder on my chest and consumes me so completely that I stand at once, startling the woman so much that she stops talking mid-sentence. I march over to Luca and grab him by the shirt sleeve, pulling him off the ground with a grunt.

"I'm going to get them back, and you're going to help me," I order, releasing his shirt with a flick of my hand. "This is my fault. If I hadn't listened to you, we would have been there to help them fight off the Reds, but instead, we were off trying to follow some useless plan of ours, and they were attacked. Is this what you wanted, Luca? Is it? I'm done with your plan!" I bellow and spit on the ground by his feet. "I'm not doing anything else until we get them out of there, you hear me? Nothing!" Luca gasps at the accusations, and my breaths are ragged with each angry inhale and exhale.

My lower lip begins to quiver as adrenaline shoots through my veins, and I push Luca out of the way and storm off into the forest. After walking several yards away so that the light from the fire faintly pierces the darkness around me, I reach up, grab a thick branch, and snap it off of its tree. I chuck it as hard as possible against a nearby pine, and it breaks in half upon impact. Crunching footsteps approach from behind, and a hand lands on my shoulder.

"Go away, Luca!" I yell, curling my hands into fists.

"It's me, August. Elisa," she says. I turn in surprise and cover my face when I see her worried eyes. Shame rolls over me.

"I'm sorry," I say, sinking into a crouch. "I don't know what got into me." Elisa's hand lingers on my shoulder, and she rubs it gently.

"We'll find them. Don't worry about it. And at least they're warm and fed somewhere. You know the Foundation wouldn't dispose of two of their soldiers. I'm sure they're fine," she says, though her voice wavers. I force a nod, but the truth is that neither of us knows if they're okay or if they're still on the Compound. But I make myself believe it.

I draw in a deep breath and stand back up, searching the

dark for her face. The glow from the fire burns in the distance, and she eclipses it so that it creates a glowing halo with her curls. I almost laugh from how stupidly perfect she is, but instead wipe the tear I'm glad she can't see from my cheek.

"How do you do it?" I whisper, stepping towards her and closing the space between us. "How do you keep from screaming all of the time?" Elisa, whose hand is still on my shoulder, doesn't respond for several seconds. I lower my head so we're inches apart.

"I just have to," she says. "If I let out the constant stream of anger and hysteria that runs through my head, I'd scare you all away." She laughs at herself, and the tension between us melts a little. "But I choose not to let it get to me so I can stay focused on whatever it is we're doing." She withdraws her hand from my shoulder, sighing.

"Then you're better than me," I murmur. I lift my hand slowly, unsure how she'll react, and brush a curl from her shoulder, allowing my fingers to linger on the smooth coil for longer than necessary before releasing it. My heart pounds, and a nervous knot grows in my stomach.

"Not better, just different. Sometimes I wish I could let it all out, but I... I guess I'm too scared to do that. Probably seems pretty stupid to you, huh?" Her breath tickles my neck as she speaks, and another chill runs down my spine.

"No, it doesn't. I'm scared too," I say, resting my forehead against hers. Her breaths speed up, but she doesn't pull back.

"Of what?" she asks.

"Everything. Failure. Success. You." I pull my head back and lock eyes with her. I cup her face with my hand, and the warming of her cheek lets me know she's blushing.

"Me?" The question lingers in the narrow space between us.

"Yeah, you. I never know what you're thinking." I bring my

other hand up to her other cheek, straining through the dark to see her better.

"Oh. I know how you feel. But you don't need to be afraid of me. Or anything else. You're stronger than you realize. You're better, too. You know that, right?" she says.

"I wish I believed you," I say and let my hands fall. I take a step back and feel colder. "We're committed now, in any case. I'm going to at least try and get Nikola and Alek out tomorrow, before it's too late."

"Okay. I trust you." She closes the space between us again and slides her arms around my neck, hugging me for a moment. Caught off guard, I stand there with my hands by my sides. She starts to turn away, but I can't let this moment go. I lunge forward and throw my arms around her thin waist, leaning my cheek on the top of her head.

"Thank you," I whisper. She places her hands on my shoulders and cranes up, kissing my scratchy, bearded cheek, before moving away.

"You're welcome, August," she says, tucking a strand of her hair behind her ear. We walk together back towards the camp. Just before we leave the trees and rejoin the others, I reach out and squeeze her hand once, and she doesn't flinch this time.

17

The Colonel stands outside the office door, dreading the impending conversation. His superior is going to be furious about the newest developments. He inhales deeply, straightens the bottom of his wool jacket, and opens the door. To his surprise, the room is empty, despite the crackling fire in the hearth. He moves through the empty space, looking for information about the Man's whereabouts.

On the desk, a file lays open, and its contents have been strewn about carelessly. Placed on the top is a photograph of a young man, a Young One judging by the dullness of his eyes. He has black hair, dark skin, a straight nose, and a strong physique. A name is printed below the picture: August Davydov. Across the photograph, spreading the width of the page, is the black outline of a triangle. The Colonel's eyes widen at the sight. How had he not known?

He flips through a stack of papers that includes information about the boy, such as the names of his parents, Jon and Rose, their address in Village D, and their occupations. At the bottom, a red piece of paper has been tucked inside. He pulls it out and reads it. ELECTED 11 MAY 2072. He balks at the words and has almost closed the folder when a voice startles him.

"Find what you're looking for?" the Man asks from the open doorway. Light spills in around him, illuminating his tall, hulking build. He wears his dress uniform, and a series of golden triangles gleam across his shoulders.

"Uh, yes, sir. I'm sorry, I didn't mean to snoop," the Colonel stammers, backing away and placing his hands by his side before bowing down in submission.

"Of course not. Tell me, Colonel: why wasn't I informed that one of the fugitives was an Elect?" he asks as he crosses the room.

"I uh, I didn't know until just now, myself, sir." He struggles to get the words out, fighting the rise of bile in his throat.

"Do you understand how dangerous it is to have someone like him on the loose?"

"Yes, sir."

"I don't believe you. The Elect are chosen as members of the Black Guard for a reason. They are stronger, faster, and smarter than every other person in this country. They are lethal."

"Yes, sir." Sweat pours down the Colonel's face and moistens his hands as he watches the man approach his desk.

"We need to bring them in. They've been gone for too long. Which brings me to something else. While you're here, can you identify the object in this box for me?" he asks as he extends a small, cardboard box in front of his chest. The Colonel reaches for the container and makes sure not to touch the Man's gloved hands when taking it from him. He pulls the folded lid back and looks inside, studying the object for a few seconds.

"It's one of the birds, sir. They found out about them," he informs the Man as he tries to keep his hands steady. Despite his attempts, the cardboard flaps bounce spastically, and he shuts them with his other hand to make the vibrations stop.

"You knew this, yes?" the Man inquires, stepping closer to the Colonel so he could watch the sweat drip over his brow from the stress of the inquisition.

"Yes, sir. I just found out and came here to tell you. We've lost them, sir."

"Lost them?"

"Yes, sir."

"Which means what?"

"They were warned about the campsite, so they never showed. We don't know where they're going. Our guess is that they're going to keep traveling. It wouldn't be worth it to them to go get the others off of the Compound." He keeps his eyes focused straight ahead avoiding the Man's narrowed gaze.

"Are you sure about that?"

"No, sir. It's what makes sense, though."

"You'd better be right, Colonel. You have two marks by your name now. Don't earn a third."

———

"How are we supposed to get inside?" Luca asks. We had parted ways with Dominick's family earlier that morning, and we now move towards the village in pursuit of Nikola and Alek.

"We're going to use the tunnel, of course," I reply as I dodge trees. Elisa and Luca flank either side of me, and our steps create a steady cadence as we move. My body warms from the exercise, which helps to offset the cold morning air.

"But it's guarded," Luca argues.

"Since when do you run from a fight? You're willing to take on the entire Foundation but not a few Reds? You're not scared, are you?" I quip, forcing Luca to see his own hypocrisy.

"I didn't say I was scared, kid. I just didn't know we'd be so open about it," he replies, and irritation shades his tone.

"How else would we do it? Sprout wings and fly?" I say, half joking.

"Cut it out," Elisa says. "You sound like children. But is there any sort of plan?" she adds. "Even if we do get into the village, we won't be able to get into the Compound. There's no way."

"We're going to kidnap someone," I say, as if it isn't a big deal. Elisa skids to a halt, kicking up chunks of earth and piles of fallen leaves.

"What?" she screeches, and Luca and I stop, too.

"In a good way. Don't worry," I reply. She doesn't blink — just stares at me with her mouth gaped open. She raises her hands out by her side and tilts her head, waiting for an explanation.

"Okay, I figured we'd grab a couple of the students patrolling the village, kidnap them, let the Crystal work out of their bodies, and then release them back onto the Compound. They'll find Joseph and help get Nikola and Alek back out."

"You can't be serious. That's your plan?" Luca asks. "How are they supposed to get back inside after being gone for days? Did you think about that?"

I nod. "We'll blow a transformer. The explosion worked last time as a distraction... no reason why it shouldn't this time," I say, feeling like I've made a valid point. Elisa's mouth closes, and she bites her lip while she thinks.

"That won't work. I'm sure they knew from the beginning that you missed your vaccine. They're supposed to keep immaculate records," Luca says.

"There's no way that's true," I protest. "They would have revaccinated us if they knew we didn't get our dose."

"They should have, but they didn't, and we don't know why.

Nobody knows why the Foundation does what it does," Luca replies. Deep down, I know he's right, and I think of an alternate reason.

"It doesn't make sense," I say. "But you're right. Kidnapping won't work. It's suicide." I take off running again, and they follow behind me.

"I'm not going to help you do this!" Luca yells. "If you get caught, the whole thing is a failure, and they'll win! This is what they want, August!" I wave off his concerns and keep running, sure of my plan. I channel the anger from last night, knowing I'll need it to fight as well as possible.

By the time we reach the tunnel, I'm in a blind rage, and like a trained bull, my eyes fixate on the color red. In one swift movement, I hurl myself into the clearing, fly through the air, and slam into a patrolling Man in Red. We crash into a tree, and the guard's head snaps backwards and smacks against the trunk. He sags beneath me, unconscious, and I turn to find my next victim. Two more Reds stand nearby, and their hands move to grab the pistols from their belts.

Before they can aim their weapons, a loud crack rings out, and one of them slumps forward, holding his face. Elisa pulls her whip back and slashes it against the same man, hitting his back this time so that he falls forward to his knees with a pained cry. Distracted by the movement to his right, the other Red barely manages to remove his gun from its holster when a rock from my sling crunches into his nose. He stumbles backwards as blood trickles over his lips, but he doesn't fall. Instead, he levels his arm ahead of him, gripping his pistol tightly. He aims it between Elisa and me, trying to decide who to shoot. His hesitancy provides me with enough time to dart forward and pummel the Red to the ground. I knock the gun from his hand, and even though the Red tries to push me off with every bit of his strength, he can't. Luca takes the shirt off of the guard and tosses it to Elisa before binding and gaging him. He sits the guard against a tree as muffled profanities flow from his gagged mouth, but we don't give him a second look as we do the same to the other two Reds.

"The shirts," I say, pulling my pack from my shoulders. I yank out the red shirt I'd worn in the South, hoping it would work as well for me here as it did there, and change quickly. Luca follows suit as Elisa wraps herself in the one acquired from the guard, and it swallows her. She pulls her hair up and shoves it under the black cap that she'd taken off of the same Red. Luca grabs the pistols from the guards, tucks one into his belt, and takes the bullets from the others before tossing the empty weapons deep into the forest after Elisa and I decline them. Our goal is to rescue, not kill.

We set off through the tunnel, moving at a fast pace through the stale air, until I burst forth into the pantry of the old bakery. I shove the floorboards out of the way and jump from the opening. I pull my knife out and push the door open enough to scan the kitchen. It's as dirty and empty as ever, so I creep forward, waving the knife in front of me as I move. The only signs of life are footprints on the dusty wooden floor. The Reds must have used this tunnel to get out to the forest.

Elisa and Luca join me in the kitchen, and we creep towards the front display room. It, too, is empty, but there's a figure on the other side of the smudged windows. I motion for the others to stand behind the front door, and once they get in position, I grab one of the broken chairs in the room and slam it against the display counter, exploding glass across the room with a crash. The front door flies open, and a guard bursts inside. Elisa dives towards him and knocks him to the ground. His pistol slides across the room, and I rush forward, intending to knock him unconscious with the splintered chair leg that I had just picked up. I can't do it, though, and slide to a stop on the dusty floors. I know this man.

"Joseph?" I ask, bending down to examine the familiar face.

"What are you doing here?" Joseph demands with his face still shoved into the ground. Elisa jumps up and lets him go, and Joseph pushes himself upright while Luca closes the door behind us. "You're supposed to be out there helping with the election."

"They took Nikola and Alek," I say, whisper-shouting back at him. I can't help but be paranoid that someone or something is filming us right now.

"I know. You need to get out of here," Joseph insists. "I'll take care of them. Don't worry." He acts like it isn't a big deal, but I still can't get over the fact that he's alive.

"I thought something had happened to you. I thought you died the night you helped us escape," I say. "I've been carrying that guilt for months."

"Nope, fit as ever. Why would you think I'd been killed?" he asks as he walks over to retrieve his gun.

"We heard gunfire that night. And then Luca said you'd disappeared or something like that. We figured..." Elisa adds.

"No. I had a different plan at first, but it worked out to everyone's advantage that one of the other Reds went insane and started attacking Clive's bunk. Well, everyone except Stern. They'd arrested him when I saw you last, but he decided to try and kill Clive. While they were busy lighting him up, I turned off the fence," he informs us. I feel sad for my old teacher, but I don't have time to linger on it.

"So you're okay? You weren't arrested?" I say. "You'll help Alek and Nikola?"

"I promise it's being taken care of," Joseph replies. He pauses and studies his unexpected company. "Actually,

August... There's someone you need to meet while you're here. Elisa and Luca, you two should go back while you can."

"I'm not leaving him," Elisa says, stepping forward.

"If you care about his safety, you'll leave. It's dangerous enough to have one of you here, but three? No way," he declares, crossing his arms.

Luca had remained silent during the entire conversation, watching from a distance. He must have truly thought Joseph had been killed, which is why he's in shock. As we walk back to the kitchen, he takes the opportunity to ask Joseph about a mutual friend.

"How's Margaret?" he asks. "She was pretty sick when I left."

"My mother's better, thanks. Father was on his way to the pharmacy when some morons arrested him because he didn't have his papers on him, but they let him go," Joseph says. I think back to the first time I'd been back to the village to meet Luca and to the man who had been arrested. I would never have guessed that the old man had been Joseph's father. An intact family inside of the village seems so foreign. It makes more sense to think everyone else is essentially orphaned like me, fighting to make their own way without the guiding hands of any true parents.

"You should be going," Joseph urges, herding Elisa and Luca towards the pantry.

"But where are we supposed to go? They found our camp-site and are looking for us in the forest," Elisa says. She stares past Joseph at me, her eyes pleading and her hands raised in desperation.

"I don't know. You can't find another campsite? There are two weeks left until the election. You can handle yourselves until then, surely," Joseph says. Two weeks. I stumble on the words, surprised it's so soon, which means our failure is so imminent.

"And what happens after the election?" Elisa asks. Joseph looks at her in surprise.

"What do you mean 'what happens'?" he asks, continuing to herd them across the kitchen.

"She means nothing," Luca says. "Just speculating."

"What are you talking about? What are you keeping from us?" I ask, reaching to grab Luca's shirt. Luca slaps my hand away before I can grab him.

"I'll explain it closer to time. Trust me," Luca says.

"What's going on?" Joseph asks. He stops moving, and Elisa and I wait. Luca turns away and scratches his head.

"Nothing," Luca mumbles.

"Bull," I spit. "He's keeping something from us, a contingency plan that takes place after the election. He won't tell us what it is." Joseph moves closer to Luca, closing the space between them. I feel for the knife in my pocket and let my fingers linger on the cool metal.

"What are you hiding?" Joseph asks. His shoulders swell and his fists clench as he tries to read Luca. "If it deals with the election, we should know about it."

Luca sighs and puts his hand up, motioning for Joseph to stop. "I can't tell you. It's too delicate right now. I trust you and all, but the Foundation already has their eyes all over us," Luca says.

"So who does know about it?" Joseph asks.

"Listen. Don't worry about it. You have to trust me. It's for everyone's good. Please believe me," he says, but none of us are convinced.

"If you're planning anything stupid, Luca, so help me..." Joseph begins. He takes a step back and looks at me, then Elisa, and then back at Luca. "If you say I can trust you, then I'll trust you. Don't break it." He glares at Luca and shoves his finger into his chest. Luca tries to force out a smile, but it hangs halfway on his face.

"You need to hurry," Joseph says. "Keep her safe, and don't do anything stupid, Luca." Elisa scowls but backs towards the pantry and opens the door. She crouches down to lower herself inside and casts one last nervous glance at me before dropping out of sight.

"We're not done with this," Joseph says to Luca. His shoulders seem less tense, but I can tell he doesn't trust Luca like I thought he did.

"I'll tell you later, when it's the right time," Luca replies and jumps inside.

18

"Where are they?" the Man yells.

"I'm not sure. They disarmed the Reds at the tunnel, and one of them said the Elect got into the village, but nobody has seen him or the two other since," the Colonel replies meekly.

"In the village? An Elect running loose in *my* village?! How did they get past the Reds? They have guns! They should *use* their guns! What is wrong with you and your ability to follow orders?" he says, spitting his words. He's furious, and the evidence sprays onto the Colonel's face.

"I'm sorry, sir. Even the Reds on the other side of the tunnel claim they haven't seen anything. It's only been a couple of hours since the last sighting. They have to be nearby. We'll find them." A knot rises in his throat as he suppresses the urge to yell in his defense. He realizes in that moment that the emotion that he feels, what he has been trying to subdue for the past month, is pure hatred for the Man in front of him.

"Get more Men in Red over there. Alert the Compound and put out a search party. I want them caught. Bring them down, Colonel, or so help me, your family is next. See that it's finished." The Colonel turns and leaves the room, pausing for a moment to gather himself before running towards headquarters.

———

"I NEED YOU TO DO SOMETHING FOR ME," JOSEPH SAYS after he puts the floorboards back over the opening in the pantry. I hang back on the other side of the room, perturbed that Elisa's going to be stuck out there alone with Luca. I fold my arms over my chest.

"What?" I ask. Joseph stands up and turns towards me.

"I need you to go see someone. Her name is Joyce, and she owns an apothecary shop on the southern end of the village. She can update you on what's been going on while you were away. You'll be glad you met her. Trust me," he pleads. It's only the second time I've spoken to Joseph, but something inside of me tells me he's okay, that I can trust him.

"When should I go?" I ask, relaxing somewhat.

"Now. I'll get you outside. Get to the rooftops and make sure nobody sees you," he says, as if this is the first time I've traveled in the village. He pushes me towards the front door and raises his hand to grab the doorknob, but he stops before twisting it. "Have you told anyone?" he asks. His eyes fixate on my right wrist as he lets go of the knob. I flinch, ducking my head.

"About what?" I reply.

"Your mark. The triangle. Has anyone seen it?" he urges.

"I don't know. I don't think so. Why is it so important to you that I keep it hidden?" I ask, wrapping my left hand around the cuff of my shirt sleeve.

"It should be important to you," Joseph says, and I resist the urge to roll my eyes.

"I get that. But why?" I continue, needing to have at least one question answered before the end of the day.

Joseph sighs. "You were chosen, August." He locks eyes with me, and my brows curl inward as I try to understand. His words alarm me, but I don't know why.

"What does that mean?" I ask.

"It means you placed at the top of your class and were chosen as a member of the Black Guard."

"The what?"

"Karlmann's personal sentinels, his warriors, protectors. They're above the Men in Red, above the Young Ones. You were meant to protect him when you turned eighteen." My thoughts churn.

"I don't understand," I mutter. I pull back my sleeve and reveal the mark. It feels like a branding now, like I'm someone else's property again.

"When people leave the compounds at the age of eighteen, they're assigned duties based on their aptitudes. If they're strong, they do labor. If they're smart, they do research and civil planning. You get the idea. The top student from every new class that enters the compounds is Elected, which means they're chosen for the Black Guard. They're marked with a triangle, predestined for service. You were chosen when you were ten years old."

"Ten? How could they make that call?" I ask.

"Things are pretty clear by that point. The Foundation knows within five years what track each of the Young Ones will take. They put you on the highest track," he says, sneaking a peek through the dirty glass window.

"So what does that mean for me now that I've escaped the Compound?"

"You are no longer a student anymore. You are a traitor, a villain. You will be hunted, persecuted, and most likely executed if they ever find you. They spent years grooming you, teaching you about Karlmann and the Foundation, and for you to leave and turn against him?" He trails off, allowing my imagination to take over from there. I want to claw the mark from my skin. "It's possible they'll just revaccinate you, but I don't know. It's not a good thing for them that you're out."

"If the Foundation knows I've escaped already, then what good does it do for me to keep it hidden? Who's going to see it and care enough to do anything about it?" I ask, feeling the rapid pulse of my heartbeat through my entire body.

"Even the closest of friends will betray you if they find out you're an Elect." An image of Elisa flashes through my mind, and I shake my head.

"I don't understand, Joseph. I don't believe you." He paces back and forth in the room now, while I stand frozen with my arm extended in front of my body, pleading for answers.

"You... you know things, okay? Things you don't realize you know. It was part of your training. You don't remember them right now, but if people outside of the Foundation find out about it, they will try to use you. They'll crack your mind open through whatever means necessary to get at that information. I worry about this with Luca," Joseph says. I drop my arm.

"You think Luca would do something like that? Torture me for information?" I ask.

"Don't get me wrong, here. He's a good guy for the most part, but he's desperate. Be careful around him. I don't know what he's up to anymore, but he's the best help I can give you right now." He returns to the door and grabs the knob. "You need to go. Remember — Joyce at the apothecary shop. Come back when you're done, and I'll help you get back."

Joseph opens the door and steps outside onto the empty street. He motions me forward, but my legs feel heavy and glued to the floor of the bakery. I'm an Elect? A Black Guard? What information did they teach me, and how can I access it? And why does everyone else want it?

I wipe my face with my hands and walk out of the doorway. After one last look at Joseph, I jump to the rooftop across the street and move southward, hidden from view beyond the edges of the buildings. It doesn't take long to find the shop. Above a faded red door hangs a gray sign that reads "Madame J. Apothecary" in whimsical, swirled black paint. When I open the door, golden light floods the street around me. I don't take the time to consider that it's a trap and head inside.

19

I shut the door behind me, causing a brass bell to clang above my head. An elderly lady — the only other person in the room — looks up from behind a glass case. Her wispy white hair is swept into a loose bun at the base of her neck, and her papery skin holds an elaborate showcase of weathered wrinkles, particularly around her gray eyes and down-turned mouth. Dried plants hang in rows from the ceiling, giving the place a heavy, sweet, floral scent. Wooden shelves line the walls, filled with countless leather-bound books, glass jars and bottles, ceramic bowls, pictures, and small, painted crates. The glass cabinets in front of her hold various canisters, each of which is labeled according to its contents and prescribed medicinal purposes. The woman wipes her hands on her beige apron, and a smile creeps across her face, accenting her creases even more. She shuffles around the counter and moves towards me.

"You must be August," she says, extending her right hand forward. I shake it with my own, somehow not surprised she knows my name.

"Yes ma'am," I say, feeling the need to use decent manners

with her. "I was told to come speak to you by a friend. Not to be rude, but who are you? I mean, I know you must be Joyce, but why did he send me to you?"

She nods, still smiling. "I believe Joseph is a mutual friend of ours," she says. "And my guess is you're here for something other than a cure for a stomach ailment." She motions for me to join her at a tall table covered in open books and surrounded by backless, wobbly stools.

"Yes, ma'am," I reply, taking the seat opposite of her. I rest my feet on the bottom rung of the stool and lean my elbows on the table, anxious for answers.

"I suppose I should start by thanking you for what you're doing," she begins. "Most others would have left as soon as they could to save their own necks. It says a lot about you that you're still here." I duck my head but don't respond. I don't need accolades. I need her to tell me why I'm here. "I assume by your quietness that you want me to skip the chitchat and get right to it. Well, okay. A substantial number of Reds are turning their loyalties. Karlmann has threatened their families one too many times, I think, and they're tired of it and willing to help you. Well, some of them are. Others will still shoot you down if they get the chance. But at least you aren't as alone in this as you were one month ago."

"Well, I suppose that's something," I mumble.

"And there's something else. Rebels are holding citizens' meetings in the village in preparation for the election. They're led by a man named Andrew. Don't let it scare you, but he's the assistant to the mayor," she says, watching my face for my reaction.

"What?" I ask, unsure if I'm impressed or alarmed.

"Just because someone is in the upper echelon of politics doesn't mean they agree with their superiors. Nobody is going to think to search the house belonging to the mayor's assistant. They assume he's with the Foundation."

"But it's still a risk. They already know so much," I reply. She lets out a knowing chuckle and adjusts her seat.

"Of course it's a risk. We all take risks every day that we defy the Foundation and even on those days that we don't. Andrew has sworn his life to protect our cause. Many of the people coming to our side, including him, have seen their own children swept off to the compounds. They know what they're getting into. Besides, Andrew is closer to the election process than any of the rest of us could dream to be. He can convince the mayor who to place inside the voting booths," she informs me, grinning slyly. "Don't you see? He can request Joseph and the other Reds on our side be put in charge of protecting the election process. But instead of intimidating the voters into choosing Karlmann, they'll secretly urge them to vote for Fletcher and will protect the identity of those who do."

It begins to click in my head. I don't know who Andrew is, but I'm glad to have him helping us out. "And are the people here going to step out and do it? Will they vote?" I ask.

"That's why the meetings are so important, as is their concealment. Seeing other people who feel the same way as they do gives voters the courage they need to speak out. Safety in numbers and all that..." she replies.

"And if they don't?" I ask. "What's the contingency plan?" Maybe she'll tell me, even if Luca won't.

"I don't know. It's a big gamble right now. We just have to do what we can and pray it works out," she answers without addressing my second question. She's either withholding the information or she's in the same uninformed situation as me. But I want to make sure.

"Joyce, they've already told me that this will fail and that there's a second part to their plan. Do you know what it is?" I inquire, feeling desperate, like this is my last chance to get this information.

"Luca told you that? He hasn't said anything to me about it." She purses her lips into a frown.

"Are you sure?" I ask, disappointed but not surprised.

"Young man, I may be old, but I'm not senile. I remember everything he's told me, and I don't remember that." She tucks a stray wisp of hair behind her ear and watches me.

"I don't mean any offense, but I don't understand why Joseph sent me to talk to you. You haven't told me anything that I didn't already know except for the bit about the meetings. Are you positive there isn't anything else?" I ask.

Joyce clears her throat and grabs the edge of the table. Without saying a word, she uses it to steady herself as she stands up and walks through a doorway and down the hall. I scan the room and wait for her to return, which she does a minute later. She carries a small vial of dark blue liquid and sits it on the table in front of me.

"This is something I've been working on for years. I still don't know if it works or not," she says as she climbs back onto her stool. I eye the bottle, curious.

"What is it?" I ask.

"I call it Topaz. It's an antidote to the serum that they give the children on the Compound. Or it's supposed to be anyways. Like I said, I still don't know exactly how effective it is."

My mouth drops open. "Are you serious? How did you come up with it?" I ask.

"A couple of years ago, I managed to get my hands on a few vials of Crystal in its pure form. I studied it and managed to create a serum that could counter its effects. I don't know if it's perfect, but it should at least speed up the process of detoxifying someone. This is the only bottle of it ever produced," she says. She picks it up and rolls it between her fingers. "Here. Take it.

But be aware that it's enough for only one person. Have them drink it." She holds it out to me. I'm astonished by her generosity.

"Are you sure? You said it's your only one," I say resisting the urge to grab it.

"I took plenty of notes on how to replicate it, assuming it works and we need more," she replies, motioning for me to take the vial.

"Thank you, Joyce," I say, filled with gratitude. I take the Topaz from her outstretched hand and study the blue serum. Behind the glass, it churns, thick and heavy. I slide it into an interior pocket of my coat.

"You're welcome." She watches me for a moment as if she's trying to decide something. "August, do you understand how much rides on this election?" she says finally. I squirm in my seat.

"Yes ma'am. I think so," I reply.

She leans forward and lowers her voice. "If only a few villages vote for Fletcher, I shudder to think of the consequences. We could all be arrested immediately. We need this to be a nationwide movement."

"I know." It's all I can think to say.

"Karlmann will know which villages voted against him. He will know which traitorous Men in Red were involved on the inside, and the consequences will be harsh. The Reds will be executed. The people in the villages will have their rations cut, assuming they aren't sent to labor camps. And he'll use the Young Ones to accomplish all of his retribution." She doesn't blink, and I feel like she's reading my fears with every word she speaks.

"I understand, Joyce. I do. It's the last thing I want, trust me," I reply.

"Things are not quite as simple as Luca has led you to

believe. I know I told you I didn't know anything else, but... it's not that I don't want to tell you. I just can't. I've been sworn to secrecy. Talk to Luca," she says, leaning back from the table.

"What are you talking about?" I ask, annoyed that she's keeping this secret from me, too.

"It's dark out now. You should go before someone sees you."

"But what about..." I start to say, but she interrupts me with an icy glare.

"I've told you everything I can. Now get back to the forest, and make sure you're prepared for what's coming." She shuffles to the door and opens it, waving me out of the door.

"Un-freaking-believable," I mutter under my breath. She cocks an eyebrow at me but doesn't say anything as I cross the room. "Thanks for the Topaz," I say and exit into the dark street.

The gentle hum of electric street lamps resonates in my ears as I jump to the rooftops and retrace my steps across the village. The weight of what we're trying to do weighs me down, and my frustration grows as I think about the gap of information between Luca and myself. I pause when I reach one particularly tall building filled with ramshackle apartments. In front of me, the moon shines so brilliantly through the sky that I have to avert my eyes. The highlighted, silvery mountain ridges in the distance before me are picturesque and heartbreakingly beautiful. I stay there for a while, falling into a trance as I try to count the glittering stars overhead.

Two weeks. I pull my sleeve back and look down at the mark. A black triangle. How could such a small mark mean so much? I cover it back up and survey the area. I'm being watched. I can feel it, but there's no one around. It's only me and my thoughts on top of the village, joined only by the lingering vagueness of Luca's plan. I firm my jaw and clench my fists. Luca is going to tell me tonight, or I'm done helping him.

20

I'm not sure at what point I begin running again — I could have stood there for minutes or hours as far as I know. Anger propels me to run faster and faster, but it also distracts me, and I leap over a street without looking below. A voice cries out from behind me.

"There's August! There he is!" I skid to a stop across the shingles and glance down at the road. Two boys — Young Ones — squint their eyes in my direction, and one of them raises a hand, pointing at me. I don't have time to think. I sprint towards the tunnel as fast as I can. I know I can outrun them, but I can't hide from them — not on the rooftops. They land with two thuds somewhere behind me and give chase. I weigh my options quickly. I can continue to the tunnel and risk being caught in a trap, or I can turn and fight, or I can risk everything and jump into the fields outside of the village. I know the first two are the better choices, but I don't want to fight the Young Ones and risk hurting them since I know they don't understand what they're doing. So I go east instead of north.

I figure I can eventually loop around and join Elisa and Luca after losing my underage trackers. I kick my feet faster, picking up as much speed as possible between jumps, and manage to put more and more distance between the boys and myself. I keep an eye out for the last building and the fence that lies beyond it. Within seconds, I approach the coiled snares of wire that are designed to keep people like me inside. The edge is near, and I suck in one last breath and throw myself forward on the last step, legs tucked beneath me and arms like wings to the side.

I clear the fence and land a third of the way into the perimeter of field. Flashlights flick on as I roll forward and absorb the impact of the landing before running again. I don't stop to look back. I'm being hunted, not by the Young Ones anymore, but by the Shepherds. The moonlight that had mesmerized me minutes ago now betrays my location. I tear a path through the long, brown grass. The forest line is within sight now, and my lungs burn with the cold air as my heart thunders, pumping adrenaline through my veins.

Just as I begin to believe that I can make it, something sharp pinches into the back of my right shoulder. A dart, I realize, has penetrated through my shirt. I'm doomed. I stumble forward as the tranquilizer floods my body and makes my legs fall numb. I drop and skid through the grass, barely conscious enough to hear the thudding of heavy footsteps behind me.

"We got him!" cries a deep voice between wheezy, gasping breaths. And then the world falls dark.

––––––––––––

I'M REMOTELY AWARE I'M BEING CARRIED, SLUNG OVER someone's shoulder. My head dangles behind his back, and his musty odor stings my nostrils. I try to turn my head in search of fresh air to clear my head but am met with unbreakable stiffness. I can't move, paralyzed. All I can do is catch glimpses of the gray walls of the buildings inside of the village. He must be taking me back to the Compound, I realize. After several minutes, he comes to a stop.

"You'll never guess who I have," the wheezy voice says. "Open up. I got August!" he bellows.

Within a few seconds, the gate beeps as it is disarmed, and it swings open with a groan. Without warning, I'm unceremoniously dumped from the Shepherd's shoulder and land in a heap on the cold ground. I still can't move, and terror slides up on me that this might be permanent. I close my eyes, hoping to convince the Reds I'm unconscious and thereby postpone whatever punishment awaits me. Vibrations shake the ground around me as several Reds run up, chattering amongst themselves.

"I'll take my reward now," the Shepherd declares proudly.

"You'll have to see the mayor for that, I'm afraid," replies another man whose voice I recognize. It's Clive, the most vicious guard on the Compound. "Get out of here," Clive orders to the Shepherd.

"Now wait a minute. I'm not leaving until I get my money. I did what none of the rest of you have been able to do, and I expect to be rewarded for it. Either you give it to me now or I take him with me," the Shepherd yells.

"Oh, okay," says Clive, his tone dripping with sarcasm. A scuffle ensues, and I resist the urge to watch. The Shepherd cries out in pain and lands somewhere behind me with a huff. The gates clatter shut, and a rough hand grabs my right arm, rolling me to the side. My sleeve is pulled back, revealing my triangular mark, and excited murmurs erupt among the Reds. Someone yanks me upright and slings me over his shoulder. Pain shoots through my body, and consciousness begins to slip from me again. After a few steps, I give in to a deep, unpunctuated sleep.

21

"We've got the Elect, sir. We caught August, and he's been given the full dosage. The situation is pretty much under control," the Colonel says triumphantly.

"And what about Luca? Where is he?" the Man inquires as he straightens his long tie in front of an aged mirror filled with brown spots and waves that make his face seem rippled and distorted. He's pleased to hear that they're nearly done rounding up the fugitives.

"He's still in the woods, hiding with the last girl. We caught some footage of them earlier, and the Men in Red are encircling the area as we speak. Don't be surprised if we've got them all by nightfall." For the first time in weeks, he feels somewhat confident in his news, and he beams when his superior turns to him with an approving sneer. He doesn't dare reveal that the security detail at the tunnel had lapsed earlier in the day. It doesn't seem important. Besides, they'd caught one more of them, and that accomplishment should appease the Man for now.

"Very good. Let me know when it's finished unless it's during my speech tonight, of course. I'd hate to be interrupted so close to the election... not that it matters," he replies with a cheerful laugh. He tugs on his black cummerbund and the lapels of his tuxedo jacket.

"Keep up the good work, Colonel," he adds and slaps the Colonel's back as he walks past him.

"Oh, and don't let me miss the trials tomorrow. I know you can't personally be there, but there's a lot of naughty Reds to deal with, aren't there?" He giggles to the point of mania, feeling confident in the success of this year's election.

The Colonel continues to smile back, but on the inside, he feels sick. The hunt for Reds who had turned on Karlmann had actually been unsuccessful, and a cross section of those who will be put on trial are in all reality still loyal to the Foundation. The whole thing is a farce, a lie. Inevitably, all of the Reds will be found guilty, despite their innocence, and the Colonel's heart falls to his stomach and squeezes the guilt through his body. But he swallows it back as he thinks of his family and the risk that he continues to put them through. He can't help but feel relieved that he won't have to deal with the anguish of losing a loved one, unlike some other families he knows.

————

A FEMALE VOICE AWAKENS ME. "THIS ONE'S AUGUST, THE Elect. What do you think?" she asks.

I realize I'm shirtless, laying on my back on a cold, metal surface. My body aches, and there's something stiff in the back of my right hand, the fingers of which I barely manage to twitch. My eyes flutter, trying to open, but stay shut.

"Can he be pulled back into service without any major problems?" a male voice asks.

"Yes, sir. We've introduced some Crystal back into his system, but he has yet to receive the full dosage. We wanted to make sure his vitals were stable enough after the tranquilizer left his system. Would you like me to administer the vaccine, sir?" she asks.

"Go ahead," he replies. Panic grips my chest, and I try to move, but everything feels sluggish and heavy. A drawer opens to my right, and someone rummages through it. After a second, I feel a cool finger press on the veins in the crook of my arm. I want to scream but can't as a she pricks the needle into me and delivers the Crystal. But it isn't Crystal, I realize, as sensation roars through my body.

I try again to sit up and succeed with one jerky movement, opening my eyes to see her shocked face as she drops the syringe to the floor. The Red behind her, who I don't recognize, grabs his gun from his holster and points it at my chest. I try to pull another intravenous needle from my hand but don't get the chance before a shot rings out and my body jerks backwards, pierced by another painful dart, and my head slams into the metal table. I try to roll to the side but can't as mental numbness returns and my body relaxes again, a useless pile of muscle and bone. The last thing I see before falling asleep is a trail of crimson blood, which runs down my arm and drips from my fingertips.

22

The Colonel wipes his mouth, removing all traces of vomit as he stands back up from the trashcan down the hallway from the Man's office. Fear has knotted itself into an unmoving mass in his stomach. He knows the worst is about to happen, and yet there's nothing he can do. He'd be caught if he lied, and he'd be punished if he told the truth. With a shaky breath, he thinks of his children playing at home with their mother. With only six days standing between today and the election, he's about to deliver some unfortunate news. After taking a few moments to gather himself, he presses forward and enters the room.

For the first time he can remember, there's no fire in the mantle, and the overhead fixtures buzz above him, showering an incredible amount of light throughout the room. Even the curtains have been drawn back and soft sunlight mingles with the harshness of the artificial light. The Colonel squints as he searches for his superior.

"Come on in, Colonel!" a chipper voice cries out, followed by the clinking of ice cubes against glass. The Man stands across the room, smiling like an idiot as he fills the glass up to the rim with whiskey. "So, is it done?" he inquires. The Colonel, caught off guard by the change in tenor and paralyzed with a new wave of fear, doesn't respond, despite his gaping mouth.

"I'm not a patient man, Colonel. Answer me," the Man insists between lengthy slurps of his liquor. He lets out a small belch and laughs at himself while patting his stomach as though it was a pet.

"Not quite, sir," the Colonel manages to say. The Man stops mid-pat with his hand in the air. He takes another swig of whiskey and wipes droplets off of his mustache with the back of his hand before setting his glass down on the heavily stocked drink cart.

"What?"

"They broke out. Well, I mean *they* didn't break out — they were unconscious. But one of the Men in Red snuck them out..." He waits for a moment, sizing up the Man's mute reaction before continuing. "We... we don't know where they are."

"You mean to tell me that twenty Reds were sentenced to death for helping them escape the first time and yet somehow it's magically happened again?" he bellows. Blood rushes to his face, and his veins bulge in his neck. "Arrest them. Arrest them all. Better yet..." He walks towards his desk and pushes a small button on the underside while the Colonel stands frozen by the doorway.

Two people appear at the door. One of them, a girl, has long, golden hair that's pulled into a tight ponytail at the back of her head, and her blue eyes are glazed over, deep under the influence of Crystal. Ordinarily, she would have been beautiful with a thin nose and full lips, but there's a hardness to her face that makes her menacing and unapproachable. The other, a young man with a bald head and smooth, dark brown skin, stands to her side. His face mirrors hers, and he holds his hands clenched in fists beside his hips. They are dressed in black from head to toe — black shoes, black pants, black coat on top of a black shirt. Even the guns slung over their backs and in their holsters are black.

"Arrest this man," he orders to them. Without flinching, the Elects grab the Colonel from behind and place handcuffs around his wrists. "Find his family, too. Get every bit of information from him that you can, whatever your method — I don't care. Then scour Village K for traitors. Arrest anyone with the slightest connection to the rebels. If their distant cousin is a known drifter, I want them taken into custody. We'll have as many trials as it takes. I want this election secure or heads will roll!"

"Yes, sir," the Elects say simultaneously. The Colonel's head drops in defeat as he allows them to take him to prison. Resistance is pointless, and a single tear slides from each eye down his cheeks.

———

SOMEONE'S TALKING. OR WHISPERING. BUT IT SOUNDS LIKE shouting. My body feels stiff and sore, and my head throbs with every pulse of my heart. I raise my hands to press my temples and my eyes flutter open. Everything is blurred, but I think I'm in a small, dark room. The ground beneath me shakes and bounces, and a roaring hum surrounds me.

"Shhh, August. You're okay. We're getting you to safety. Rest, now," a woman says, and someone's fingers caress my cheek. The sound of her voice is like a warm blanket, and I drop my hands down by my side again. I try to stay awake and ask questions, but I can't focus. The harder I try to keep my eyes open, the heavier they feel, so I allow myself to drift away again.

———

I DON'T KNOW HOW LONG I SLEEP. CONSCIOUSNESS COMES back slowly, and I don't focus on anything but the aching in my body. Everything hurts, from my toes to my head and out to my fingertips. My shallow breaths seem too big for my chest. I don't know where I am or what's happened to me, but at least I'm not dead. Death shouldn't hurt this much.

After several minutes, I sit up, using my hands to support my upper body, and realize I'm shirtless beneath a wool blanket. I have no clue where I am, where I've been, or why I'm here. I scan the room and have no memory of this place. It has four, plain, towering walls, one of which holds two large windows through which a golden, dust-filled glow shines. Two doors sit in the wall opposite the windows — one on the ground that looks like the main entrance to the room and another on a singular platform that floats several stories above the ground. Above the platform, numerous metal beams weave from wall to wall and support what's left of the crumbling ceiling.

I wrap the blanket around my shoulders and curl over my knees, trying to conserve my body heat. As I tuck my arms in around my chest, a black mark on my wrist catches my eye. I trace the shape with my fingers but don't know what it is and decide it isn't worth focusing on at the moment. Despite the protesting pain that rips through my muscles whenever I move, I stand up and shuffle towards a heap of fabric in a nearby corner, hoping for something wearable. I'm a few yards away when the pile moves. I stop mid-stride, aware now that I'm not alone.

"Who's there?" I ask. I instinctually plant my feet apart, prepared to run to the nearest door. A giggle emanates from the corner, and I cock my head to the side, confused.

"It's just me. Elisa." A girl sits up and removes the covers from her head. Her brown curls are in disarray, and her eyes are shrouded in dark circles. My heartbeat speeds up at the sight of her, hoping she's a forgotten friend and not someone of whom I should be afraid.

"Do I know you?" I ask. She's wearing a brown shirt, which hangs loose over the top of her matching brown pants. Both pieces are worn and faded, like she's been wearing them for a long time.

"Yeah, you do. You don't remember me?" she replies as her smile fades. I shake my head, and her shoulders drop.

"Not at all?" she asks.

"No," I reply.

"They must have given you something strong back there," she says, and I tilt my head, unsure what she means by that.

She rummages through her pack, pulls out a coat, and tosses it to me. "Here, put this on." I don't hesitate and slide my arms through the sleeves and button the front, taking note of a circular, dark bruise on my chest.

"How do I know you?" I ask. "And who gave me what?"

"Eat this first, and then we'll talk," she says. "And before you ask me what's in it, just trust me. It'll make you feel better." She holds out a brown package from where she remains on the pile of fabric, and I creep forward to retrieve it, watching her the whole time.

"It'll make me feel better?" I ask in disbelief as I take the bar. Every step I take feels like a shockwave up through my body.

"Please eat it," she says as she unwraps her own bar, breaks off a piece, and pops it into her mouth. I relinquish my caution, peel open the package, and take a bite. Within seconds of swallowing, the pain eases and strength returns to my limbs. I stuff the rest of the bar in my mouth, eager to speed up the recovery process, even if I don't know what I'm recovering from. When I finish, I brush the crumbs from my shaved face and hear Elisa chuckling under her breath. Without a word, she hands me her

canteen, and I don't hesitate to drink, feeling sudden desperation. I force myself to quit gulping and hand it back to her,
ashamed I only left a few drops. But she smiles in return.

"So, can you tell me where I am and how I got here?" I ask.
Elisa opens her mouth to speak and then stops. Her body stiffens, and she cranes her head towards the door to our side while
her widened eyes flick around the room. Without hesitating any
longer, she stuffs her belongings back into her pack and jumps
up. She holds her hand out to me, urging me to take it, which I
do, and she tugs me towards the door.

"Where are we going?" I ask, stumbling behind her.

"Someone's coming. I heard the truck. We have to get out of
here before we're caught," she answers without looking at me.
We're a few yards away from the door when it bursts open and
floods the room with light.

"Run!" she screams and pulls me in the opposite direction. I
do as she says and follow after her and then realize — I am not
just running. I'm practically flying as my feet kick beneath me.
We approach the opposite wall, and I scan the area, looking for
an exit, but there isn't one. I pull back on Elisa's hand, trying to
slow her before we run into the wall, but she squeezes tighter as
she picks up speed.

"Jump, August!" she yells, and I look up, searching for a
place to land. The only elevated surfaces around are those of the
ceiling rafters that cross far overhead. "You can do it!" she cries
and releases my hand.

She takes three more steps forward and propels herself
upwards. With the grace of a bird, she lands, poised and steady,
on a beam that intersects the wall. It doesn't seem possible, but I
have to trust her. I press my heels in and spring towards the
rafters, aiming a few feet to Elisa's left. I land perfectly,
crouched with my head down, and my chest heaves with aston-
ishment as a chuckle slips past my lips.

"Follow me to the door!" Elisa orders, snapping me back to reality as she runs and jumps from rafter to rafter as though it was nothing. I take a second to sneak a glance at whatever it is that has her frightened and see a man watching us with a predatorial smirk that accentuates his bulbous nose. His arms are crossed over his chest, and he wears dark pants and shoes topped with an undersized gray shirt that stretches across his broad stomach. On his right hip hangs a black gun, and a faded gray cap perches atop his head.

"You can't get past me this time. One way in, one way out," the man yells, casually reaching to retrieve his gun from his position inside the main door. I don't know why we're running from him, but I'm guessing it has something to do with his weapon. I follow after Elisa, mimicking her leaps as fast as possible until we reach the platform. She kicks the door open with a bang. From below, the man curses loudly, unaware there was a second exit from the building. Elisa grabs my shoulders, locking eyes with me.

"We're going to have to jump again. See the tree line out there?" she asks. I nod, scanning beyond the empty dirt lot that surrounds the building. "Jump as hard as you can and start running as soon as you hit the ground. Don't stop running until we've lost the Shepherd, okay?"

My eyes flick between her and the forest, and I nod again. Honestly, I don't know how far I'll get. It's one thing to jump straight up and a different thing to leap across a fifty-yard clearing, but I've already surprised myself twice in the last minute and will at least try. Elisa scoots back to the edge of the platform and takes two massive strides, throwing herself through the open doorway. Gunshots fire from below, but Elisa lands and darts to the forest. I don't give myself the opportunity to second-guess my decision and follow Elisa. It feels less alarming this time to fly through the air, but I still flail my legs throughout my descent until I hit ground and roll to a stop.

Unharmed, I stand up and find Elisa a few yards from the forest. I am about to run after her when the pounding thuds of the Shepherd's footsteps grows louder behind me. I turn in time to see the Shepherd aim the gun at my chest.

"Don't move!" the man yells. I respond the only way I know how. I push into the ground and jump over the man, knocking the weapon from his pudgy hands. The gun flies to the side and disappears in a clump of thick, dead grass, and I land behind him in a defensive crouch with my fists raised. He turns towards me, his face contorted into shock. He straightens his back and extends his right hand like he wants me to take it.

"Come here. You can trust me. It's the girl who you need to fear. I can help you," he says with a soft, innocent voice. The inside of his brows turn up and a faint smirk creeps to the corners of his otherwise puckered mouth.

I remain crouched, unsure what to think. Before I can make up my mind, a loud CRACK echoes through the clearing, and the chubby man crumples to the ground. Behind him, Elisa recoils a whip from his ankles and prepares to strike again. The Shepherd rubs the back of his legs and groans between shallow wheezes.

"The trees, August!" Elisa cries as the Shepherd begins crawling frantically towards the discarded gun. That's all I need to see. Together, Elisa and I race through the remainder of the clearing and dive deep into the forest. Behind us, shots fire from the ivy-covered shell of the building, but none of them strike us. We're safe... for now.

———

"So we were soldiers?" I ask. We've settled for the

night on the side of a mountain, surrounded on all sides by ancient, sprawling trees, the empty branches of which fill almost every empty space like blackened fingers against the star-filled sky. Elisa has spent the past hour telling me who I am and what all we've been doing for the past several months. I don't remember any of it, but she says it will come back. I hope she's right, but even she doesn't seem too confident, despite her attempts to appear so.

"Yeah," she replies. I mull over the words, unable to digest them. It doesn't seem real. Broken images flicker through my mind on occasion as we speak, but nothing stands out.

"And how many Young Ones are left back on the Compound?" I ask. From beneath the wool blanket draped over her shoulders, Elisa looks up and frowns.

"There's no telling... tens of thousands across the entire country at least," she says.

"And the election is the best way to free them?" I ask, trying to connect the dots.

"That's what we've been told. I don't know enough about Belstrana's politics to verify it, but I guess we have to trust Luca, especially since we've already spread the word to pretty much everyone in the country," she answers.

"Even though he keeps saying it's going to fail?" I ask, rubbing my temples as I try to find the logic.

"Yeah..." She sighs, and her frown deepens.

"And this doesn't seem strange to you? You don't know what else he's planning?" I ask.

"No, not exactly," she begins and then pauses. "Actually, I don't know if you can remember, but a week or two ago, after we snuck you and Luca into Village B to see his wife, we ran into an older woman, a drifter." She waits to see if I know who she's talking about. I shake my head, so she continues.

"Well, she was pretty scary, and she kept warning us that we are on the brink of disaster, that we are going to cause a civil war. She said those comments, and you and I didn't think much of them, but then Luca said something. He said 'that might be what we want' or something like that. It was hard to hear, but I swear I think he said those words. Any memory of that?" I squeeze my eyes shut, yelling at my brain to remember something, anything, but it's a void.

"No, I'm sorry," I say, hanging my head. "But he said those actual words? You're sure?"

"Yeah, I'm pretty sure," she replies, tucking the blanket around her folded legs and under her chin.

"Maybe he has an army somewhere?" I suggest. "Or maybe he's gathering people to march to the capitol and fight the president — what's his name?"

"Karlmann," Elisa replies. "I've thought about that, too, but it seems like such a huge risk."

"Why?" I ask.

"Well, because of who makes up the Foundation's army — children, remember?" Her words from earlier in the conversation come back, and my heart drops at the thought. I don't know Luca, but I can't believe he would assemble an army to knowingly fight against children.

"Can you think of any other ideas?" I ask.

"Besides killing Karlmann, no." I tug my own blanket around my shoulders, scooting a few inches closer to the small fire in search of warmth.

"I want to find out what Luca knows as soon as possible. How far away do you think he is?" I ask.

"I'm not sure. He's been taking care of Nikola and Alek since they were rescued from the Compound, so I doubt they've gone too far. We could reach them tomorrow unless we run into some sort of problem."

"Nikola and Alek?" I ask.

"Our friends. They escaped the Compound with us months ago but got captured before you did. Joseph rescued them, too," she says. I try to picture them but can't.

"So they're safe?" I ask. Even if I don't know who they are, I'd like to know that they're okay.

"Yeah. I'll take you to them tomorrow, okay?" she replies between yawns.

I lie back on the ground, wrapped as tightly as possible inside of my blanket. She shifts in her own makeshift bed and then the forest falls silent aside from the crackling of the fire beside us. I figure she's already asleep, but regardless, before I close my eyes, I whisper, "Thanks, Elisa."

23

"Once again. What did you do with them?" the Man asks, pacing in a circle around Joseph, who, bruised and bloodied from the inquisition, holds his head up in defiance and says nothing. His head throbs, and he's sure his nose had been broken. He remembers the crunch from the boot's impact well. But he won't speak. The Man lunges forward and grabs the collar of Joseph's shirt. His clothing is ripped in several places and smudged with a mixture of blood and dirt.

"If you don't tell me right now, I swear I'll make this the worst day of your life. And it won't just be you who suffers." His voice is low and steady, filled with the violence of his threat. Joseph meets his gaze but doesn't flinch.

From the corner of the room, the Colonel, bound by his own set of cuffs and shackles, watches helplessly as the Man lands a series of vicious blows on Joseph's back and stomach. Until recently, the Colonel had felt nothing but loyalty towards the Foundation, unwavering in his belief that they would save Belstrana from the crippling influence of the outside world. But now, as he watches the bearded man tremble with pain, blood trickling from a cut over his eye and purplish bruising erupting across his jaw, he knows they had been betrayed, and hatred boiled in his veins.

"If you won't speak," the Man says, "then so be it. Take him downstairs and see what you can do." Two Elects with distant eyes step forward, jerk Joseph up to his feet, and drag him out of the door and down the hall.

"As for you, Colonel, or should I say *former* Colonel," the Man says, turning his attention to his other prisoner, "this is what's in store for you if you don't open your mouth and tell me what you know about their plans." The Colonel's pulse quickens, and he struggles futilely against his bonds as the Man comes to stand in front of him.

"I don't know anything about it! I swear!" he cries, forcing tears back.

"Of course you do. You've been overseeing this operation the whole time and yet *somehow*, despite all of your grand plans to capture them, they're still out there. Don't tell me that's a coincidence," the Man says. The sour smell of liquor hangs in the air between them, and the Colonel fights back a wave of nausea.

"I'm telling the truth, sir. I have been nothing but loyal to you! I have served you faithfully since the beginning of the Foundation!" The Man throws his head back and laughs sarcastically.

"You mean to tell me that when I threatened your wife and children, you never wanted to betray me and help them? Don't lie to me," he replies, his voice turning soft. "I would have done the same thing."

"But I didn't do anything! I followed every order you gave me!" the Colonel protests on the verge of mania.

"Then why are they still out there?!" The Colonel yelps as a blow lands across his cheek, and he drops his head.

"I don't know, sir." Pain surges through his jaw and lands in his chest where it wraps around his heart and squeezes.

"I believe you *do* know. And we're going to find out everything. Mark my words," he warns. "Get him out of here," he directs to another set of Elects by the door, the same ones who had arrested him the first time, and they tug the Colonel downstairs, where they place him in an empty prison cell across from Joseph.

———

WHEN I AWAKEN THE NEXT MORNING, THE SUN HAS BARELY kissed the sky, sending a swirl of pinks and purples and oranges out as its ambassadors that stand in stark contrast to the wiry, dark branches that reach out overhead. Enough light fights its way through the branches that I can see Elisa's covered figure on the other side of the smoldering ashes. I don't move, afraid to let the frosty air meet my skin. Instead, I watch her sleep while thinking about everything she told me yesterday. After a while, my muscles begin to ache with tension, so I sit up and stretch my arms out, grimacing at the cold. Beneath me, dead leaves crinkle and crunch, and Elisa groans.

"Are you awake already?" she asks, yawning.

"Yeah. Sorry," I reply, as a shiver runs down my back and raises goosebumps on my arms.

"Well..." She sighs as she pushes herself upright. "I might as well get up, too. We should have already left, but I think we both needed the sleep." She grabs her pack, which she had used as a bulgy pillow, and sifts through it.

"Breakfast," she says and tosses me another one of the bars.

"Is this what I ate yesterday?" I ask as I tear at the seam, exposing the brownish-gray food within it.

"Yeah. They're what the Foundation gives to the Young

Ones to make them extra strong and healthy. Joseph helped us sneak them out. Too bad they taste like dirt," she replies and then stuffs her own bar into her mouth. I nod in comprehension and wipe the crumbs from my lips, feeling the bristles on my cheeks.

"Do I have a beard?" I ask, rubbing my face.

"Well, you did. It was pretty long, too, but they shaved it while you were back on the Compound. It's coming back, though," she says, and the sparkling in her eyes makes me blush.

After a quick drink of water from a nearby stream, we cover the ashes with dirt and leaves, and Elisa slings her pack over her shoulders. As she moves, I catch a glimpse of her wrist. There's no mark on it. Insecurity creeps over me, and I pull my sleeve down around my palm to cover mine. She adjusts the strap of her bag and then stops.

"Oh wait," she exclaims. "You'll need this." She tosses me what looks like a pile of leather strap, and I examine it closely. It's my sling. I run the leather through my fingers and the memory of how to use it comes back to me. I bend over, pick up a small rock, place it in the pocket of the sling, and swing it around my head. I release one of the thongs, and the stone flies out, striking the tree I had selected as my target. A smile stretches so widely across Elisa's face that her dimples appear. I grin back at her.

"It's coming back to you," she says knowingly. "I think this belongs to you, too. Joseph said they found it in your pocket when they captured you." She hands me a small glass vial full of thick, glossy blue liquid.

"What is it?" I ask, rolling the vial between my fingers.

She frowns. "I was hoping you could tell me." I shrug and drop the container in my pocket. We walk in silence for a little while, but I want to know more. I have too many questions.

"How did you rescue me?" I ask.

"Well, it wasn't me. It was Joseph. He told the nurse that Karlmann had ordered you, Alek, and Nikola to be taken to Apex. He had faked the paperwork and everything," she says, grinning.

"That's it?" I say. "They just let him leave with us?"

"Well, not exactly. Clive, the head Man in Red, challenged him pretty well. One of the nurses had to intervene and back up Joseph's claims. He knew once his lie was discovered, they'd hunt us down, so Joseph risked his own safety and drove you out in a delivery truck. He dropped Nikola and Alek off with Luca and brought you to the warehouse, where I was waiting. We figured we'd be safer if we split up," she says, ducking under a low branch.

"So where's Joseph now?"

She purses her lips and tucks a strand of hair behind her ear. "I don't know. He said he was going to head to Apex to prepare for the election. I hope he made it," she replies. I step over a fallen log but don't ask anything else, feeling guilty at how much he had had to risk to get me to safety. After a few hours, we detect the scent of smoke from a campfire and follow its trail.

"Over there," Elisa says, pointing towards a narrow hollow in the trees. The stream of smoke is visible now, and we pick up the pace.

"Someone's coming!" a female voice shouts. Elisa waves me back, and we stop in front of an overgrown shrub. I peer around its edge and jump back when a blonde girl stands up a few feet away. I reach for my knife, but Elisa stops me, pressing her hand into my arm.

"It's us!" Elisa cries. She walks out from behind the foliage, revealing herself to the blonde. A lean teenaged boy with shaggy black hair drops down from his hiding spot in a nearby tree. They're both wearing the same brown clothes as Elisa and me.

"Nikola, it's me, Elisa," she says, holding her hands up and talking to the other girl. Nikola's sharp eyes narrow on Elisa's face and then dart to me as I show myself. An older man, maybe in his thirties or forties, walks up behind Nikola.

"It's true, Nikola. These are the people I told you about," he says. Nikola clenches her eyes shut for a moment and shakes her head. When she reopens her eyes, her expression changes, and she blinks furiously, looking back and forth between Elisa and me. Elisa hands her a folded bow staff.

"My staff?" Nikola whispers, fingering the object and turning it in her hands. "I remember this. How'd you get it?"

"It got left behind when you were arrested at our old camp-site. A drifter found it and gave it to me," Elisa says. She turns to Luca. "Did they forget everything, too?"

"They remember most of it now, but it's slow-going." He rubs his chin, and his eyes are dark and worn.

"Hey, Alek," Elisa says. He watches her with curiosity and then relaxes.

"Hey, Elisa. It's good to see you again," he murmurs, smiling at her. Frustration rolls through me.

"So, wait. You both have memories back, but I don't yet?" I ask, folding my arms over my chest. "What's the deal?"

"You must have been given a much stronger dose of what-ever memory-suppressant they used on the others," Elisa says, trying to calm my worries. But it doesn't work. I turn away from the others, who now chatter like old friends, and resist the urge to shout. The clearing here is small, and the ground slopes towards the middle, where a crackling fire burns. I scoot close to it and lie down, trying to block out the murmuring of conversa-tion around me. I lace my fingers behind my head and close my eyes.

"Here," Elisa says. "You look like you're freezing." She sits cross-legged beside me with a blanket in her outstretched hand. I accept the cover gratefully.

"Thanks," I mumble and force out a grin. She returns it, and I take the opportunity to study her features. She's pretty, very pretty, even with a dirty face and wild hair. We're friends, judging by how she treats me, but how friendly are we? Are we more than friends? She twirls the stem of a dry leaf between her fingers and sighs.

"Well," she says while she pushes herself upright, "I'm gonna let you get some rest, I guess." She dusts the earth from her pants and takes a few steps towards the others. I curse myself for not being nicer to her and reach for her before she can leave.

"Wait," I say. I run my right hand over my hair. "I don't know if you heard me last night, but seriously. I appreciate everything you've done for me." Her lips turn up slightly, and she nods and walks away, leaving me to fall asleep.

———

SOMETHING GOES OFF IN MY HEAD, LIKE A BLAST OR A siren, and I jerk awake. Everything I've been missing since I was rescued comes back to me in a rush. The election. Elisa. My parents. Joseph and the Men in Red. The Crystal. The mark. The Topaz. I pat my pocket to make sure it's still there and then jump up. The others sit gathered on the opposite side of the fire.

"Luca!" I bark, bent on getting the truth out of him. Luca jumps at the sound of my voice.

"Welcome back," he says. "You're just in time."

"For what?" I ask, walking around the fire to reach them.

"The election is four days away now, and we're finalizing plans. Unfortunately, we don't know anymore how things stand inside of the villages since we've pretty much been cut off from our allies inside, but we'll have to assume things are going as planned. We're going to head towards Apex in case things go downhill."

"Why would we do that?" I ask. I recall Joseph's warnings about Luca and remember that he has been concealing a second part of the plan.

"I know what you're asking, but not yet. It's not the right time to tell you," Luca replies. He picks at a loose thread in the seam of his pants leg and fidgets under the pressure of our collective gaze. It's more apparent than ever — I'm not the only one who distrusts Luca.

"And when will be the right time? As people are casting their ballots?" I question, sneering at his cowardice when he doesn't look at any of us. I lean towards him, putting my face inches from his, daring him to avoid my gaze again.

"You woke up feeling snarky, didn't you?" Luca mumbles under his breath.

"I woke up wanting answers," I respond, holding my position. Luca clenches his teeth and folds his arms.

"I can't tell you yet, for crying out loud. How many times do I have to say it?" he replies. He locks his gaze with mine.

"I'm going back to the village to see Joyce," I say, standing up again so I tower over him.

"Are you kidding?" Luca replies.

"No. I'm not kidding. If you won't tell me, she will. She said she didn't know, but she's lying."

"And what if you get caught again? There's no way to get you out a third time. It's too risky," Luca says. Elisa and Alek both shuffle with discomfort. Nikola smirks, twirling her staff through her fingers.

"Then leave me there. I won't ask you to risk yourselves for me again." I can't look at Elisa when I say the words.

"It's suicide," says Alek, "and it's not worth it. Don't do this, August."

"I'm not going to sit around anymore and wait for Luca to decide we're trustworthy enough. We have a right to know," I say, jabbing a finger at Luca.

"But you don't know where you are or where the village is from here," Elisa says, pleading. My resolve quakes for a fleeting moment at the sound of her voice, but I shake my head.

"Then I'll find out," I reply, ending the discussion.

24

"We caught a glimpse of footage of them earlier today and have placed a dozen Reds on either side of the tunnel. The Elect is coming back to the village," a fidgety Lieutenant says to the Man. "We'll find him, sir."

"You had better. The last person in your position failed miserably and well... I don't need to explain anything else, do I?" the Man replies.

"No, sir. I understand. He said he's going to go visit a woman named Joyce at the local apothecary shop. Should we have her arrested?" The Man stares across the room, deep in thought.

"No. Assign two Reds to follow her. If he doesn't make it to her, maybe she'll find him."

"Yes, sir."

———

"I'm going with you," Elisa whispers, startling me awake beneath the layers of blankets that pretend to keep me warm. I open my eyes, and there she is, leaning over me, and my breath catches in my chest. Her hair falls in a curtain around her flushed cheeks, and her emerald eyes sparkle in the morning sun. Had she not just told me that she wants to join me on this trip, I would have considered brushing my fingers across her smooth skin. Instead, I sit up.

"What? No way," I say, running my fingers through my hair. "You're not coming. It's too dangerous."

"Yeah, well, you went alone last time and look what happened. I'm not going to let you risk your safety again, not this close to the election," she replies. Her voice is firm, and I grimace from her reminder. "Plus, you're going to need someone to show you the way back to the village." She smiles boldly, revealing her dimples, and my resolve dies away. Her argument is valid. Plus, I'd like the company.

"Fine," I say and then try to stifle a yawn with the back of my hand. "You can come." She beams, delighted, and I can't help but mirror her expression. It's nice to see her happy again, even if it is due to her eagerness to join me in what could be a catastrophic trip.

We roll up our blankets and eat our bars in three quick bites. After saying our goodbyes, we set off towards the village. The sun rises gradually to our left as we run, and somehow — despite the circumstances — our moods are light, like they were when we first left the Compound months ago. We joke with one another, taking turns recalling bits of our earlier excursions across Belstrana, and the time passes quickly. After an hour or so, Elisa falls quiet.

"Is everything okay?" I ask, noting the downward curve of her lips and her puzzled eyes.

"Yeah, I think so... did you ever remember what that blue stuff is?" she asks. I weigh the risk and decide to tell her.

"It's called Topaz. It's supposed to be an antidote to the

Crystal. Joyce made it and gave it to me," I say, and the vial feels like a five pound weight in my pocket.

"Too bad you couldn't have remembered that earlier," she says, still frowning. "But that's awesome that she gave it to you." Her hair bounces behind her as we run.

"Yeah, but I guess it's only useful if we can remember to use it. And chances are if we remember to use it, then we don't need it," I say, appreciating the irony. She snorts.

"Can I ask something else?" she says.

"Sure," I reply, dodging around a large spruce tree.

"I... I saw something while you were asleep back in the warehouse and wanted to ask you about it," she says, clearing her throat. Her hair bounces behind her with every step.

I think I know what she's going to say, but I ask, "What are you talking about?"

"The black triangle on your wrist. Why do you have that?" she asks, glancing over her shoulder at me.

My chest tightens. Surely when Joseph warned me about people outside of the Foundation, he didn't mean Elisa. It should be safe to tell her, right? Or should I keep it from her? I agonize over the decision, aware that she's expecting an answer soon. I doubt she would ever use it against me, but what if someone else asks her what it means? I don't want to put that responsibility on her, so I decide against it.

"I don't know," I say, lying.

"Seriously?" she asks, and her tone betrays her doubt. She doesn't believe me, but I stick with my story.

"Yeah," I say, and to my relief, she doesn't push me on it.

I feel like such a jerk. I bite my lip and focus on the quick cadence of our crunching footsteps. With the songbirds gone from the forest, we continue along in an uneasy silence that weighs on me. The longer we run, the more my conscience wails against my decision, but I swallow back the urge to tell her the truth. Not yet, not until I'm sure she's safe and the information can't be used against her.

By the time the sun shines overhead, we reach the edge of the clearing that contains the tunnel entrance. We slip from tree to tree, looking for signs of patrolling Reds. I pull down a fluffy branch of a fir tree and peer through the evergreen window. Elisa presses forward so that her face nearly touches mine, leaving enough room for a breath between us. She clasps her hand over her mouth to keep from gasping audibly. At least ten Reds wait with guns in hand around the tunnel. We don't stand a chance, not against ten guns. We're fast, but bullets and darts are faster.

"We need to get out of here," I whisper in her ear. I release the branch as gently as possible and grab Elisa's left hand. We step backwards, and every noise we produce makes me more and more worried. Maybe the murmur of the Reds' voices and movement is loud enough to conceal ours. We go back north-wards, fingers intertwined, and scan the woods around us. Sweat builds on my forehead, and I draw my sling with my open hand. Elisa unhooks her whip, and it uncoils so the tip of it grazes the forest floor. A whip and a sling would be no match for ten Reds, but they'll at least slow them down.

We've made it about seventy yards when we see a Red to the west of us. Elisa yanks my hand, and we both drop to the ground. My heart slams into my chest, and I hold my breath, listening for noise of the Red's approach. His footsteps draw nearer, deliberate and targeted. I release Elisa's hand and wrap the straps of my sling through my fingers.

"Psst," a low voice calls. "Hey. August. Come on out," the soft voice continues in a scratchy whisper. Elisa and I exchange alarmed looks, and she shakes her head fervently.

"August, I know you're there. I have news for you," the man persists. "I'm a friend of Joseph." The sound of Joseph's name alarms me more, and Elisa's expression turns frantic. I'm torn between the desire to flee and to see if this man truly is a friend.

"No!" Elisa mouths, still shaking her head. She grabs my arm and squeezes, tight. Her eyes plead with mine. The last thing I want to do is risk her safety, but something presses me to respond to the Red.

"If something goes wrong, don't try to help me. Run as fast as you can and get out of here," I whisper to her.

Her mouth drops to a frown, and her eyebrows narrow, but she lets go of my arm. I stand up, spinning my sling to my right, and my left hand rests on the top of my knife. A man, who by all indication could have been Joseph's twin, waits a few feet away. He has the same dark skin and black hair, and the build of his muscular body is nearly identical. Even the same jaunty nose and warm eyes have found their way on to this stranger's face.

"Shh!" he whispers and raises a finger to cover his mouth. "We don't need to attract anyone else. I've been waiting out here every day, hoping you'd be stupid enough to come back."

"Well, here I am. Who are you?" I ask, lowering my sling.

"I'm Joseph's brother. I can't stay, but I wanted to let you know that everything is set for the election, and we'll start reversing the Young Ones' lessons in two days." My head cocks to the side, and I scrunch my brow in confusion.

"What are you talking about?" I ask. "What does that mean, reversing their lessons?" He balks at me, mouth open as his eyes search my face.

"Do you not know? I figure Luca would have told you..."

"Know what? What are you planning?" I probe. Elisa stands up from her hiding spot and slinks forward, eyes on the Red.

"Uh," the man stammers. "I thought he would have told you since you're supposed to lead them."

"What? Lead who? The Young Ones?" I ask. My cheeks grow warm as my heart rate picks up. I step forward, debating whether I should tackle the Red — Joseph's brother or not — and pin him until he tells me the truth.

"You should talk to Luca," the Red says, stepping away from me as I advance.

"What difference does it make who tells us?" Elisa asks. She's following me, I realize.

"Listen, I shouldn't have said anything. Forget I was here, okay?" He turns and hustles back towards the tunnel. I stare after him and decide not to give chase. Elisa looks as irritated as I feel.

"This isn't good," she says. I don't respond. I grab her hand and dart back towards our camp, propelled by anger. She runs with me for several yards before yanking back on my arm so hard that my shoulder almost dislocates.

"What are you about to do?" she asks, grabbing my shoulders.

"I'm done waiting. Luca's either going to tell me on his own, or I'm going to kick his butt until he tells me. I'll leave it up to him," I say louder than I should.

"You can't let your anger get the best of you, August. You know he won't respond to that," she says.

"How can you be so calm about this?" I ask, irritated with her. "Did you hear that guy?"

"Yeah, I did, and I told you it doesn't sound good. But beating up Luca isn't going to help things," she says. I can't help myself, and a sarcastic laugh slips through my lips.

"We'll see," I reply. "Now come on." I feel guilty for being short with her, but I'm done getting used and run over by Luca. It ends now. Elisa follows behind me as I tear through the forest. She doesn't try to stop me again, and we reach Luca together within the hour.

"Luca!" I bellow as we approach the clearing. "What have you been keeping from us? Tell me about the children inside of the Compound!" I break through the trees and slide to a stop. He sits on the other side from me, and I storm towards him, clenching my hands into fists. Luca's eyes widen, and a pile of belongings — including the gun he had taken from a Red — drop from his lap as he jumps up, scattering across the ground.

"Who told you about that? You haven't been gone long enough to see Joyce and get back," he stammers.

"Never mind who told me what. You tell me," I demand, bowing my shoulders, "or I will beat it out of you." Nikola and Alek run over and stand between us, and Alek presses a hand into my chest, trying to calm me. They glower at Luca, who recoils from their gazes.

"Okay," he replies. He opens his hands as though he's surrendering and sits motioning for us to join him. We don't. The four of us tower over him and wait. He fidgets with his jacket and clears his throat.

"You want the truth? Here it is." He takes a deep breath and smooths his palms over his legs. "We have more people on the inside of the compounds than you realize. We're going forward with the election, of course, regardless of the risk of failure, because it will send a message to Karlmann that we're not going to take it anymore. We want change." He pauses to scratch at his unruly beard and continues. "You know all of this, of course. You've been an integral piece in that component of our revolution."

"Revolution?" I ask, raising an eyebrow. "Elections are not revolutionary."

"Yes. Stage one will be completed in four days, when the election takes place. And stage two starts in two days." He doesn't look at us.

"What is stage two?" Nikola asks, and her hand rests on her folded bow staff.

"Reds loyal to us will begin reversing the orders given to the children by Karlmann — civilians will no longer be their targets," Luca replies.

"What does that mean? Why would they do that?" Elisa asks and wraps her arms around herself. Only Alek maintains a placid expression.

"Because when Karlmann sees the people voting against him, he's going to send out the armies of Young Ones to put down the movement. They'd be used against their own people, against their own families, and we don't want that to happen," he says.

"So what good will changing their orders do? They'll still be doped up on Crystal, and you can't just let them run free. Who's their new target?" I say, feeling like my chest is filling with water.

"Well... this is why I didn't want to tell you until later," he begins. I shift my weight from one leg to the other, never looking away from his shifty posture. "We're going to use them as our reinforcements. They'll still be strong — as strong as any of us — and they'll be lethal. But we'll change who they target so that they go after Karlmann and any Reds still loyal to him instead of the people in the villages. He'll never see it coming."

25

His words suck the air from the clearing. The wind doesn't blow, the trees don't sway, and my heart doesn't beat. My breath catches in my chest, and I can't speak. Luca speeds up, fumbling over his words to get them out.

"We don't *want* to use them, but we will if we need to. Karlmann has to go, and this will get the job done," he stammers. Nikola's staff clicks out beside me — *tat tat tat.* My hand moves to my knife, but I dig my nails into the meat of my palm, resisting the urge to use it.

"*That* is your plan?" I say. My voice is rigid, stiff. Elisa covers her mouth with her hands and shakes her head.

"We're doing the best thing we know to do!" Luca cries. "This way they aren't used against their families, and we remove Karlmann! Two birds, one stone and all."

"But they're children," Elisa murmurs. "We were supposed to rescue them, not use them."

"Listen, you may not want to believe me now, and you may think we're doing them an injustice, but we are rescuing them.

Once Karlmann is gone, they'll be returned to their families, and everything will be okay," Luca replies.

"Not all of them, Luca. Some of them will die if you go through with this. The Foundation won't spare them. You know it's the truth," Nikola says, tapping the tip of her staff against the ground. "Is there any way to stop this from happening?" Her tone is icier than the air.

"No." His answer is frank. "Everything's underway already. They should be prepared to march on Apex the day of the election. The Reds on our side will deal with those amongst them who are still loyal to Karlmann, and then they'll direct the Young Ones on their new mission. You'll see. It's all been taken care of."

"You want us to thank you for this?" I ask, flexing my fingers to get my blood flowing through them again.

"We want you to lead the soldiers to Apex," he replies. I balk at his audacity.

"I'm sorry. What did you call them?" Alek asks.

"He called them soldiers, Alek." Nikola sneers.

"They're not soldiers, Luca. They're children. If nothing else, think of your son!" Elisa cries.

"You want us to lead them into battle?" I ask, taking one step closer to Luca, whose legs quiver as he pushes himself upright and stands eye-level with me. He nods.

"You lying son of a... how could you do this? The only reason we stayed around here was to make sure they never had to fight again!" I yell, shoving my finger into his chest.

"Listen!" Luca responds, and he puffs his chest and pushes my hand away. "If you don't want them to be used, then come with me to Apex and get to Karlmann before they have to."

"What are you talking about?" Nikola asks, now digging the tip of the staff into the ground.

"If you won't help lead the Young Ones to Apex, then I'm

going to solve the problem myself and kill Karlmann." The threat in his tone is tangible.

"You never said anything about killing people. You just said you wanted him removed from power..." Alek says, stepping forward. His chain clinks from where it hangs on his belt.

"You don't understand, and I don't expect you to," Luca responds, looking at each one of us. He seems calm. Too calm.

"I understand. I understand that you and I are different, more different than I'd realized. I know I may not have been jumping at the chance to help when I first escaped, but I'm not that person anymore. If you want to perpetuate the violence used by the Foundation, then do it on your own," I say.

"You're a coward, Luca. I like smacking around the bad guy as much as the next person, but this isn't right," Nikola says.

"None of it is," Alek adds.

"Go to Apex and kill Karlmann. Or don't. But you're not getting any more help from us," I say, stepping back from him. "And we're going to do everything we can to stop this plan of yours from happening. You'll have to kill me before I let you use them like this." I mean it.

"Don't do this, August," he says, dropping his voice. *Is he threatening me?* My hand moves back to the knife. Elisa must see my intentions, because she shoves in front of me and goes toe to toe with Luca.

"Go," she says, raising her arm to point towards the east. Nikola twirls her staff up to rest over her shoulders, behind her neck. Alek's chain clinks nearby.

"We're done," I say. I reach down and grab Luca's bag and then shove it into his chest. He steps back and wraps his hands around the straps and then bends down to gather his scattered belongings.

"Leave the gun," I say when he reaches for it. "Face him like a man if that's what you're going to do." Luca pauses with his fingers inches above the barrel, and I tense, ready to fight him if necessary. He removes his hand and stands back up. With one last look — a mix of disappointment and anger — Luca saunters through a break in the trees and disappears.

I watch him go but don't speak. None of us do. We keep to ourselves and try to digest the turn of events. Nikola takes out her aggression on several innocent trees which she destroys limb by limb with her staff and her bare hands. Alek jumps up to the top of a feathery spruce. Only Elisa and I remain in the clearing.

"I'm sorry I got you into this," I say.

"You didn't get me into anything. I'm the responsible one. You wanted to cut and run when you had the chance, and now you're caught up in everything. Please don't apologize." With flushed cheeks and bloodshot eyes, she doesn't look like herself. I want to reach out to her and wrap her in my arms, but my hands feel weighted and numb.

Something rustles behind me, and I glance sideways at Elisa, who also hears the noise. I stand up slowly, loading a stone into my sling while Elisa reaches into her boot and withdraws her knife. Before she can flick it open, I release the stone. It shoots towards a clump of pine needles and collides with something. A small, brown object falls from the tree. Crap. I run over and stomp on the bird and curse — loudly.

"I should have seen this coming. And I should have known better than to trust Luca. The Foundation will know everything now," I say, pacing. "We have to do something. We can't sit here while it falls apart, especially since whoever is at the end of that camera just heard our entire conversation."

"What can we do? We can't get to every village in the next two days, and Apex is the last place we need to go," Elisa says.

"We at least need to try to stop it from happening on our Compound so our village might not suffer. This is your chance to help the children, Elisa. Come with me." Part of me hesitates at asking her to join me in this, but I know her. She's strong and smart and can take care of herself. She reaches forward and cups my face, stopping me in my tracks.

"Okay," she says. "But we need Alek and Nikola, too." I don't try to hide the pleasure that grows across my face. I grab her hands from my cheeks and kiss the tops of them. She blushes, smiling back at me.

"Alek! Nikola!" I yell. "Get your butts over here!" I clench Elisa's left hand in my right one, and it gives me the strength I need to move forward.

26

"So they think they can use our own soldiers against us?" the Man yells, slamming the phone down onto its receiver, and it cracks from the impact. He storms through his office and out of the door. By the time he reaches military headquarters, which is a block away from the capital building, his chest burns like it's been set on fire. He bursts through the front doors and enters the main hall. Rooms line either side of the entry, revealed by windows and open doorways. Men and women dressed in dark green military uniforms sit in front of computers in each of the rooms, monitoring the villages and conducting research.

"Call down to Apex and get as many men as possible sent out to the villages! I want them swarmed!" he hollers between winded gasps. Several officials rush from their offices at the commotion and see the Man standing red-faced in front of them. A red-headed secretary wearing a black pencil skirt and white blouse pushes a rolling chair towards him, and he kicks it away. She falls backwards and slides across the black marble floor. General Volkov, one of the country's top officers, steps forward and bows to the Man before speaking.

"Is everything okay, sir?" he asks.

"No, everything isn't okay! They're turning on Karlmann, that idiot puppet of ours, and they're going to take out our main line of defense if we don't stop them. Get the Reds out there immediately. Quarantine those already in the compounds. Lock them away — they can't be trusted. And lock the children up, too. I will NOT let this happen so close to the election!"

"Yes, sir. Is there any particular village you want us to concentrate our forces on?" General Volkov asks.

"Yes. Village K." The Man feels as though his heart is seconds away from exploding, and he searches for a seat. The same secretary from before approaches him — slower this time — and offers him the desk chair again, which he sinks into. Another secretary runs up with a glass of water and hands it to the Man, and he slurps it down so quickly that it dribbles from the sides of his mouth and darkens his green shirt.

"Should we tell Karlmann what we're doing, sir?" General Volkov asks.

"Of course tell him. He's about to be plastered on every television screen in the world as a tyrant. He might as well know about it. But tell him if he speaks to anyone about the truth, if he tells a single soul about our involvement, then the deal's off," the Man replies.

"Yes sir, Mr. President," General Volkov replies.

"And Volkov? Give them twenty-four hours and then bomb the forest. It'll send the rats scurrying right into our laps."

———

I PERCH IN THE BARE BRANCHES OF A LARGE TREE, LOOKING out over an expansive clearing towards a huge rectangular building made of tan cinderblocks and sprinkled with windows. Around it stands a tall metal electric fence topped with barbed wire. Towers stand at each of the corners, and Reds perch on top of them, holding large, black guns. More Reds are scattered around the perimeter of the building. This is the right place. This is Karlmann's Complex inside of Apex.

My survey of the building's defenses is interrupted when several small bodies dash across the field from the tree line all around me. Blood freezes in my veins as I realize who they are — Young Ones, dressed in brown, like those on the Compound. They yell their hardest, trying to muster the intimidating sound of grown men and women, and charge the Complex with their weapons raised in their hands. Before my eyes, the Reds transform, turning into young adults dressed in solid black uniforms. The members of the Black Guard lift their guns towards the insurgents and order them to stop, but they don't.

The pecking sound of gunfire lashes out, and one by one, the Young Ones begin to fall, their small bodies slumping to the earth as they're peppered with bullets. I yell for them to turn around, but more and more children pour out from the trees below me. Bile rises in my throat as a young girl with braided pigtails, no more than seven years old, screams in pain and drops to the grass, holding her stomach.

The field, which had been covered in the dead, brown grass of winter, turns red with blood. The level rises higher and higher until it laps at the edges of the walls and swallows its victims like a crimson lake. I scream and scream, but no sound comes out, and then I fall backwards, limbs flailing and eyes wide.

I jolt awake. The weather is freezing, but sweat drenches my clothes as I gasp for air in the dark. The fire has died down only a little since I first drifted to sleep, which must have been only a few minutes ago. How could I dream something so terrible so quickly? Is this some sort of premonition? Am I leading everyone to slaughter? My pulse continues to race as I lie back down and wipe my brow with my coat sleeve. I can't get the dream out of my head and have to focus on counting my breaths in order to relax again. It takes hours, but eventually I settle back down enough to fall back to sleep.

———

WE WAIT UNTIL THE NEXT AFTERNOON BEFORE LEAVING for the Compound. Friction fills the clearing, scaring away even the wind, so the forest is oppressively quiet. We stow the remaining packs behind bushes and sit there, contemplating the attack and knowing it isn't going to work. How can four people overtake an entire compound? We can't, of course. But we'll try. We have to try.

That night, I watch the Reds from a distance. The others and I have hidden ourselves several yards back, and I creep forward as bursts of icy wind rustle the trees and conceal my footsteps. Approximately fifty yards sit between us and the tunnel, and at least ten Reds (maybe more) guard it with weapons in hand. I motion for the others to scale the trees for extra security while I take my position, pressing my stomach against a thick tree trunk. A few yards away stands the Red we've been looking for — Joseph's brother. I load a small stone, a little larger than a pebble, into my sling and strike his shoulder.

"Psst!" I whisper as the Red jumps, searching for the source of the projectile. He sees me motioning towards him, and checks over his shoulder to make sure nobody else is looking before walking over to speak with me.

"What are you doing?" he asks under his breath. I can barely see his features in the pale moonlight.

"We need you to get us into the Compound," I reply.

"How am I supposed to do that?" he asks, looking up to see Nikola, Elisa, and Alek perched in the trees.

"Arrest me," I suggest with a crooked grin. "Get us into the Compound. Please."

"Why?"

"There's something we have to do. Luca okayed it, and we need to get in there as soon as we can," I answer, unashamed of my lie. I hold my empty hands in front of my chest. "Cuff me, please." The Red huffs at the request, waiting for me to laugh at my joke, but I'm not joking. The others drop down and do the same with their hands.

"You have to be kidding me..." he says. He rubs his bald head and shrugs. "I don't have enough handcuffs for all of you. You'll have to pretend like you're wearing them behind your back." I can't hold back my grin. This may work.

"Thank you, uh..." I say, realizing I don't know his name.

"Elijah," he replies. "Joseph's brother, remember?"

"Yeah," I say and then use the opportunity that's available to me to find out about our ally. "Have you heard from Joseph lately?"

"All I've heard is that he was arrested after helping you escape. Now come on. If you want to do this, let's do it," Elijah says and motions us forward. He aims his gun at our backs and begins yelling for us to stay in line as we break through the trees. Immediately, every other weapon in the clearing is targeted towards us. Elijah's going to have to pull off a convincing act if we want to get out of this in one piece.

"Where did you find them?" one of the Reds asks, holding his pistol between his hands at eye level.

"They were up in some trees. I spotted them and threatened to shoot if they didn't surrender. I'm taking them to the Compound as we speak," Elijah says. "Move on!" he yells at us, and I act as dejected as possible as I stumble ahead, hands behind my back.

"I'll go with you," another Red says as he steps forward. The majority of them are so aghast that Elijah caught all of us by himself that they don't think to check us for handcuffs.

"And split the reward with you? I don't think so. You stay here and look for your own fugitives," Elijah says with a nervous chuckle.

"Aw, come on Elijah, don't be stingy," another Red says, edging close to us with a menacing sneer.

"Back off, man," Elijah says.

"What'd you say?" the Red replies, lifting his gun again.

Elijah pauses and sighs. "Alright, Ivan. You can come. Stay in the back though, behind the blonde one. She's a flight risk." Alek coughs to cover a laugh.

"Hey, what about me?" the first Red cries, shoving his way to the front.

"Look at your shoulder, Erik," Ivan says, and the Red looks down at his shirt. "See two bars? Thought not. Step back." The other Reds murmur in frustration but don't challenge him again.

I've reached the tunnel by now and Elijah uses the barrel of his rifle to nudge me inside. Someone behind me offers to call up to the Compound to let Clive know we're coming. I don't hear his response, but I hope no one lets him know. We need the element of surprise on our side in order to get in and guard the Young Ones.

I let my hands drop and rush through the tunnel quicker than ever before. A scuffle breaks out in the dark behind me, and after a few seconds, I hear Nikola sing-song, "Problem solved!"

I burst into the bakery's pantry and find the store empty. Elijah takes the lead, and I re-clasp my hands behind my back after double checking that my sling and knife are still attached to my belt. He opens the front door and steps outside, relaying the same story that he'd told back in the forest to the Reds on patrol here. He summons us forward, and we march through the streets. I feel vulnerable on the ground, especially when we pass our "wanted" posters taped to several store windows. To my relief, we arrive at the Compound without incident. The gate is unguarded, but I don't have time to question it.

I grab the identification card clipped to Elijah's shirt and yank it off. "Thanks, Elijah!" I say as I run to unlock the gate.

"Hey!" he yells after me, but I don't stop. I slide the card through the black security box and fling open the entrance. Elisa, Nikola, and Alek follow me inside, and I swing the gate shut behind us and toss the card back to Elijah through an opening in the fence. He catches it and gives a solitary nod before disappearing behind the corner of a building.

"We'll each take one of the barracks," I say, reviewing our plans. "Lock the Reds inside of their quarters. If they can't get out, then they can't hurt the Young Ones, and it'll give us time to tell them what both sides have been up to."

"This is suicide," Nikola says. "Even if we tell them every-thing, what's to stop them from attacking us?"

"Um, nothing?" Alek replies, shifting his weight back and forth. "Does anyone else find it strange that this whole area is empty?" he adds, looking around. And he's right. The entrance to the Compound should be buzzing with guards since it's dark out, but we're alone.

"Yes. It's weird," Nikola adds. "Something's up. I have a bad feeling about this."

"You sure we still want to go through with this?" Alek replies, running his fingers over the links in his chain, which is still clipped to his side. He looks at me.

"It's a long shot, okay? But we all agreed it would be better to do something than nothing, right?" I add. Nikola nods and unfurls her bow staff.

"Right," Elisa replies. Her jaw is set with determination,

and I reach out and squeeze her hand one last time. It's cold and stiff with fear, and I don't want to let her go. But I do.

"If things go wrong, head north back to our camp," I remind them. "Best get going. Good luck." With that, I race towards my old barrack. I kneel down beside the corner of a building and crane my head around to scan the street. Nikola leaps to the rooftop of the Reds' mess hall and runs forward like a cat with her staff extended to her side.

I continue down the alley and tear through the empty streets until I reach the first of two boys' barracks. I pull back one of the heavy red doors and slip inside. Hundreds of sleeping boys fill the room. On the other side of the building stands another door, which leads to the Reds' sleeping quarters. I slip around the bunks, looking for something useful to secure the handles of the Reds' door. My eyes land on the trunks that sit at the end of each bunk. A chain has to be stored in at least one of them.

I bend down in front of the nearest one and yank the lid open, but all I can find is a bow staff. I close it back and scoot to the next trunk over. After searching through four more, I locate a chain. I withdraw it carefully and carry it to the door.

Just as I start to loop it around the handles, blinding flood-lights burst through the windows to my right, and the awful scream of sirens fills the air. I hurry, twirling the chain around the handles. Behind me, the boys begin waking up. They know the drill. When a siren sounds, they grab their weapons and proceed outside to stand in formation and await orders.

27

I watch in horror as hundreds of boys pull themselves out of their cots and open their trunks. I hold my breath and begin sliding down the wall towards the main entrance. I hope I can slip out unnoticed, but that plan shatters when the doors leading to the Reds' quarters clatter in protest against the chain. They yell on the other side, muffled somewhat by the sirens and heavy door, and the boys look around, alarmed by the noise.

"It's August!" a voice hollers from within the barrack. Small figures, illuminated by the searchlights outside, turn towards me. A colorful variety of profane words slip from my lips as I search for an exit.

"Stop him!" yells another, and they all move towards me with slow, calculated steps. I'm cornered and outnumbered. There's no way I can fight my way out of this, so I try pleading with them instead.

"I'm here to help you!" I cry out. "Stay back and listen to what I have to tell you!" But my pleas are drowned out by the ongoing sirens. I'm met with blank, glossy stares. Behind the students, the main doors to the barrack slam open and Men in

Red swarm inside. Crap. This has now gone from bad to worst-case-scenario. I search the room for an exit, knowing I'm on my own. The Young Ones are too drugged to do anything but follow orders, and unfortunately their orders are to apprehend me.

"Don't let him get away!" a Red bellows from the front of the building, and the boys surge forward. There's no more calculation in their movements — it's mania, a hunt. I lunge towards a bunk, set beneath a window, and shove the mattress off into the floor so I can grab the metal frame and hurl it through the glass. It works, and the window shatters on impact.

I'm too slow, though, and several of the boys land on me, hitting me with various weapons. I drop to my hands and knees as another kick lands against my stomach and another against the back of my head. I deflect them as best as I can, and the more they hit me, the angrier I become. With a surge of strength, I stand up and spin my elbows out from my chest, and boys stumble back from me in all directions. I glance towards the ceiling and spy a narrow pipe that runs beneath the rafters. Before they can reach me again, I leap up and grab it, swinging over the crowd towards the broken window.

The tip of a whip slashes against the left side of my face, burning my skin and causing my vision to blur. Somehow, I keep my grip as Reds raise their guns and point them at me. I rock my legs back one more time and then swing forward, release the bar, and fling my body feet-first through the shattered window. A jagged edge rips into the top of my right forearm, but I manage to land on my feet outside of the barrack. Blood soaks my sleeve and runs down my arm, dripping against the broken glass on the ground. I hiss through my teeth and run forward, propelling myself onto the nearest rooftop as I head towards the north side of the Compound.

Below me, chaos erupts, and students swarm out of their

barracks. I sigh in relief when Elisa joins me on top of a building, and I search for Nikola and Alek while we run. Sirens continue to wail around us, and floodlights illuminate the entire Compound. I don't see either of them anywhere. Elisa and I hurdle forward as Young Ones jump onto the roofs behind us and give chase.

"Over here!" Elijah yells from below, waving his arms at us when we reach the edge of the Compound. We leap off the side and run towards the gate. Before I can reach it, though, someone tackles me and sends me skidding across the ground.

"You're not getting away this time," Clive says as he struggles to pin me. He smashes his arms against my face and grasps for my wrists, but I arch my back and roll him off to the side. We scramble to our feet, and I drop into a defensive crouch with my fists raised in front of my face. Pain surges through my body in several spots, especially my bloody arm, and my left eye is swelling shut.

"Go, Elisa," I yell, catching a glimpse of her from the corner of my eye. When she hesitates, Elijah opens the gate and pulls her through. Clive snarls at him.

"So you're one of them, too?" he asks, casting a glance at Elijah through the fence. I take the opportunity while he's distracted to grab my sling and a stone from my pocket.

"Don't worry about him, Clive. I'm the one you want," I say, trying to ignore the burning pain in my arm. I load the stone and spin it beside my shoulder. To the side, I see Young Ones running towards us, and I know my window for escape is closing. Clive unfastens the clip on his gun holster and removes it, tilting it up in my direction, so I release the stone. It slams into his broad jaw, and he drops the gun. I tuck and roll forward, grab it, and toss it against the fence. It hisses and pops on contact. Clive coils back and releases a punch, directed at my face, but I intercept it with my good hand and squeeze his fist, grinding the bones. He drops to his knees and screams.

"You won't get away with this," he spits as his face contorts from anger to agony and back again. He reaches into his back pocket, pulls out a switchblade, and flicks it open. "You're going to die, August. So will she, you traitor." He points the blade towards Elisa, and I lose control, crunching down on his fist as hard as possible and then sailing a right hook against his face. His eye socket and nose fold from the impact, and he slumps over, unconscious. Blood trickles from his nose.

"Hurry!" Elisa screams. I fly towards the gate. Elijah slides it open just as the Young Ones reach Clive's body. He slams it shut behind me, and the electric hum comes on, barely audible above the siren.

"Have you seen Alek or Nikola?" Elisa asks Elijah as Young Ones hurl threats at us from the other side of the gate.

"Yeah, they came through already. What happened in there?" Elijah asks, sizing up my wounds.

"Later," I say and then push Elisa forward. "Thanks for your help, but you'd better leave, Elijah."

We take off running, and when I steal a glance over my shoulder at him, he's gone. We've gone a few blocks when several pairs of headlights approach. I dodge to the side into an alley, pulling Elisa with me. I press her back into the side of a building with my good arm, trying to conceal her body with my own. Four large, red buses roar past us towards the Compound. After they're gone, I bound up a fire escape and jump onto the roof overhead. Elisa follows me, and together we look back towards the Compound.

"Oh my God," I mutter. Dozens and dozens of Men in Red armed with tranquilizers and pistols pour out of the buses and storm the gate. Students fall, one after the other, pierced by what I hope are darts, not bullets.

"We have to do something!" Elisa screams, grabbing my shoulders. Her eyes are frantic, and a sob follows her words.

"We have to go," I say, and touch her face with my left hand, forcing her to look at me and not the Compound. "We can't go back. There's too many of them." Her eyes search mine for a second, and her mouth hangs open in distress. Below, Reds start searching the streets for rebels, kicking in doors and breaking windows. Frightened screams cut through the siren's call.

"Oh, God. What have we done? Did we cause this?" she asks. I consider her question and shake my head.

"No, I don't think so. This can't just be a response from us breaking into the Compound. They got here too quickly," I say. The metallic clang of footsteps on the fire escape rings out.

"Go!" I yell, and we spin around and run northwards. We're reckless, not taking the time to check for empty streets. Shots fire at us, whizzing past our heads.

"We're going to have to jump!" I holler over my shoulder at her. She nods as we approach the final precipice. A wave of déjà vu comes over me — the hunt, the feeling of weighted limbs and paralysis — but I shove it back. We have to be faster than the Shepherds and their weapons.

Without wavering, we plant our last step on the shingles and throw ourselves off the edge, flying over the fence. Below us, Shepherds flick on their flashlights, and more shots sound out, but they miss us and we land deep inside the field. Floodlights shine behind us, and we duck our heads as we sprint towards the trees. A bullet snaps into a tree to my right as we enter the forest, and I curse under my breath. Our legs pump harder than ever before, and we don't stop until we reach the campsite, where Alek and Nikola wait for us. Their faces are white with fear as I drop down, feeling faint. My arm is bleeding faster now due to my racing heart, and I clamp my hand over the wound, trying to stop the flow.

"What happened back there?" Elisa asks, and my eyebrows rise at her tone. She's livid.

"It was me. I'm so sorry. I tripped and slammed into the door of the nurses' quarters. It's my fault," Nikola says. She looks more vulnerable than I've ever seen as her chin quivers and tears pool in her eyes.

"It's not your fault, Nikola. One of those stupid birds was hiding in the bushes yesterday when Luca was talking about the plan. I didn't see it until afterwards. The extra Reds must have shown up to stop us," I say and groan at the pain in my arm.

"Oh man, I forgot about your arm," Elisa says. She tears a piece of her shirt off at the waist and wraps it around the cut. Blood soaks through almost immediately. Her lips purse, but she doesn't say anything, only locks worried eyes with me. And she doesn't have to say anything. If I keep losing blood at this rate, I don't know how long I'll last.

"So what's our next step?" Alek asks. He gives Nikola an awkward side-hug, trying to comfort her, but she shrugs it off and wipes her face with the back of her hand.

"I guess we hide out in the forest and wait for the election," I answer, looking at him through my one un-swollen eye. "They're going to need our help. The Foundation is going to punish them for everything we've done, and we can't let that happen."

Elisa walks away, and I stand up to follow her, ignoring how light-headed I feel. Her eyes brim with tears, and I pull her against my chest with my good arm. She wraps her arms around my waist and releases her tears, sobbing into my shoulder. Her disappointment rages through her.

"I'm so sorry, Elisa," I whisper into her hair. "I'm so sorry."

"We failed. We never should have trusted him. Now Karl-mann will win again, and he'll use the Young Ones to punish everyone else, and it's all our fault," she says between sniffs. I don't reply. There's nothing I can say that will ease the pain of our failure. She pulls back and wipes her face with her sleeves.

Alek clears his throat. "I don't think we should stay here. We're too close to the road," he says. I nod.

"Agreed," Elisa says. "But where can we go?"

"What about the camp of drifters that the old guy told us about months ago? They should be close, and maybe they'll have information that we don't," Alek proposes.

Elisa, whose face is red and blotchy, forces out, "Okay."

I hesitate. I wasn't here when they met the guy, and I don't know anything about these people. Joseph's warning runs through my head. I will be hunted, captured, and tortured if the wrong people find out who I am... or what I am, rather. Blood covers the tattooed mark right now, but I won't be able to conceal it if anyone tries to clean me up, especially since my sleeve is in shreds now. On the other hand, what better choice do I have? None, I realize, and agree to go with Alek and Elisa.

"I'm not going to go with you," Nikola says. She folds her bow staff and clicks it on her belt. "I have to go find my brother. I told you I'd help, and I've done as much as I can. And since this whole plan has been blown to pieces, I'm going to go find Stephan while I still can."

I balk at her. "You're leaving now? Seriously?" I say.

"Yes." Her response is matter-of-fact.

"What if you're captured?" Elisa asks, picking up her whip from where she dropped it earlier and curling it on her hip.

"I guess I won't remember enough to care at that point," Nikola says with a shrug.

"There's no talking you out of it, is there?" I ask. She keeps a straight face and shakes her head so that her braid swings behind her. "Okay," I say. It's settled.

"I guess we don't have to worry about you defending your-self," Alek says with a smirk. "One look at you and anyone crazy enough to come after you will leave the country." Nikola forces a laugh, but the nervousness in her tone makes it sound more like a croak. She has good reason to be nervous. We're enemy number one now to the Foundation, and she's only seventeen and setting off by herself to find one man in a sea of thousands. I don't envy her, but I do respect her.

Elisa bends down and opens her bag, which she'd stowed here before going down to the Compound. She retrieves the remainder of her bars and hands them to Nikola. "Take them. You'll need them more than I will for where you're going," she says.

Nikola stammers, shocked by Elisa's generosity. "What will you eat?" she asks, hesitantly lifting her hands to take the bars.

"I'll get the drifters to teach me how to forage or something," Elisa says, forcing a grin. "Seriously. Take them."

Nikola shakes her head and says, "I won't take them all. You have to keep some, especially if things are about to get even worse." She takes fifteen of the bars, enough to last her five or six days, and puts them in her own pack. I watch her, surprised at her selflessness.

"Thank you, Elisa," she says, and they exchange a quick hug. As Nikola pulls away, a scream breaks through the forest. She doesn't wait for answers and slips away to the east before we can say goodbye.

"August!" the voice cries. It sounds like a woman. "August!"

"Over here!" I yell, spotting the glow of a flashlight about a hundred yards away. Snowflakes begin to fall around us, and I shiver as I wander towards the light. It takes a few more minutes of yelling back and forth, but the woman reaches us. Wrapped in several layers of wool, it's Joyce. Her face is smudged with dirt, and snow gathers on the hood of her coat.

"Joyce?" I ask. "What's wrong?"

"It's... it's the village," she says between sobs. "They knew what the rebels were planning, that we were going to use the soldiers against Karlmann. Reds stormed the village tonight and arrested everyone involved, including Andrew. They put the whole place on high-security lockdown. No one in, no one out." She pants, and her breath makes puffs of steam in front of her pale face.

"So, how'd you get out?" I ask.

"I have a permit to travel since I'm the pharmacist for the village. I heard the siren go off on the Compound and figured something had gone wrong, so I got on my bike and rode to the gate. They let me out for some reason. I guess people think I'm too old to cause any trouble. I took the road up, hoping you'd be here. This was one of Joseph's favorite places when he was a boy, and I knew he'd have told you about it." She sniffs and wipes her nose with her sleeve.

Something seems unusual about her story, and I hesitate to believe her. She said they locked down the village, but they released her? One of the leaders of the rebellion? It doesn't add up.

"We're on our way to speak with some drifters further up the mountain," Alek says before I can stop him. "Come with us."

Joyce smiles and nods. "Thank you, young man," she says.

Her wrinkled eyes are so kind that I feel bad about doubting her, but after the truth came out about Luca, I have a hard time trusting anyone. I think back to the Topaz she gave me and decide to give her the benefit of the doubt.

Alek leads the way, following the directions the old man had given us. The snow falls heavier and heavier, collecting on every surface, and I hug my arms to myself. The only thing that keeps my mind off of the searing pain from the cut is thinking about what's going on in the village. The election is supposed to take place in three days, which I guess is more like two now since it's so late. I wonder if it'll happen, and I dread to think that it will. Guilt weighs heavy on me, and blood drips down my fingers and onto the fresh snow. I can't tell if it's from the dark, or if the edges of my vision are going black as I stumble forward. This is so not good.

28

"The villages are on lockdown, sir. The Reds are quarantined, and the children have been subdued," General Volkov says.

"And the other thing I asked you to do?" the Man asks.

"The planes should strike this evening."

"Good."

————

WE'VE WALKED FOR FIVE MINUTES WHEN ALEK STOPS DEAD in his tracks. He turns around and whispers, "Get down!"

We drop where we are. Behind us, figures move in the dark, but I can't tell who they are.

"Come out with your hands up," a man's voice orders. Joyce had been followed. Or Joyce had betrayed us. I whip my head around to question her, but I decide against it when she whimpers.

"I'm sorry! I didn't know I was followed," she says, and her frail voice sounds sincere.

"We'll take care of it, Joyce," Elisa tells her, squeezing her shoulder.

"How many of them do you think there are?" I whisper to Alek, trying to decide if we should fight or run.

"No telling. Sounds like two, but I can't be sure," Alek replies.

"We've got your little friend, the blonde girl who left your group," one of them yells. My heart jumps. "It's only a matter of time before we get you, too."

"We have to do something," Elisa says. "We can't let them keep her. There's no telling what they'll do, how much they'll torture her to get information about us."

"They won't have to torture her when they load her full of Crystal," Alek says. I try to formulate a plan.

"Okay, here's what's going to happen. I'm going to create a diversion. When I do, Joyce, you should turn on your flashlight and toss it towards the Reds. Alek and Elisa, you both disarm them. Don't kill them, though. We'll need them to tell us where Nikola is," I say. I don't give them time to ask questions before I get up and run as fast as possible. Gunfire echoes behind me, but I continue to fly between trees in a wide circle around the Reds. I come up behind them and jump into the branches of a tall pine.

I arch my back and yell as loud as I can, "Over here, you trolls!"

Joyce's flashlight clicks on and provides enough of a glow that I can see Elisa and Alek scuffling with the Reds below. Elisa lashes her whip across the face of one of the men and knocks off a set of goggles. Alek and the other Red are engaged in close combat, swinging fists and feet at one another. But the Red is no match for Alek's strength and speed, and Alek lands a resounding blow to his stomach, causing him to double over in pain.

Out of nowhere, a shot rings out, and Elisa crumples to the ground. Before I can stop myself, I jump out of the tree and race towards the Red who's holding the pistol. I recognize him as Ivan, the Red who Nikola had knocked out earlier. I pick up speed and tackle him. Something snaps beneath me as we skid to a stop, and I hope it's his back. I pin him, placing one leg on either side of his chest, and land blow after blow against his face. Pain shoots up my right arm, but I ignore it and keep punching, mixing his blood and mine in a grizzly crimson pool. Even when the Red quits resisting, I continue to punch.

Alek pulls me off of the unconscious guard, and I stumble backwards, spitting blood from my mouth. I can barely lift my arm now, and my knuckles are swollen and red. I pull myself over to Elisa, who looks as though she's sleeping. Her chest rises and falls slowly, and her pulse is strong. I search her body, feeling for darts or bullet holes, and find a dart lodged in the thigh of her left leg. I pluck the little black feather from her skin and flick it to the side. I pull her into my arms, so thankful that she'll be okay.

I lie her back down and refocus my attention on the two Reds. Alek had managed to tie up the hands of the one with whom he had been fighting, and I stumble over to face him. The man's nose pours blood, but he maintains an indifference as Alek shines the flashlight into his face.

"Where's Nikola?" I ask. I crouch down so my face is level with his, but he doesn't respond. Tired of tight-lipped jerks, I unclip my pocketknife from my belt and flick it open, pressing the blade against the Red's cheek.

"Where is she?" I ask again.

"We don't actually have her," he says, stifling a laugh filled with bloody spittle. "It was a bluff. We were told to follow the old lady and saw the group of you talking. We saw the blonde leave, but we didn't follow her. You're worth more." I back away from him as relief crashes over me. Only then do I realize what I've done — threatened this man with violence and almost killed the other one. I close the knife and shove it in my pocket, shaking my head as relief is met with guilt.

"What's going on in the village?" Alek asks while I try not to fall over. My vision swims in and out of focus, but I try to pay attention.

"Why?" the Red replies, still maintaining a tone of apathy.

"Because those are our friends! They're our people, and you're hurting them!" I force out between heavy breaths.

The Red sighs and responds, "We were sent here to monitor the election in the village and prevent the rebel coup."

"So why are you all the way out here on the mountain?" Alek asks.

"We were told to arrest anyone with ties to the rebels, including drifters. Like I said, we followed the lady to see where she went, planning on arresting the people she met up with and then getting back out of the forest as soon as we could."

"Why?" Alek asks.

"Because you're traitors. All of the drifters are, and you're all going to be punished tonight."

"Punished how?"

"I don't know... something about bombs or fire... I'm not sure. I just do what I'm told, and I was told to follow the lady, arrest anyone she meets, and then get them back to the village for questioning before midnight. They gave us twenty-four hours to round up as many valuable people as possible," the Red replies.

"Twenty-four hours until what?" Alek asks. Joyce has fished a bandage out of Elisa's bag and takes my arm, wrapping the bandage over the cut and the tattoo. I'm bleeding less than I was, but it still flows.

"The bombing, kid. Don't you listen?" the Red asks, slumping forward and shaking his head.

"When did you get your orders?" I ask, alarmed. "When did the twenty-four hours start?"

"Yesterday around zero six-hundred hours. It was early in the morning."

Joyce secures the wrap on my arm, and Alek and I exchange looks. If what this man has told us is true, then we have just a few hours to leave the forest. The closest border to a neighboring country where we might be able to seek amnesty is thirty miles to the north, on the other side of the low mountain ridge. There's no way we can make it that far before Karlmann rains down his vengeance, not with Joyce's slow pace and while Elisa is unconscious.

"Tie his feet up," I tell Alek. He retrieves a roll of twine from Elisa's bag and weaves it around the man's ankles.

"You'll be able to get out of this before we've gone a mile away, and I suggest you go back to the village and take your friend with you before this place gets bombed. If you follow us, I'll make sure you don't walk back out," Alek tells him, and his tone is deadly.

I force myself to my feet and pick up the two guns that had fallen during the fight. I hand one to Alek and throw the other deep into the forest. I want nothing to do with it. I walk over to the Red who I'd beaten. His face stands in bloody contrast to the snow beneath him, and he groans and moves his legs slightly. I'm relieved his back isn't broken, though the crooked angle of his left arm indicates that it isn't so lucky. Yes, he had attacked Elisa, and I rewarded him in kind. So why do I feel so guilty?

I turn back to Elisa and lift her body, cradling it to my chest. "We need to leave immediately," I say. "We have to get to the camp of drifters and warn them."

"Why don't you let me carry her?" Alek asks. He's otherwise uninjured, but I shake my head. I can't bear the thought of giving her up. He seems to understand and opens a bar of food.

"At least eat this and get your strength back up," he says. He shoves the whole thing in my mouth, and I chew it gratefully as he leads the way without another word. It helps immediately, but I still feel much weaker than normal.

A silent hour or so later, we encounter the familiar scent of a smoky campfire followed soon by the rumbles of conversation. We enter into a meadow similar in size to the one we used for so long. Twenty drifters of varying ages stop what they're doing and stare at us.

"We've come to warn you," I say. Elisa is still unconscious in my arms, and I bend over and gently set her down.

"Warn us about what?" asks a middle-aged man. He's backlit by the fire, but I can see him well enough to take notice of his giant beard and shoulder-length hair.

"Karlmann. He knows we've been trying to organize a mass vote against him, and he's blaming it all on the drifters," I reply.

"What? We heard this whole election thing was *your* idea, kid. We didn't have anything to do with it," answers one woman. She has a hood pulled over her head, shielding her cheeks from the snow.

"I'm so sorry. Trust me, we didn't know what Luca had planned until last night or we would have stopped it," I say, feeling guiltier than before. Our choices would cost these people their homes at minimum and their lives at most.

"Luca? Luca Karlmann?" another drifter asks. "That's the president's son!"

The air rushes from my lungs. "His son?" I ask, looking at Alek, whose face turns white.

"Yeah, his son. From Village K, right?" the drifter asks. I nod. "We grew up together. Those two used to be thick as thieves until something went wrong years and years ago. Luca's had it out for his dad ever since he became president. I didn't trust either of them, which is why I left the village when Karlmann got elected." It had never occurred to me that Luca could have such a personal relationship with the man he wants to kill. Anger rolls through my body, deepening my sense of betrayal.

"It doesn't matter who his father is. He deceived us, and now everything's imploding. The forest is crawling with Men in Red, and they're arresting anyone they find. We came here to warn you and to ask for your help," Alek says, sensing that I'm too livid to speak at the moment. "Unfortunately, Karlmann knows everything, and he's retaliating. He's going to bomb the forest."

"This is your fault!" shouts the woman from before, pointing her finger at us. "You did this!" The other drifters join her, yelling threats and insults at us.

"Shut up, everyone," orders an older man who steps forward to speak, and the crowd goes silent. "There's no sense in arguing about it right now. If what they say is true, then we need to leave. Gather your things and bring only what you think you'll need," he directs. Everyone proceeds to run around, gathering laundry, food, and homemade weapons. It takes them less than five minutes to prepare.

"Where are we supposed to go?" asks the same older man.

"Best bet would be to go north towards Staridruch," says another. "It's about twenty miles away, and the closer we get to the border, the less likely it is that we'll be bombed."

"That's what we were thinking," I say, picking Elisa back up. The others murmur in agreement, and despite their hateful glares, they follow us.

Alek helps Joyce navigate the steep, icy rocks of the mountain while I huff and puff with Elisa, trying to keep her body warm against my own. We don't stop for anything and climb further and further north. Conversations are few and far between as everyone tucks their heads down against the biting snow. We've walked as fast as possible for almost four hours when I break the silence.

"How much farther away is the border?"

"A couple of miles, I think. Maybe less," answers one of the drifters between labored breaths. "We've been moving at a pretty fast clip, considering how many people are with us."

I look down at Elisa, wishing she would wake up. I could use her support now more than ever, but her eyes stay shut. After several more minutes, we finally reach the crest of the mountain. Below us, the glimmering, electric lights of a city shine out through the snow, a beacon guiding our descent. Before we can get much farther down the other side, a faint roaring, rumbling noise grows from behind us. I search the sky for the source of the noise, but I can't see anything against the black sky.

"Bombers," says one man. "I can tell already. Planes haven't flown over Belstrana for years, but I'd recognize that sound anywhere. You never forget the sound of a bomber..."

Suddenly, the earth shakes with explosions as planes begin dropping Karlmann's vengeance on the forest to our south. Several people scream, and everyone starts to run down the mountain away from the approaching planes. Even running as fast as I can, I know I can't reach the city before the planes reach us.

A few drifters trip on the roots of the dark forest floor and slide down the mountain for a little way before getting back up to run again. No one speaks as we concentrate on getting away from the bombers that are racing up on us. Explosions behind us light up the sky, and I run for what seems like forever before seeing a break in the tree line. There's a road less than one hundred yards away and a row of buildings on the other side.

The sound is deafening now, and I fool myself into thinking

we've reached safety when an explosion blasts out behind me. I'm thrown forward as the impact shakes the forest. Splinters and pieces of bark rain down around us, and I scramble forward to shield Elisa's body with my own. Right as I reach her, something pierces into the back of my thigh, and I scream in agony, though I can't hear my own voice for the ringing in my ears. The bombers continue past us, and I lay motionless, stunned by the pain, as they retreat away from the border.

I can't see or hear anything, and pain screams through my body. I move my hand to press the back of my leg, and find it wet and hot with blood. My fingers tremble. I can't afford to lose any more blood. My vision comes back somewhat, and I pull myself over to make sure Elisa's okay. Her face is scratched in a couple of places, but she looks otherwise untouched. Relieved, I rock back on my knees.

"August?" a voice asks, but it's muffled and distorted. Alek drops down in front of my face. He looks okay, too. Behind him, though, a woman screams as she leans over a body. Her hands trace the man's limp figure as she tries to find signs of life, but he doesn't move. Bile rises in my throat, and I turn away from Elisa and vomit, trying to expel the last few months from my body. But they stay with me, pressing in on my conscience again. I try to stand up but fall onto my back in a bank of snow. Flashlights erupt into the scene, accompanied by anxious voices.

I think someone hollers, "Are you okay?" I want to scream back that I'm not, that nothing will ever be okay again, but I can't. At least a dozen people in white uniforms run among us, checking for survivors. One of them eclipses my vision. Her lips move, but I can't make out everything she says. All I hear is "help" and "Staridruch." Relief floods over me as the forest swims and spins in circles. Someone else leans over Elisa, and when I'm sure she's safe, I allow my mind to protect itself and surrender to the darkness.

29

"Your color is coming back," Elisa murmurs from somewhere close. My eyes flick open, and I search the brightly-lit, sterile room for her face. She's there, at the edge of my bed, and she smiles when I see her. I move to sit up, but something tugs on my left arm — tubes. I'm hooked up to a bag of fluid that hangs over my shoulder. My right arm is wrapped in clean, white bandages, but I don't feel any pain.

"Where am I?" I ask as memories click into place.

"In a hospital in Staridruch," she replies. She takes my right hand and squeezes it gently.

"We were attacked," I tell her, waiting for confirmation. She nods, and I sigh. "Are you okay? What about Alek?"

"We're both fine. Alek told me how you shielded my body from the blast with your own. I have no words to thank you," she says, trailing off. Her hair hangs like a curtain over her left shoulder as she studies my face, and her emerald eyes sparkle beneath thick lashes that are damp with spilled tears. Wearing a navy-blue dress with a scooped neckline and fitted waist, she looks more beautiful than ever before, and her cheeks blush under my gaze.

"You don't need words," I say. "The last thing I want is to see you get hurt." Now it's my turn to be shy, and I duck my head. She leans in and places a soft kiss on my cheek. Her warmth mixes with the painkillers in my body, and I let out a deep, throaty sigh.

"How long have I been here?" I ask, searching for a safer topic.

"You've been asleep for three days. You cut your arm pretty bad back on the Compound, and a piece of tree got lodged in the back of your thigh from the blast. You passed out from blood loss. The doctors were able to clean both wounds, though, and you should be back to normal in a couple of months."

"Months?" I ask. "We don't have months."

"Don't worry about it now. Let yourself heal," she says, brushing her fingers through my hair.

"What about the others? The drifters?" An image of a bloody woman flashes through my mind.

"For the most part, everyone's okay. Not many people were hurt as badly as you, and those who were are here in the hospital, too," she says.

"Nobody died?" I ask.

"Well, nobody from the group that was with us," she tells me, frowning. My relief dissipates as she picks up a newspaper from the floor by my bed and places it in my lap. "Turns out we weren't the only ones who made it across the border."

A familiar face stares back at me from the front page. It's the round, beady-eyed man from my childhood, the same image my parents had worn on their buttons years ago. It's Karlmann. I snatch the paper, wrinkling the edges with my fingers, and read the headline.

BELSTRANA UNDER SEIGE BY PRESIDENT KARLMANN:

THOUSANDS PRESUMED DEAD AS REFUGEES FLEE TO BORDERING COUNTRIES

I feel sick. Thousands of people died that night? *Thousands?* It doesn't seem real. Elisa picks up a controller from my bedside table and aims it at a black screen mounted into the corner of the room. It snaps on, and I watch as different videos of the bombings play one after another. Pictures of mangled forests and of bloody refugees, lined up at official border gates, scroll through. A tan woman speaks from the screen. Her glossy black curls are piled high on top of her head, and she's dressed in a white shirt, bright pink blazer, and shimmering, silver earrings.

"The images you see here are evidence of an ongoing situation that began three days ago on the eve of Belstrana's presidential election. Known as the Black Sheep of the West, rumors have swirled for years that Karlmann has spent the majority of his time in office participating in research and experimentation deemed illegal by all standards of the modernized world, but there's never been definitive proof until now. His violation of human rights is shocking, and today we see more victims of his iron fist as thousands of Belstranan civilians continue to flee the country after a massive bombing raid took place throughout the North. The cause for the attack is yet unknown, and villages are said to be on lock-down as Karlmann, who has named himself president again, deploys his Men in Red to maintain martial law in response to an organized rebellion.

"Three young Belstranans in particular, known solely by their first names — August, Elisa, and Alek — have garnered quite a bit of international attention as symbols for liberty after they escaped one of Belstrana's youth compounds and led a group of refugees to safety during the initial attack. The whole world now waits with baited breath as they recover, hopeful to meet them and learn how they got free and what's been going on behind the secure gates of Belstrana's compounds for the last fifteen years," the woman concludes.

I stare in shock as my picture disappears from the television screen. The image cuts to a video of a rotund man with short, dark hair and a mustache. His skin is pallid, almost sickly, and the darkness in his eyes causes me to flinch, even though he's shaking the hands and smiling with a group of refugees. I feel as though I can smell liquor on his breath by watching him through the screen.

"That's the President of Staridruch," Elisa says. "Despite what the drifters said about resistance from border countries, he's been welcoming. He came to the hospital to visit you while you were unconscious." She clicks off the television and places the controller back on the table.

"Sorry I missed it," I mumble. "Why did he come here?"

"He said he wanted to make sure a hero like you was well taken care of and to let us know that we're safe." I frown, and Elisa's expression drops when I don't seem impressed by our visitor. I don't want to disappoint her, so I change the subject.

"So everyone knows who we are, huh?" I ask, folding my hands in my lap.

"Apparently so. Karlmann locked the borders of international communication years and years ago, and nobody knew anything for sure about life inside Belstrana until this week when we all flooded their borders." I rest my head back for a moment, absorbing the information, and Elisa brushes a lock of hair from her face. My leg is starting to hurt again, and I try to roll to my side to relieve some of the pressure on it, but I can't without hurting my arm.

The door to the room opens suddenly, and a light-skinned woman in wildly colorful matching shirt and pants walks in. She uses a little pen to mark something down on a thin, black electronic tablet she carries in the crook of her left arm.

"I see you've woken up, August," she says with a smile that shows off her straight, white teeth. "Welcome to Staridruch. How are you feeling?"

"Okay, I guess. A little confused," I reply, watching her tap away on the screen.

"That's to be expected. Any pain?" she asks, looking up for a second.

"Yeah, a little," I reply.

"Well, we can take care of that right now," she says, pulling a syringe of clear liquid from the front pocket of her shirt. I jerk upright and throw my blanket off, scrambling to get away from her.

"Don't come any closer!" I yell, struggling to untangle myself from the web of tubes biting into my arm.

Elisa grabs my shoulder and yells, "August!" loud enough to get my attention. I stop and look at her, and her expression pleads with me. "It's okay. It's not Crystal. She's going to give you something to take the pain away." The nurse stands frozen with her eyes wide and the syringe suspended in midair.

"I'll deal with the pain. No more needles. No more medicine of any kind, actually," I decide and yank the intravenous needle from my arm.

"Are you sure?" the nurse asks, re-capping the syringe and sliding it back into her pocket. I stop moving and look her dead in the eye.

"You don't know what they did to us back there," I say. "No. More."

Blood trickles across my skin, and the nurse pads to a set of drawers, retrieves a piece of fluffy gauze, and presses it gently to my arm. She secures it with tape, watching me in quiet observation until she says, "I'm so sorry this happened to you."

I slump back on the bed, stunned by her confession.

"You're so brave, you know, the three of you leading all of

those people to safety. They would have died without you," she continues with a half-hearted grin. She glances at my leather sling, which I assume Elisa had placed on my bedside table. "Going up against President Karlmann like that? You're like David," she says, broadening her smile.

I glance at Elisa and ask, "I'm sorry, who?"

"David, from the Bible. You must know who I'm talking about," she replies, raising an eyebrow.

"What's the Bible?" I ask. Her mouth drops as she searches our faces.

"It's the story of God," Elisa says, and I turn to her in shock. "We had one when I was a kid. My mom read to me out of it every night. I remember the story."

"What's the story?" I ask, looking back and forth between the two of them.

"Suffice it to say that David was a nobody, a castoff from society who the world looked down on. When his home and his people were attacked by Goliath, a giant warrior who was feared by everyone, David went off to fight him all on his own, despite everyone telling him that he'd get himself killed," the nurse says, retrieving her tablet and scribbling some notes.

"What happened to him?" I ask, intrigued.

"He knocked down Goliath with a single stone from his sling and then cut off his head," Elisa says. She slides her fingers between mine.

"That's right," the nurse adds. "He saved his people and became a hero. Well, I've got to go finish my rounds. I'll be back later to check on you. You're probably going to be in a lot more pain soon, so let me know if you change your mind about the medicine." She shuffles out of the room and closes the door behind her.

Elisa's distracted, chewing her lip and staring blindly at the door. "You know we have to go back, right?" I say to her. Her eyes come back into focus as she looks at me. "We have to find Nikola, assuming she's still alive. Not to mention our parents. They're out there somewhere, too. We can't let them all suffer because of what we did."

She nods and says, "We will. But right now, you need to get some sleep." When she says the word, I realize how exhausted I am, despite having slept for three days. My leg throbs, and I close my eyes, trying to ignore it.

Elisa moves to stand up, and I tug back on her hand. "Don't leave," I beg, looking at her. I scoot over on my bed, and without a word, she lies down, tucking her body around my side and wrapping her arm over my chest. Her head nestles into my neck, and her warm breath kisses my skin with each exhale. I shut my eyes again, trying to soak in every second.

I don't know what the future holds for either of us. It seems like all we did was make things worse, and I resolve to fix it, whatever the cost. Karlmann has to be punished for what he did — for what he's doing. I think back to the story the nurse told. Am I really like David? Can I defeat our Goliath? Time will tell, I guess. I promise myself I'll do whatever I can to free the Young Ones, and not only the Young Ones, but everyone. With that, I allow myself to recede from the hospital room into a dark, dreamless sleep.

ABOUT THE AUTHOR

Laura Wadsworth Carter is a native of Oxford, Alabama, and is a graduate of the University of Montevallo. When not teaching American history to teenagers, hunting for caffeine, or writing fiction, she spends her time with her musical husband and their hilarious toddler whose energy knows no bounds. Together, they live in Huntsville, Alabama. You can visit her website at https://laurawcarter.com and follow her on Twitter @MrsCarterWrites.

lauracarterwrites.blogspot.com/

ACKNOWLEDGMENTS

First and foremost, I would like to thank God for his provision, his inspiration, his grace, and his mercy. I am nothing without Him.

To my husband, Evan, who spent many, many nights listening to me read my story aloud, discussed plot changes and character development with me, and was nothing but supportive through the entire process. Thank you for being my biggest fan, my sounding board, and my best friend.

To my parents, Daniel and Susan Wadsworth, who instilled in me a love for learning and writing and encouraged my curiosity. Your love and support has meant the world to me, and I am beyond grateful to have parents like you.

To my son, Dylan, for being my motivation and inspiration. I love you more than words can say.

To my students, current and previous, for being amazing young adults and for supporting your whacky history teacher. You all are so much smarter and kinder and full of potential than many people in our society give you credit for. You inspire me with your thoughtfulness, your jokes, and your hearts for others. You are a major reason why I write, and I love watching you grow each year.

To my editors, Christi Corbett, Jacob Bedel, Kimberly Wheaton, Trina McCulley, and Renee Quaife. You all are awesome.

To my missional community group and church family at Summit Crossing, for your prayers and support throughout this process. It has meant so much to me, and I thank God for you every day.

To my publisher, Stephanie Taylor at Clean Reads, for taking a chance on me when I least expected it. You've made this dream come true and brought my story to life. Thank you, thank you, thank you.

CPSIA information can be obtained
at www.ICGtesting.com
Printed in the USA
LVHW091256300520
657006LV00005B/1365